OUT OF THE RUBBLE . . .

Naldosa didn't know what happened as he was pulled past his partner, but he saw Amunsen ahead of him, suddenly and inexplicably being sucked into a hole. Head first, Bjorn went deeper and deeper into the falling rubble, snagged at one point as if caught on a nail, but then ripped forward, his left arm dangling behind. In the next split second Naldosa saw an enormous pair of dark claws clamp over the bigger man's neck and shoulders. Moments before falling debris buried Amunsen and the claws, Naldosa saw two burning red eyes against a deformed, blackened face.

Was it illusion? A horrible waking nighmare? He saw something·in the rubble that slithered toward him, something that mimicked human cries in order to lure him and Amunsen here, something scratching at the debris on all sides of him, trying desperately to get at him as it had Amunsen.

Something that fed on the trapped, on the dying, on the already dead . . .

Other books by Robert W. Walker

BRAINWATCH

SALEM'S CHILD

AFTERSHOCK

Robert W. Walker

ST. MARTIN'S PRESS/NEW YORK

AFTERSHOCK

Copyright © 1987 by Robert W. Walker

Library of Congress Catalog Card Number: 87-60623

ISBN: 0-312-90906-3   Can. ISBN: 0-312-90907-1

Printed in the United States of America

First St. Martin's Press mass market edition/November 1987

10 9 8 7 6 5 4 3 2 1

This book is affectionately dedicated to the one beautiful constant in my life, a woman who knows the shocking truth about me and loves me anyway, Cher . . .

Acknowledgment

In a career checkered with the shocks that plague all writers, where projects often become mutants, at long last I found an editor on my "wavelength" who works harder than I. All my gratitude goes to Jack Caravela whose keen eye and incredible energy made this novel into the best it could be. As if he were a character in the novel, Jack set out to play a major role, and I'm so glad he did . . .

prologue

Marie Vorell Robel needed only to slide her hands into the oversized protective gloves, with their metallic knuckles and fingers. With headgear in place, she appeared ready for a walk in space. But her stroll into a chamber only a few feet away was potentially more dangerous than any contemplated by NASA. Her visit would take her into close proximity with an invisible, deadly killer, a virus she had helped to bring into being.

Marie and her husband, Arthur, comprised Dr. Leo G. Copellmier's special project team, and their work was of such a highly sensitive nature that they had agreed to be buried alive with it. The underground laboratory had been built to Leo's specifications and it rested below his own Center for Disease Control, the Copellmier Center in Downtown Los Angeles.

It was a vault, sealed from entry and exit by a magnetic door that opened on an elevator. Only one man held the key—Leo. Inside the high-tech crypt the two scientists had everything they had asked for.

"Help me on with the gloves, please, Arthur," Marie said, her voice calm, resolute.

"I don't like this, not a bit of it."

Marie's firm jaw was set. She stared at the inner

1

chamber through an eight-foot high, sixteen-foot wide, four-inch thick panel of acrylic glass. The experiment chamber was framed in thin pillars of black steel. "Please, Arthur, for God's sake, no more debate."

Arthur frowned, looking hard into her eyes as he worked at getting one of the gloves snapped and zipped. An undisguised look of anger hardened his features, but Marie chose to ignore this. "You're only making this more difficult for me," she added.

Arthur responded by giving a good yank to the glove, forcing it high up her forearm and twisting.

"Easy, you make me feel like a horse being cinched. I already feel like a blimp in this thing."

Arthur replied almost under his breath, "Has to be secure for the relays running through the material to work. Each snap is a conductor for the synthetic arteries carrying impulses from the fingertips. According to Leo, it's more foolproof than your own sense of touch."

"We'll see."

Behind the visor, Marie's face was almost lost in the glare of the overhead lights, but Arthur knew her heart-shaped visage so well, he imagined he saw it clearly anyway. He had to work a bit harder to find the stylishly short-cropped raven hair, her shapely eyebrows and elegant lashes. Arthur liked looking at her when she wasn't watching or when she slept. There was a slightly frightened, vulnerable pout to her lips when she was asleep or deep in thought, a look that appealed to him much more than her usual stern, determined conscious glare. Her eyes were sometimes aqua blue and sometimes emerald which fascinated him further. She was almost twenty years his junior, and he'd known from the beginning she had married him as much for his prestigious name as any professed love—to advance her own insatiable desire to achieve a name for herself in the newly developing field of recombinant DNA and genesplicing. But he loved her anyway.

Theirs was not a perfect relationship, but he was not so alone as before, alone in his work, his mind, his laboratory, his bed.

Marie seemed more driven by the work than even he was, as if she were the old one instead of him, as if time were running out for her. Impatience of youth, he had called it, but she called it ambition.

Arthur shivered involuntarily with the thought of losing her. One way or another, he assumed, one day he would lose her. Maybe that was why he had agreed to this madness, this confinement. They were no better off than prisoners in a cell block here with hardly as much in the way of creature comforts. And it was always so damned cold.

Arthur's thin, wild red tufts of hair were brush-stroked with gray. Although hunched at the back, he remained a tall, imposing man. Age spots showed on his scalp where the hair was gone, and of late, he feared, his mind was also showing gray and bare spots. He wondered at times if he were a candidate for premature senility; he dozed easily, sometimes in midconversation. He rankled more easily than ever before. He was getting more forgetful than ever.

On the other hand, he wasn't too senile or careless to have missed what had occurred between Marie and Leo Copellmier. But she was young and he could not always give her what she needed, and he believed she did, in her way, love him.

"Amazing how maneuverable the fingers are," Marie said, breaking his reverie, the robotlike gloved fingers doing exercises in front of his eyes. "Look," she added, picking up her watch from a console. "I can feel how hard, how light and dense it is . . . like . . . like it's an extension of my hand."

"Precisely how it should work."

"Oh, get the other one connected. This is fascinating."

"Marie, I'm worried. For the last time, please, let's wait until we can get help."

"Arthur, do you have to be so . . . so contentious?"

"Contentious? You call concern for you contentious?" He pointed to the chamber as if it were an open grave awaiting an occupant. "I don't for a moment believe it is our responsibility to fix Leo's plumbing. The very least the man could have done was to provide properly functioning equipment. No one's supposed to have to go inside there, not at this stage of the experiments."

"We have the problem, Arthur. Not Leo, us!"

"Brought on by his cyborg in there!" Again the long, bony finger pointed to the chamber at the center of which stood a squat, robotic form with a computer-screen face as emotionless and blank as a dead picture tube. Extending from the shoulder dangled the now useless single limb, with a hand, identical in appearance to the glove Marie now wore on both her hands. "Damned suit," Arthur grumbled. "Damned Leo, damned Manfred."

Manfred was the name Arthur had given the cyborg, having tired of calling it by a number. The cyborg had, up until recently, a fully operational computer brain that communicated directly with the computer outside the chamber. But it had suddenly gone dead in the night. The arm, hand and fingers which did the actual handling of the toxic chemicals contained real human tissue below the protective outer shell of specially formulated alloys called plates.

The spindly arm, controlled by a synthetic sense of touch and the computer eye, was in essence more careful with the deadly materials than any human could ever hope to be. Inside the sterilized, rarefied environment of the chamber, no human could safely work. Marie and Arthur, until now, had done all the tests by remote control.

Manfred's hands were designed like those on Marie's protective suit. Beneath the armor of the plates lay human nerve tissue connected by synthetic arterial tubes finer than fibers, which ran the length of Manfred's arm to his brain. Like Marie's suit, the cyborg's exterior was supposedly impenetrable, but something was wrong.

"I think I know why you're so determined to go through with this, Marie," Arthur said suddenly, his voice spiteful.

"You know very well—"

"To impress Leo, isn't it? *Isn't it?*"

"Oh, Arthur!" She feigned dismay. "Don't be ridiculous."

"He already promised to come down to have a look himself!"

"When do you suppose that might be? We haven't time to sit idle here."

"Say what you will; I *know* you, Marie!"

She took hold of him by each arm, squeezing hard, feeling the strength of the metallic hands, causing him to wince and pull away. "Arthur, we are either committed to this or we are not!"

"Of course . . . as always . . ."

"Now, go to the monitor. The kindest thing you can do for me now is to be vigilant and stop worrying."

Arthur looked dejected as he went to the monitoring station directly in front of the chamber, where he would control Marie's entry and exit from the chamber. As he called up the command to open the door to the decompression area, he thought about his past accomplishments. He was once heralded as a genius by none other than the president of the United States, but it had all been done in secrecy, behind closed doors. His Medal of Honor was known only to himself, Marie and a handful of people in the Pentagon. His discovery had not been meant as a weapon in itself, but an alternative to the catastrophe of a nuclear attack. But since the U.S. had his weapon, it raised the risk of nuclear war all the more—since the U.S. could at least, in part, render a nuclear disaster controllable—controllable in that the dreaded nuclear fallout could be greatly reduced.

Since he was totally without religious sentiment, Arthur felt no qualms about creating new life forms *per se,* but the heads of state and Leo G. Copellmier now wanted something more than a "bug" that fed on atomic-waste particles. They wanted something truly terrible to add to the country's chemical-biological arsenal.

Arthur had been happy enough in his Bethesda, Maryland, lab, understanding better than any American the need for underground nuclear testing in the desert areas of Arizona and Utah. He knew that with each nuclear blast his new life form was also being tested, with startling results. It had even worked on a neutron blast.

He wondered how he had been talked into working with Leo Copellmier, whose government contacts seemed endless. He wondered how Marie had persuaded him here.

"The door, Arthur, close it," said Marie.

"Oh, oh, yes." Arthur tapped the keys and the door was sealed. A blinding light followed, so intense Marie's entire form disappeared in it.

"Enjoying your bath?" he asked.

"No, not particularly."

Arthur wanted to keep her talking, to monitor voice inflections. His eyes scanned the dials and indicators before him. Marie's heartbeat, blood pressure, voice and vital signs could be watched easily from here.

"Talk to me, Marie."

"I'm doing just fine, Arthur, really."

Arthur saw that she was right. She was again proving herself a most capable and strong-willed individual. The monitors all registered her as perfectly calm, a bit skittish on the heartbeat but otherwise just fine, as if she were going to a tea party with Manfred as the Mad Hatter, and looking forward to it.

So far as they knew, only Leo was aware that they were both here. They had been in their cell for almost seven uninterrupted months, working toward a goal that had begun to seem like madness. Leo had secured everything they requested of him, including the diseased brain tissue that had started them on their first truly exciting discoveries. Arthur had thought it fascinating that from the minds of long dead men and women, with his and Marie's intervention, there might arise, Phoenixlike, a new life form.

Copellmier had provided the Robels with one large magnetic card, a key to the single exit out of here, but Arthur had discovered that it did not work. The key was meant as a placebo, but Arthur had kept this knowledge to himself. He knew that if there were an accident, there could be no escaping it.

"Opening the interior chamber door, Marie," Arthur announced. "Unless you've come to your senses and wish to come back out, in which case—"

"Please, stop treating me as if I were a child, Arthur! I know what I'm doing."

"Door opening," he replied without another word.

Inside, Marie glanced about the concrete floor near the cyborg. She saw nothing out of the ordinary, nothing to indicate a problem existed, only the silent, dead screen face and lifeless gray metal arm.

It wasn't for Leo's benefit that she insisted on entering here, she told herself. Sure, she wanted Leo to be impressed, but he was like Arthur, a means to an end. This project could advance her career tremendously. It had been her ideas that had gotten it off the ground. She had suggested they use tissue samples of the diseased brains, and she had syphoned out the virus which was now the cornerstone of the new life form that could render an army, or even an entire nation, helpless to an organism that literally devoured people. The next honors extended to Arthur Robel would also be extended to his wife, Marie. She would see to it.

As for the killer virus itself, it might be applied overseas or in outer space for all she cared, but either way it rendered strategic defense systems in both the U.S. and USSR useless and obsolete. All that remained to be determined now was how to control the virus, render it ineffective to oneself.

You could win a war, any war, all wars, if this could be accomplished. The CBW, or chemical biological weapon, they were developing could more selectively wipe out an enemy than anything dreamed of before.

"I'm going to conduct the test," she told Arthur.

"You will do it carefully, do you understand?"

"Understood." She stooped to where the virulent strain of virus was kept in a concrete coffin below a counter.

As she took hold of it, her eyes registered something odd around Manfred's hand. Blurry yet distinct brown splotches encircled each small plate.

The plates were scales, like snakeskin scales, only metallic, covered in a synthetic sealant. They overlapped one another in layers like the feathers on a bird or shingles on a roof. On the underside of each was an electronic sensor and behind these sensor chips was the real human nerve cells that made this particular robot a cyborg. It was capable of processing information at an incredible rate and handling toxic materials, thus freeing humans of danger. But why it had suddenly refused to work remained a mystery.

The brain and nervous system in Manfred coordinated all information which was then used to determine the course of future decisions and actions. Without Manfred, they could not have accomplished so much in so short a time.

"Perspiration's up, along with heartrate, Marie," came Arthur's voice over the microphone. "Is everything all right in there?"

"Fine . . . no problems, Arthur," she lied, her eyes still on the odd brown rings.

"Don't like the blood-pressure reading I'm getting on you," he protested. "Like it or not, the computer's giving you away."

"Just a little healthy fear," she countered. "You wouldn't have it any other way. You taught me the value of caution, remember?"

"Indeed. You sure you're all right?"

"Arthur, we have to prove to Leo he was right to put his faith in us! Is that simple enough for you? Is that clear?" She was standing again, staring out at him with her outburst.

He tried to ignore her anger. She seemed to be having difficulty breathing. Vital signs had risen but seemed to be leveling off. She crouched and continued her search for the materials she wished to work with. She was muttering to herself but it came clearly over to Arthur. "For God's sake, be a little supportive."

Marie tried to go about the work, to ignore the brown splotches on the gray metal, to assume it was some sort of corrosion. But in a sterile environment corrosion could not occur.

She put the concrete coffin on the countertop.

Her eyes wandered back to the brown splotches. *What is it?* she asked herself. *What does it look like? Lesions? Robots don't get lesions. But Manfred's not a robot in the strictest sense,* she reminded herself, *he's a cyborg.*

Get hold of yourself . . . just a malfunction in the wiring. But she knew Manfred's "wiring" was not copper, that his conduit was as close to actual human arteries as science could duplicate. Through them ran nerve impulses, from human synapses.

She stared again at the cyborg's blank screen face, a single huge eye gone dead. *Through his—its—arteries impulses pass, no different from my own,* she thought, *and now he—it—is paralyzed, frozen, mind dead . . . and now those damned lesions.*

It's just a robot . . . no matter the inner workings, she argued with herself.

But then Manfred stirred. Not a lot, just a glimmer of movement, almost rocking in place. Then she felt movement below her feet, a rumbling, unnerving feeling.

"It's the ground below, Marie!" Arthur shouted, but by the time he said it, the tremor was over.

"It's past," she said.

"A tremor, a damned earth tremor. That does it, I want you out of there, now. Suppose you had removed the—"

"No," she replied instantly. "I'm in here now and I'm going to run the tests."

"I'm calling it off, Marie. I forbid you to go any further, to take any more chances!"

"Leo assured us the building is quake-proof, and I'm not about to be dictated to by—"

"I'm senior in experience and authority here, Marie! You forget that too often!"

"I'm finishing what I started."

"Absolutely not!"

"We run the tests!"

"No! Come out!"

"As planned!"

"I had no part in these plans!"

"Damn you, Arthur!"

"The risks are just too great!"

"I know the risks! I accept the risks! I've always accepted them!"

Marie turned her space-suited back to him and returned to the table. She breathed deeply and proceeded as casually as possible. She lifted the seal from the container and lifted out a thick decanter of olive brown liquid. Beside it she placed the additional viral culture which Manfred should have introduced to it some twelve hours before.

"Marie," came Arthur's pained voice, "please, listen to reason."

"I'll be out in fifteen minutes."

"If your heartrate continues at its present climb, you'll be dead in fifteen minutes!"

"Scare tactics won't work on me, Arthur."

Somewhere far below Marie and Arthur Robel, the earth rumbled.

one

6:50 A.M., second tremor

Aboveground, Los Angeles's four hundred and sixty-four square mile landbase, nestled snugly around the Santa Monica and San Pedro bays, moved again. It was slight, almost unfelt, like a deeply released, contented sigh from a lover in warm slumber. It was quick but it was there, a gentle reminder of the plates scientists spoke of as being belowground, which at times acted like the vertebrae in the backbone of the San Andreas Fault, moving ever so slightly, until one slipped.

People on the streets, in cars and buses, on their way to work, felt little or no sensation. Vibrations from the earth had less effect on moving objects, and the autos of L.A. moved like quicksilver down the avenues and freeways. Only stationary people and objects registered the tremor. No one was too terribly alarmed, no one became hysterical. In fact, the population showed remarkable calm.

After all, it was only one more tremor, certainly not as common as smog or traffic jams in the city, but almost as acceptable a phenomena of life in L.A. as the rest.

On the breakfast terrace at the L.A. Hilton, Dr. Michael McCain was growing steadily more impatient and angrier with his unarrived guest, a Dr. Casey Sterns.

McCain watched for any sign of Sterns at the entrance-way, past a cashier who seemed to think he was interested in *her*. Sterns was the doctor he had come to think of as The Last Holdout, the single member of Leo Copellmier's floundering AIDS research team whom McCain had not met.

The Acquired Immune Deficiency Syndrome nowadays had staggering business implications, the fact just dawning on most drug companies and investors. As crass as Leo was, he was correct in saying that a cure for AIDS meant millions. As for Leo's already major investment toward this end, things seemed to have soured since his initial speculation into the field. But as far as Mike McCain and many another virologists were concerned, the cutthroat competition between giants in the pharmaceutical field had a positive side, allowing for more research than ever before. He could recall a time when he—*and this guy Sterns very likely*—worked on AIDS only during their spare time, on their own, if at all.

When the second, stronger tremor pinged glassware together around the room, Mike reacted a bit more strongly than those around him. He was a Chicagoan by birth, and he had seen tornadoes and lightning storms that had frightened him more than he liked to admit, but he had never encountered the bizarre, unnatural feeling of rumbling earth. This was something out of his ken, and it only added to his already agitated state. *Where the hell was this guy Sterns?* he wanted to know.

Just then he saw a stunning, immaculately dressed honey blonde come into the dining room, searching from table to table, her arms loaded down with thick books. The CCDC insignia was clearly visible on her jacket. Mike had not worn his own patch; he felt a first meeting ought to be informal. Now it appeared Sterns had ducked Mike again, sending his secretary instead of showing up himself. Mike could hardly believe the man's audacity.

He waved the tall blonde toward him when their eyes made contact.

"Dr. McCain," she said as he got to his feet, extending hands to take her books. "I recognized you from your photo in the *Gazette*."

"Yes, thank you, but I expected Dr. Sterns himself."

Her topaz eyes bore into him. "Sorry to disappoint you but—"

"Not your fault! Care to have breakfast with the newcomer?"

"Dr. McCain, *I* am Dr. Sterns," she said between clenched teeth.

McCain bit his lip, dropped his eyes a moment as if searching for something clever to say, but all he could muster was, "I'm sorry. I . . . didn't know you were . . . I mean, I guess . . . I assumed."

"Is that your idea of an apology?" Her hair was remarkably soft-looking and her features were fine, yet her eyes and manner were fiery. "I might have expected better from so prominent a man."

"My mistake, but I assure you it was not intentional. No one told me, and since you were such a *holdout*—"

"Ahh, I see."

"Please, sit down, *help me*," he pleaded as calmly as he could.

This slowed her down. She nodded and sat in the chair opposite him, studying him but not allowing his cobalt blue eyes to pin hers down. "Naturally, you assumed anyone as successful as I must then be a man. I can understand that."

"Leo didn't say you were a . . . a woman, Dr. Sterns, and neither did anyone else for that matter, and I didn't get a file on you."

"No time for homework, you mean?"

"You understand why I am here, Dr. Sterns?"

"I believe so: to run interference for Dr. Copellmier, to boost production, get results, all that sort of thing.

Get a test to detect the AIDS virus itself, perhaps a total cure in the next few weeks? I'm sure a vaccination wouldn't suffice for Leo's ego."

"I know."

"You know? Well, good."

"I know Leo's reputation."

She was surprised at his response, slowed by his total agreement, but she gritted her teeth and continued in more control now. "Two years of my life's gone into my research and I won't compromise that by announcing premature results just for the sake of seeing Leo's stock rise. Since AZT went on the market—"

"Hold on now," he interrupted, "no one's asking that at all. And your being defensive has only slowed any joint effort to rein in all the findings of the past two years in a team that, under Dr. Marcus Weintraub, has pretty well disintegrated. *That* is my understanding of the picture."

"So, what happens? Dr. Weintraub is history, the other doctors on the project in a complete disarray, feeling unsure about the future . . ."

"Anyone who feels insecure about my presence is going to react badly under any circumstances, doctor, but I assure you now—"

"I've had two years of assurances from Leo. His favorite line is, *If you have an idea, I'll give you the freedom to develop it.* Only one catch in the fine print: *show me results tomorrow.* You know very well it takes six or eight years to bring a new drug to market."

"Indications are that you log more lab hours than anyone on the project," he said, examining her records at a glance. She took a deep breath of air, saying nothing. Mike did a quick study of her features as they softened. She was striking, her eyes filled with energy.

A waiter came to the table with a cart filled with fresh baked croissants, heaping pots of jellies, jams, and butter, and a selection of juices and fruits.

"We're supposed to be enjoying a business breakfast, Dr. Sterns, to get to know one another. As it happens, I am very interested in your research—not to rob you of it, but to help see that Leo doesn't cut off his nose to spite his face. He *is* upset with the timetable and looking to cut his losses, true."

She didn't respond.

"I see my job as salvaging what's best out of the entire effort and, if in the process I introduce a new idea or two, point to a new direction, and build better relations between staff members, all the better. I'm not looking to destroy careers."

The speech was good, the voice as sincere as any she had heard in a long time, but her mind kept saying *it's all talk*.

"Breakfast?" he asked now, sounding boyish, a smile lighting his face. She noticed he was tall, broad-shouldered, in need of a tan. His dark hair framed a cream-colored complexion and highlighted the ocean blue of penetrating eyes.

She nodded. "Breakfast." With that word they had called a shaky truce.

As they drank coffee and ate, Mike glanced over some of the material Dr. Sterns had brought. She had predicted that some 3.5 million people would be infected with the AIDS virus by 1991. At the back of his mind, partitioned off from what he was reading, he was giving additional thought to her. He hated having perfect strangers angry with him for no good reason, and she was a *perfect* stranger.

"From what I see here," he said, "it appears I'll be going to bat for your research, doctor. Of course, I'll want more time to go into it in depth but I think you may be on to something. And I like your honesty."

"That is encouraging."

"Since taking this job I've seen everything *but* honesty and . . ."

"Anger?"

"It didn't help that my first words to you were so chauvinistic. But impressive work, Dr. Sterns, speaks for itself. It's obvious you're very talented, very . . . thorough."

"Well . . . too bad Leo doesn't see it quite that way."

Casey thought for a moment of her last confrontation with Leo Copellmier, of his sexual politics, his loathsome blackmail attempt. Leo would keep a hands-off policy on her research *if* she'd allow a hands-on policy between them. Casey had shouted her contempt and stormed from the man's office, prepared to leave the center, but the work was too important for her to simply walk away. She preferred to fight it out with Leo and anyone he sent after her, knowing Leo would not have the courage to confront her again.

"I'm here to do Leo's house-cleaning for him," Mike admitted, "but I am a doctor, a researcher, like yourself. I'm not an administrator. I'm a virologist, Dr. Sterns, like you."

"Like me, Dr. McCain?"

"Our goals are the same, the salvation of an important research project, gaining additional funds for that purpose. If you could keep that in mind. Some of the others seem more preoccupied with a higher rung on the newly fashioned ladder, but you appear genuinely concerned about the future of the project itself."

"Now I'm supposed to thank you for the compliment and that's supposed to ease the situation?"

He caught a glint of malice in her eyes, but her voice had softened. "The tension, maybe. Look, Casey—can I call you Casey?" He dared not wait for an answer, and plunged ahead. "For years before AIDS became a well-publicized disease, you and I were hard at work investigating it, seeking a cure for it. A cure, not a highly toxic retardant. I can see by your work that you're still committed to that, by the sheer number of hours you've sacrificed . . . the number of cultures done, your insistence on examining the pathological effects of the disease—"

"Your point, doctor, just what is it?"

"That we're on the same side, like it or not."

She shook her head. "I refuse to release information too early, without proper, thorough clinical work preceding it, assuring me of its validity. You and Leo may fear you're going to be ruined if the center is not in the marketplace first with a cure, but for me it has to be a certainty, the work foolproof, evidence on the table. Even if someone else beats us to the punch, I must know I did all in my power to be right. A few test cases does not make a drug a miracle."

"We're in a footrace, Casey, and time is important to Leo—"

"And you!"

"I see Leo's side of the picture, but I also understand your concerns, believe me. The CCDC is one of the few large centers committed to an AIDS vaccine, and our success boils down to—"

"Money, I know," she said.

"—Money, yes, Casey, in a situation fraught with incredible potential for liabilities of every sort. The risks to people receiving treatment here at the AIDS experimental drug program are staggering. Overnight, we could all see our careers ruined by rushing in with something ineffective or dangerous."

Casey was listening intently now. McCain *had* done his homework after all.

"I'm on your side, Casey, really. I'm interested in proper methodology, proper testing, caution as much as you, *and* to one day find that vaccine or cure. I'm also on Leo's side, because he's betting his company on you and me and the others. We scientists have to accept the facts for what they are, take the challenge. *Time* is at a premium, true, but I can recall when virtually no one was researching AIDS, and virtually no money was going into research."

"Understood," replied Casey, knowing that what he said was true. Since the passage of laws limiting liability for AIDS vaccine manufacturers, the footrace had become a Grand Prix. Those who tested possible cures without sufficient research or caution could cause great harm to their patients *and* their reputations, however, and Casey agreed with Mike that too much haste would eventually backfire. "Guess I'm of the old school, the starry-eyed type who still worships Louis Pasteur."

"Nothing wrong with that . . . not at all. In fact, it's my guess that some young scientist whose mind is open to the possibilities of imagination will one day confound us all, recognizing a cure the rest of us have been stumbling over for years. I believe that kind of attitude still exists in our profession, Casey."

She laughed lightly, without scorn. "You're a dreamer, aren't you?"

"I suppose, at bottom, yes. Dreams are important. Couldn't be in our profession if we didn't hold on to them, don't you agree?"

Casey's eyes softened. "I've seen lots of dreams shaken." She now looked at him with something knew in her gaze. Was it curiosity? Mike tried not to stare at her, but with sunlit hair the color of cornsilk and her eyes a deep, devastating topaz with flecks of gold, it seemed an impossibility.

"Can't imagine why Dr. Copellmier didn't warn me about you," he said.

"Warn you about my temper?"

"I meant the fact you're so attractive." Mike caught himself. "I mean, he might've told me you were a woman."

A blush and she was again in control. "Leo may well become your biggest problem at the center, doctor."

Mike laughed, nodding.

"Remember one item about Leo and you might not get hurt."

"Yes?"

"Leo maintains control, always. Just when you think he believes in your judgment, trusts you, has faith in your ability, he cuts you deeply. You're never without big brother Leo looking down at you. He doesn't allow that. At least, not for long."

Mike sensed the hurt in her words. Leo had obviously cut *her* deeply. He wondered if he would ever hear the story. He decided to change the subject to counter the downward spiral her mood seemed to be taking. "Can't say I haven't wondered what I'm doing in L.A.," he said, sipping his coffee. "I'm a Chicago boy, not at all comfortable with groundswells like the ones I felt this morning. Happen often?"

"Oh, the tremors? They scare me, too!"

"People here are so . . . so calm about them."

She smiled. "People living under a volcano either laugh at it or deify it. I suppose we Californians do the same. Tell me, Mike, do Chicagoans ever laugh at God?"

"Sure, absolutely, but only in the daylight."

Her smile was radiant and he wanted to tell her she should use it more often. The check was brought to the table, the waiter asking if there was anything further he could do for them. They both grabbed for the bill, their hands touching briefly, until Mike pulled away with the paper.

"Reflex," she apologized. "Been a while since anyone's paid my way."

"I find that hard to believe."

"Believe it. Spend all my time in the lab. In fact, I've just come from there. I've been working all night." It sounded like a confession.

"You certainly don't look it, Casey."

"I showered and changed. You'll find everything at

the CCDC, including a pool and a workout room to keep in shape. Leo likes his people in shape. It must work if you mistook me for a secretary."

"Oh, hey, I'm sorry about that, really."

"Apology accepted," she said as she eased from the table. "Oh, no, don't get up. I really must get home, get some rest. I'll see you again, after you've had time to familiarize yourself with these records." She indicated the books she had brought with her.

Mike took her hand in his and shook it, saying he would examine her work closely, but thinking how impoverished Western customs were for indicating feeling. He didn't want to shake her hand. He wanted to hold her hand, to somehow subtly imply his attraction to her in some acceptable manner. But there was none and she was gone.

7:02 A.M., lights out

Dr. Leo G. Copellmier moved away from the floor-length window overlooking Los Angeles in his private suite atop the CCDC, and with a resolute motion he placed a key-card into the wall behind his desk. The magnetically sealed door swished open in response. Leo was annoyed and upset as he stepped into the elevator which would take him down to the experimental lab. He had a plane to catch for D.C., and he didn't place much credence in Arthur Robel's story about a goddamned defective cyborg that had cost in the hundreds of thousands of dollars to build.

Leo wasn't buying it, although he had been careful not to allow the Robels to sense his distrust when he had spoken to them via the intercom in his office. Leo's nature was given to suspicion, and he had suffered from it on more than one occasion when so-called partners wised up. There seemed to him only one way to view the

Robels' claims. All the cyborg crap was an elaborate scheme the husband and wife had cooked up during their long, solitary confinement. A pure fabrication.

The elevator began its slow descent.

One thing he remained certain of since their last reported results: the Robels were on the verge of something truly stupendous. Still, if they could be believed, they remained far from a controllable viral weapon.

The elevator passed silently down through the hidden shaft.

Marie Robel had tried before to get Leo to come down. She was understandably lonely. She might do anything just to have another man acknowledge her existence at this point. She may even have persuaded Arthur that she would go mad without some contact from the outside. Leo had no doubt of her power over Arthur.

The elevator was better than halfway there.

Certainly, being married to Arthur, she shared certain traits with him; determination, for instance, and ambition which was too great to contain in so small and secret a place. Marie could have planted ideas in the old man's head. Perhaps the two of them had decided it was time they band together against Leo, that it was time to make more demands on him. He had seen it happen before. The geniuses get halfway through a project and decide they want more of a share in the profits, and to hell with the kudos.

The elevator continued to whir, very quietly.

A large, bull-shouldered, stern-faced man, Leo was almost totally bald, sporting a well groomed, thick, gray beard. Over his tailored suit he wore a lab coat. His shoes shone in the single light of the elevator, expensive imports from Spain.

He hadn't given the tremors any thought. They came and went, like the weather. But then the single light overhead went black, and he felt a twinge of fear in the darkness. No one knew of the elevator shaft or the secret lab, not even those who funded it. When federal grants weren't enough for the construction, he had done some creative accounting. He found money everywhere he looked, as he always did. By inflating building costs through friendly contractors, he had gained more money from investors and the government. He then turned this gain around and managed to slash actual costs, disallowing what he considered, in the end, unnecessary expenses. One of the cost-cutting tactics was to ignore plans for the so-called "quake-resistant construction."

The shaft seemed to be bottomless now, an effect of the dark, and the whirring turned to a roar in Leo's ears.

Copellmier had believed for a long time he would never see a return on his investment in the underground DNA lab; then he discovered the Robels. Everything went smoothly, as if it were all meant to be. Marie had been a longtime admirer of Leo's early work in virology, and Marie knew how to play on his vanity for all it was worth; he knew this, and still it didn't matter. She brought it all back, made him feel like a younger man, and on their first night at Leo's Beverly Hills estate, with Arthur sleeping off jet lag, they had made love in the greenhouse amid crushed orchids.

Leo grinned at the memory. He had been bullshitting about the marigolds, having taken her to the greenhouse on her request, and only slightly aware of her motives. She had surprised him there, taking off her clothes, standing naked amid the steam and mist, huge palm fronds lying across her breasts. When he turned it was like an erotic dream, and he hadn't expected the urgency he felt to take her. It had been fast and torrid. Beneath her simple exterior, there lurked a woman whose desires were insatiable . . . but insatiable for what?

The elevator came to an abrupt, settling stop. In the dark he had to feel for the slot where he must place the key-card. In his breast pocket he fingered a scalpel with a familiar gesture, an illogical but habitual precaution.

The door swished open and he stared out at Arthur, who turned and looked at him. "Leo! You've come! Thank God, maybe you can talk sense into her!" He gestured to the chamber, and Leo realized Marie was inside, suited up and working, her concentration so total she didn't know he was there.

Christ, Leo thought, *if these two are trying to pull something, they're good . . . damned good. Marie in there, precisely at the time he comes to check the cyborg, and Arthur's face ashen with a look of fear.*

"Arthur," Leo said to him, "what's this all about?"

"Talk to her, Leo, before there's another tremor, or a quake."

"Just a little land settling beneath us, Arthur. Now, show me what you have on this defective cyborg. Then we'll get Marie the hell out of there."

Arthur's color began to return. "Yes, Leo, whatever you say." He rushed to the computer for information on the defective cyborg, information that had been inconclusive and useless. But if it would speed things . . .

Marie noticed the activity outside and realized with rising excitement that Leo was gazing at her with renewed respect. He got on the communicator and gently asked what stage of preparation she was at.

"Almost completed, only a few minutes now, Leo," she replied. "Let me finish."

"Of course, Marie, but you must know how terribly concerned Arthur and I are for you."

She smiled behind the visor but he could not see it.

Then there was an enormous shaking.

The acrylic glass between them shimmied in and out

between the black steel supports. The countertop vibrated. Manfred shook. Marie felt the force swim through her suit like an eel had been let loose inside her every organ. She caught sight of Arthur shouting, pounding against the console as he lost his footing and fell. Leo was holding tight to a table, but it bobbed and shook with him.

Concrete explosions began at the walls, loud enough for Marie to hear. Steel girders groaned like dying men.

Both Leo and Arthur were gone, disappeared, perhaps pinned to the floor, perhaps crushed beneath the heavy equipment, perhaps dead. Marie felt she was alone, truly alone.

She felt trapped inside the suit, inside the chamber that might be her only hope of survival. But she would only survive if there were someone left alive outside to get her out.

She screamed for Arthur, trying to get a response. She screamed for Leo.

The rupture of the concrete floor outside the chamber was her only answer, pushing up boulders that slammed against the acrylic glass which, so far, held.

Then she saw the ripple of a small crack move across the interior of the chamber floor like a lightning bolt and she knew the chamber was already being infiltrated by air and bacteria that was combining with the virulent material on the countertop. She saw a stream of smoky air spurting in through a seam between the acrylic glass and the steel girder over her head. The crack on the floor ruptured wide, Manfred tilting over into it. The deadly new life form on the counter jumped up and down like a child's wind-up toy, reaching to the edge and striking the floor as Marie screamed for help.

Only the noises of destruction answered. The ceiling falling, walls caving in, the floor bursting. There was nowhere to hide, no place to run. She backed into a

corner of the chamber, cringing, already seeing that the
bright yellow of her suit was turning crimson, saffron,
brown, that it was being eaten away by the virus which
was trying desperately to get at her.

In a blur of time and fear she saw movement amid the
smoke outside the chamber. It was Arthur, his forehead
gashed and bleeding, his face white, fists pounding at the
chamber's controls. But all was blotted out when an
enormous weight of concrete and steel came down, a
girder slashing diagonally through the top of the chamber and splintering the acrylic walls into shattered
pieces.

Through the enormous hole Arthur came for her, but
she could no longer see him. She called out to him, but
had lost the ability to say his name or anything else
clearly, the speech centers in her brain already affected
by the new strain of the virus the accident had created.
All around her a thick cloud arose as the olive brown
liquid on the floor turned to gas which eventually
enveloped her. The last thing she saw before passing out
was Manfred's single claw sticking from out of the
ground where the cyborg was buried.

Outside the chamber, Arthur had stopped Leo in his
frantic attempt to get to the elevator. Arthur knew his
escape would take the deadly virus out with him. He
had used a chair to send Leo crashing to the floor, and
he tore the key-card from his hand. Now his full
attention was on Marie. He couldn't see her through the
blackened, smoldering outer skin of the suit. He rushed
to where the second suit should be, but found it trapped
below a pile of rubble where the wall had come down.

When he returned to Marie, he had already realized
that they were all going to die here, buried with their
awful secret. He was resolved to accept this now, and he
climbed through the broken glass toward Marie, who
had suddenly stopped screaming and calling out his

name in her pitifully twisted speech. He knew he had only moments before the virus invaded his own mind, cutting off his senses, feeding on him.

All that was left was to be with Marie at the end.

Suddenly, an awful cry of indescribable pain escaped from Marie, deep in the chamber. Her death agonies.

Arthur stumbled forward, crawling on hands and knees as rock and concrete continued to rain down like the last parting shots of the gods. He went below the worst of the thick, amorphous cloud inside the chamber. Somewhere behind him, he heard Leo cursing his name, then pleading for the key-card.

Leo stopped cold before the chamber, however. The noises coming from inside sent a chill along his spinal cord.

"Aaaaawwwwwgggggggaaaaaashtc! Wwwwwaaaaaallll! Kkkooonnntz!" Could that be Marie? Arthur?

Leo pulled the scalpel from his breast pocket and, against all reason, rushed into the chamber and found Arthur's ankle, pulling him back. "Where's the key-card? The key-card! I'll cut your throat!"

Arthur laughed as if he were retarded. His skin was a dull copper, circles of brown linking before Leo's eyes.

"Wook-at-your-own-face, Leo," he said like an idiot. "Your-hands."

Leo was holding the scalpel to Arthur's throat, and he saw clearly that his own hand was showered with the brown lesions. Leo let go of Arthur, staring, unbelieving, as the awful sulfuric odor assailed his nostrils. Finally, he was gripped with the utter hopelessness of his plight.

"Butter-use-this-on-my-self," Leo said, staring at the scalpel, aware that his own speech centers were now being affected. Just thinking of how to point the damned thing was a chore, now that the controls from brain to

hand were almost as severed as those from brain to
tongue. Inside his head he felt electrical charges of light,
as if so many loose wires were sputtering sparks.

Horror-stricken, his eyes registered Arthur holding
Marie's blackened carcass in his arms. Leo slowly
turned the scalpel toward himself, but his grip was
weak, uncontrollable. The killer he had financed into
the world was killing him quickly, softly, turning him
into a human slug. Soon he wouldn't have control of his
backbone, his arms or legs. Squeaks, rattles, and sucking
noises escaped from Leo as if he were an infant,
incapable of any but the most primitive sounds. Then his
bowels emptied themselves of their own accord. In front
of him he heard Arthur and Marie carrying on a
conversation that sounded like so many rats feeding,
bubbling and gooing over a favorite prey.

Leo tried to tighten his grip on the scalpel but failed.
He tried to concentrate, perspiration beading his forehead, until the effort made him cry. Then he collapsed,
his legs giving out. He was only sorry he hadn't fallen on
the scalpel. Instead, it skittered to within inches of
Arthur.

Arthur had propped Marie in his lap, turning her to
face him, and gasped for breath when her still helmeted
head turned, unprepared for what he saw. The visor had
literally been grafted onto her face, as had much of the
suit against her limbs and body. She looked like the
victim of an atomic blast.

Marie's body jerked with spasms, making him hold
tighter. Her head jerked to face him and her eyes, which
had rolled back in their sockets, dropped back like
blood red cherries in a slot machine. Marie's mouth was
twisted in a tight snarl of tortured pain, the lips ripped
over the gums in a paralytic seizure. Her skin was the
color of ox-blood; hundreds of circular lesions had
combined to color her complexion. The lesions swelled

and contracted, up and down, as if there were ring-worms below the skin, slithering about.

Arthur had witnessed her transformation into a help-less, grotesque caricature of herself, a spineless doll in his arms, but he had hoped that deep inside the visor he would find her face. Arthur busied himself before the inevitable end by plucking away dangling parts of the suit she wore and trying to force off the helmet, his eyes blinded by smoke and tears.

"The scowlpel, Arrrrthhhoorr," said Leo.

Arthur looked to where the helpless man pointed. For the first time he realized he had the capability of ending Marie's torture at his fingertips. "Ya," he agreed with Leo. "Fer Maaaarieee."

"Keeeel me furst!" pleaded Leo.

Arthur strained for the scalpel, within easy reach of a man with all his senses, but Arthur's were as poorly lacking as Leo's, perhaps worse. He could not rely on his backbone and his legs were completely dead. He stretched uncooperative fingers toward the scalpel and felt a rush when his fingers wrapped about it and brought it up and over Marie.

"Doooo it!" Leo kept shouting. "Then doooo meeeee, pleeeease."

Arthur's own incapacity was causing him great pain, his mind still trying to understand the situation while his hand tried to grip the scalpel properly. He could not feel the nasty gash on his forehead any longer, as if it were anesthetized. But an insufferable, poisonous pain leaked steadily into his inner organs like acid. At times the pain gripped his abdomen with such force he felt he was in the grip of a powerful forklift. It made no sense; the outer extremities felt nothing, the senses severed at the source, but he was experiencing such excruciating pain from within. He had not wanted it to be this way. He had been aiming for a virus that would shut down the mind then shut down the body. A momentary question fought through the haze of his mind. Had Marie used the *cannibal* virus when he had expressly forbidden it?

No matter now . . .

He brought the scalpel down but it didn't penetrate the thick layer of the suit. He hadn't the strength to force it hard enough.

Arthur fought to rip back the helmet and he managed to pull away the top portion. He could stab through this way, put his wife out of her agony. He worked to the sounds of Leo's gibberish, attempts at curses and threats.

"Arrrrrfaaaaa?" Marie groaned.

Her nearly calling his name made him look into her seared eyes. They didn't seem to be eyes at all anymore, and Arthur vaguely wondered if she were even more grotesque than she appeared to his fevered senses. The lump of flesh in his arms seemed to be something other than a human being.

"Doooo ittttt," he told himself, but to firmly hold the scalpel and penetrate the blackened skull in his arms, might be more easily accomplished by an Alzheimer's patient. He realized his only hope was to somehow put the force of his own weight behind the knife. Then, somehow, he must attempt to turn it on himself.

Leo was slithering toward him, wormlike, his face grotesque, a mask of hatred and the disease. He was beyond reach but moving closer.

Arthur realized he had time for only one action, that only one of them could escape this torture chamber by way of a quick death. Perhaps he should use the scalpel on himself, now and quickly. Marie was all but gone, her suffering nearly over. Don't be a fool, he told himself. The scalpel would be wasted on her and he would have to live the agonizing death she had just gone through. Time was already lost on her. His love had *always* been lost on her. Was his pity lost on her as well?

Outside the chamber and overhead, the combined weight of tons of debris from the forty-odd stories overhead effectively decided the matter for Arthur, sending down a rain of stone, glass, girders and asphalt. Leo, Arthur, and Marie were buried with the secret they had all so briefly shared.

two

Michael McCain had just begun a final cup of coffee; his thoughts were on Casey Sterns. Slowly, a tiny rattle of cups all over the Hilton Hotel's breakfast terrace began an eerie symphony. Next, tables wobbled and pictures on walls trembled, then fell. Plate glass windows pulsated, and the pitch of all the noises, combined with the shockwaves running through his body, convinced McCain to drop to the floor only moments before the windows all around exploded.

On his stomach, Mike felt the tremble of the earth rising as if an enormous bubble were trapped below it. He felt as if he were at the center of the disturbance, as if the coming quake was directed specifically at him. But he fought this irrational fear, concentrating on Casey Sterns instead, who had left him only moments before and was probably on the street, standing between monolithic glass and steel mountains about to crush her.

"Casey . . ." he gasped, getting to his feet and crawling through a shattered window. Looking left and right, he opted for the direction of the CCDC where she had likely left her car.

Mike's cheek had been slashed by a shard of glass, and his navy blue suit was dusted with asphalt particles the moment he entered the smoke-filled street. Blocks of concrete were dropping from the building next to the Hilton, as if the structure was shedding its skin. The building was going limp, melting as if in a Dali painting. Steel reinforced concrete walls, rising skyward, were warping, bending, curving. Mike and a group of others raced to escape the shimmy-dancing skyscraper, which was now threatening to topple the Hilton, sending enormous slabs of concrete through its windows. The creaking sounds of stress on the girders seemed amplified by speakers. It was a sound like no other he had ever experienced.

As he ran, he heard the groaning become a roar, as if the building was being demolished by experts. Its collapse sent up a choking, dense smoke cloud of asphalt fumes that enveloped Mike, dusting him gray-white.

He continued to race through the chaos in search of Casey, focusing on a single mission amid the horror. He'd traveled only half a block, but it was through a dungeons-and-dragons landscape where the least mistake was fatal. Metal lampposts rose, toppled and fell toward him like giant, venomous snakes. Fire hydrants ripped apart, spewing forth water. Telephone poles turned and twisted like enormous ball bats, snapping electrical wires which fell across cars, buses, and corpses, fire-spitting at their frayed ends.

No place was safe. Buildings rained glass and stone around him, as one huge block of murderous concrete exploded into hundreds of ricocheting, deadly pieces, one stabbing and numbing his leg, while another fragment of shrapnel sliced a deep cut across his chest, cutting through his suit coat and shirt like a razor. Below him the street waved as if it had turned to liquid, and there was a big ripple coming at him. He dodged to his left and saw an underground gas line rupture into a flaming geyser where he had stood a moment before.

It was as if the city were committing suicide and wanted to see everything human die with it.

Filled with terror and panic, people ran mindlessly, some right into the path of the falling debris. Mike saw men and women crushed as if they were insects, and he knew he may well be next. He was only holding himself together, fighting back the overwhelming fear and helplessness, by searching for Casey. He refused to believe she was beyond help.

Then he saw her through the asphalt dust that had so obscured his vision, stinging his eyes and lungs. Casey stood in a group of people at the revolving doors to the Copellmier Center, trying desperately to get the doors moving. She was urging the others to remain calm, while trying to evacuate the patients from the center. Overhead, the terrible groans of stress from the complaining building grew louder. Mike recognized the sounds only too well.

"Casey! Casey!" he shouted, rushing toward her. A tide of people swept against Mike, pushing, falling, frantic to get away, the CCDC bombarding them with icicle shards of glass and concrete. Mike saw an entire group fall facedown, all instantly killed by a burst of shrapnel.

Perhaps fifty yards separated him from Casey, who remained near the doorway, shouting orders, until they all saw the concrete plaza and steps in front of them suddenly buckle and lift. Stone spewed everywhere, leaving the plaza looking like a field of toppled headstones. Mike saw Casey fall, hit by a small chunk of concrete. She was laying at the foot of the building, which was dangerously close to collapsing. He climbed over jutting stones, determined to reach her, and leaped over gaping pits like open jaws from some earth monster trying to swallow him whole.

He finally reached her, and took her in his arms. She was only semi-conscious. He looked in every direction

for an escape route, but could see none. Then his eyes
followed a group of escapees from the CCDC, who were
fleeing out another set of doors. Lifting Casey, he joined
this crowd, praying against all odds they might possibly
survive.

Mike saw the crowd was moving in the direction of an
excavation site nearby. Hundreds had already found
momentary protection behind corrugated metal fences
that defined the site. Others cringed behind heavy
machinery.

It could be a trap, Mike told himself. *But it may be
our only chance.*

Just then the entire CCDC imploded, creating a force
that sent Mike and Casey falling into the excavation site
on top of the others. The entire medical complex
stacked down on itself, each floor a waffle of useless
material falling atop another. The collapse sent up a
dark mushroom cloud of thick dust, the cloud rising to
where Leo Copellmier's suite had been only moments
before.

The noise was deafening. Over the roar of falling
skyscrapers, however, could be heard a human wail, a
terrible torrent of voices betraying distress, fear, sadness
and loss. More screams signaled the fall of yet another
building, this one opposite the end of the excavation site
where Mike lay draped over Casey in a desperate
attempt to protect her. Girders, concrete, flying rubble
smashed into a crane, sending the huge machine toppling, trapping and crushing people beneath it.

Mike tightened his grip on Casey who shuddered
beneath him. He felt like a frightened child amid a
horrible war, conscious of every breath, every heartbeat,
believing each his last. More hysterical screams came
from nearby. The far end of the excavation site and all
the people who had huddled there were buried in
another mountain of rubble.

Then there was silence . . . broken by the horrible

human cries, the tortured wailing of human beings
reduced to the most primitive level of grief.

Everyone was suddenly mourning for dead, the dying,
and themselves. For most survivors were left with eyes
to see the carnage, with minds forced to assimilate it.

Mike sensed that Casey, although injured, was going
to be all right. She was safe, but she remained shivering
in a fetal position of hiding beneath him. He could
somehow smell the perfume in her hair, and he touched
her blond locks gently, as he had wanted to do in the
restaurant. He'd like nothing more than to bury himself
in her hair, to hide along with her, but instead he called
her name, softly, trying to draw a response from her.

"Casey? Dr. Sterns? You all right? It's over."

The quake had seemed to last at least a half-hour, but
when Mike looked at his watch, he realized it must have
come and gone in just under two minutes.

"I'm . . . I'm all right," she said at last, slowly rousing.

"I don't think so. You have a pretty deep cut on your
forehead."

She touched a dirty, asphalt hand to the blood and
looked at the red stain on her fingertips. "Didn't feel a
thing. Is it really . . . over?"

"Has to be." Mike's response was as much a prayer as
a statement. He tried to guide Casey to her feet and up
toward street level, to avert her eyes from the other side
of the excavation site where arms, legs, and torsos were
half buried in the killing debris. But Casey caught a
glimpse of the nearby devastation and covered her face
in Mike's chest.

"Come on, Case," he said softly, guiding her by the
arm.

What remained of the CCDC was a mountain of
trash, a monument of concrete blocks the size of tract
houses, huge steel girders twisted in, out and through
the blocks like enormous straws. Smashed cars had slid

off in every direction from the climbing parking garage. One area was draped with scattered, dangling surgical gowns and bedsheets torn and discolored, decorating the awful trash heap as if tossed there as a nasty afterthought. Pipes and plumbing spewed water over the garbage dump, where even the most common objects were no longer quite recognizable.

"You . . . you saved my life, Mike," Casey said, as they both stared at what was left of the building.

"I rushed out after you the moment I realized you were out here . . . then I saw what you were trying to do . . . knew you were in danger."

"All . . . those lives," she said, her voice cracking, her strength waning as she stared at the devastation. "Helpless children in their sickbeds, doctors, nurses . . ."

They held onto one another for a moment, and stared at the scenes all around them. Downtown L.A. looked like a war-torn landscape. Buildings were down everywhere, which meant hundreds of thousands of trapped people, dead or dying. The survivors were wailing, crying or muttering, walking about aimlessly, their sensibilities shattered. Buses, trucks, and cars were overturned or crushed. From far away, Mike heard sirens rushing toward the giant gravesite. Atop the heaps of rubble, some men worked with bare hands, straining at immovable objects, cutting the flesh from their own hands in a mad, defiant act. Others cried for help at the top of their lungs, trying to reach a loved one who was surely beyond help. Some were severely injured, but unaware of their terrible wounds, having given in to shock.

"We're going to need every doctor in the city," said Casey, who was overcoming her shivers and tears.

Mike stared at her, and saw the fight in her eyes. "That's right, we will."

"The excavation site is the best open clearing. It could make a perfect emergency station. Help me organize this; we should get started at once. We'll need tents, surgical supplies, blood, plasma, lights, tables—"

"Set up an emergency *triage,* sure, but we'll need ambulance assistance, communications equipment . . ."

"Food, hot liquids . . ." Casey broke off from the list. "We . . . we would've been inside, Mike, if you hadn't held our meeting at the hotel."

"I'll get the help we need to set up here," he assured her. "But first you should have that cut looked at." He touched her cheek, and looked deep into her eyes.

"I'm okay, really." Something caught Casey's eye, and she looked up. She rushed toward an ambulance that weaved in and out of the debris, lights flashing, looking hopeless against the carnage. But Casey was right; with the proper use of the facilities connected with hospitals still remaining intact, they might establish a useful front line against the effects of the destruction.

Mike rushed after her, feeling some little comfort in the idea of taking action against the effects of the quake. He still felt guilty that his first thought at seeing the center destroyed was that he had lost the most exciting opportunity of his career. Overshadowing all his feelings, however, was a fascination for this strong, caring, lovely woman he had found.

It was a hell of a story. The biggest in L.A., all of California, the entire nation, and Tony Qunin knew that such a disaster built careers as easily as it destroyed them. Tony was a large man, so tall he drew stares, and his features were subdued yet exotic. His skin was coppery and sleek, his complexion clear beneath the teasing, dark Oriental eyes and thick, natty Spanish curls. He was the son of a Japanese father and a Mexican mother, who had both died when he was very young. Much of his life had been spent in foster homes, and as a boy he had learned that through words he could gain power, build his own identity, even achieve fame.

But for much of his adult life, Tony Qunin had bitterly maintained that TV newsmen in America had to be—or at least appear to be—white middle-class Americans. The few ethnic reporters on the tube that made it to anchor news desks were of the "acceptable" white-type; they spoke, acted and presented a white manner. But lately, much to Tony's surprise, real minority people were "in," and Tony was riding the crest of the wave for as long as it lasted, for as far as it would take him.

He had long lived with the fact that 3-CTV news executives believed his dark features could only hamper any rise to television popularity in L.A. But now, perhaps it was *because* of his unequivocal plan to be himself on camera that he was fast becoming the Number One newsman in the city. He was L.A.'s hottest rising star in the youngest and fastest growing television news team the city had ever seen. The station had undoubtedly taken a great risk with Tony, but now, as the popularity grew, so did his Tony Danza smile and his belief that it was due to his own determination and hard work.

It was true. Tony worked harder. He was driven by fear, fear of failure and a return to his beginnings. For this reason he was on the street minutes after the quake, forcing his camera crew to get shots of everything possible. The battered van they rode in carried a concrete slab across the hood, riding piggyback as they weaved from side to side, attempting to follow the ambulance that neared what was left of the CCDC. Tony was determined to be at the center of the action, wherever it took him. When he saw the ambulance turn in and Casey Sterns, followed by Mike McCain, flag it down, he wanted to know only how they fit into the story.

Members of Tony's crew were in a mutinous mood,
deeply concerned about family and loved ones. Jose
Ortiz, his only true friend among them and driver of the
van, turned to speak to Tony. The crew had already
filmed enough footage for a week's worth of news time,
and still Tony wanted more. Jose had taken their lives in
his hands, weaving around disabled buses, overturned
trucks and cars, narrowly avoiding rubble of all description that lay in sprawling piles. The 3-CTV van had cut
through parks and down sidewalks where necessary.
Ortiz knew every alternate route in the city he had loved
since childhood.

Jose Ortiz was almost as tall as Tony and twice as
bulky, but his voice was soft when he spoke. "You got
no family, Tony, 'cept for me. They all got family,
Tony." He indicated the other two men, who were
anxious to leave. "Let me take them to their homes, and
I'll come straight back."

Tony frowned, but didn't allow the others to see it, at
first muttering his reply to Jose and then shouting to the
two men crouched in the rear of the van. "All right, you
guys! Jose's going to run you home, then. When you see
everything's all right, come back. Foley's probably
getting more stuff from the sky than we can from here
anyway. Let me try one last time to get him."

Tony went to the radio and clicked it on. "Foley!
Foley! Air-3, do you copy?" Tony tried again and again
to raise Carl Foley, the 3-CTV copter pilot. "Still no
answer."

"I don't like it," replied Jose, his big, pudgy face
creased with worry. "I mean, we can't get Davis at the
station and we can't get Foley."

"Christ, Tony," interrupted Dave Thomas, the youngest member of the team. "What about our families? We
shouldn't be here, we should be with them."

Tony looked at the kid, betraying no emotion. "In a
minute."

There had been only static and silence from CTV headquarters. Qunin looked into Ortiz's eyes. Ortiz took a deep breath. "You don't think . . ." Ortiz began.

"You usually know what I think."

"Could be the radio is just knocked out."

"Could be," Tony replied. He sounded unconvinced.

For the first time Tony considered the possibility that Channel 3 News and the Continental Building were no longer there and that perhaps the chopper was also not out there. The dead air on the radio seemed to confirm his fear. He wanted to curse. Maybe the quake had ended his own career.

"We need this van!" Someone had shouted at him, and he looked out a window to face Michael McCain. "I'm a doctor. We're going to require every vehicle we can get until we can get emergency help."

"Wait a minute," Tony began, but Casey Sterns rushed up behind Mike and pleaded for the van as well, causing Tony to look at the other men and at Ortiz.

"You're just after a story," said Mike, angry at Tony's hesitation. "We're asking for help to save lives."

"All right, all right," Tony agreed, "empty our equipment. You guys'll have to find other transportation to look in on your families. Meantime, I'm sticking to this area."

From all appearances, as the TV crew had neared Downtown L.A., the real devastation was in the heart of the business district. Tony's mind raced with questions. How extensive was the damage? Was it confined to the massive hotel district and convention sites flanked by the Santa Monica Harbor and Hollywood freeways? The chopper was the only way to be certain of the extent of the destruction, and Foley appeared grounded, if not dead.

"We need you to ambulance the injured away," Mike said to Jose. "Will you do it?"

Jose looked to Tony before replying, "Yes, sure."

Tony had grabbed up a mini-cam and began the work he knew best, allowing the others to do as they wished for now. Some people were working to put out burning buildings, while others were working to free trapped victims inside what was left of battered cars.

All around Tony people walked about with blood-stained arms, legs, and foreheads. Tony felt a wave of purposelessness come over him, as if mesmerized by a disease transmitted by the others. Perhaps he was simply hypnotized by the awful extent of the carnage, the crushed, exposed limbs, the wounded people being herded into common waiting areas. Whatever the reason, the result was to drift, a detached sensation. Perhaps it was the only way he could deal with what his eyes were registering.

Tony saw a woman holding onto the remains of a child in her arms, her eyes glassy, terror-struck. He saw men on their knees, tears freely flowing, hands tearing at rubble until they became bleeding stumps. He found children searching for parents, one black-haired urchin clinging to him as if he were her father. Through a great distance, he realized he held the camera at his side.

Qunin, dazed, the lost child holding his hand, found himself back at the van. It was now being loaded with injured, moaning victims, and was about to take off for the nearest hospital. McCain was using the radio, shouting over the general noise of the firefighters, the sirens and the screaming all around.

"Downtown L.A. hit the hardest," McCain was saying. "Estimate loss of life in excess of . . ." he paused, unable to believe his own words. "Of thirty, perhaps forty thousand. We need all emergency help we can get. I'm Dr. Michael McCain and will be headquartered at the remains of the Copellmier Center for Disease Control."

Casey, seeing the child clinging to Tony's leg, took her aside for treatment, placing an arm around her shoulders, speaking gently to her. Tony saw the makeshift tent hospital taking shape in the sunken excavation site which had suffered less damage than the surrounding area. He realized for the first time that the real story was staring him in the face, and it was not a story of despair, destruction, corruption or crime. This was a story of heroes.

For most of the rest of his day Tony watched Doctors Casey Sterns and Michael McCain work tirelessly to organize their "resistance" to the quake's aftermath, to help people amid the death and disorder. At the emergency site they put to work every available doctor, nurse, and paramedic they could collar to deal with the trauma victims and the wounded, to save as many lives as possible. Wherever he could be of help, Tony pitched in.

At one point, between the ambulance runs which Jose Ortiz was making for the doctors, Jose came to Tony and asked in a conspiratorial tone, "What's up, Tony? Why're you still here? I see something cooking behind your eyes. What is it?"

"Need more shots of the doctors, maybe a few interviews."

"Then what?"

"Maybe get out to LAX. Get a flight to Nevada so the film in the cans can spread the news for us . . . maybe get our doctor's back here some real, high-powered help, like the federal government, right?"

Ortiz was skeptical. "Suppose L.A. International's as hard hit as downtown? Suppose you can't get a flight out?"

"Then we take a Piper Cub out of Hollywood-Burbank. We find a way . . . before the wire services have the story on the CCDC. This is big, man. That building was supposed to be built quake-resistant, you know that?"

"Oh, I see . . . still out to fry Leo Copellmier's ass?"

Tony hadn't given the prestigious Dr. Leo Copellmier a thought in over a month, having quietly given up on ever "frying his ass," but now this sounded like a new possibility. He'd been given a tip about the cost-cutting measures Copellmier had taken when building the CCDC. The latest in quake-resistant construction now appeared to have been sacrificed as one of his economical measures. Finally, after so long investigating the curious Dr. Copellmier, a misstep of major importance had come to light, one that could send him where he belonged.

Just then a sudden rumbling began without warning, the earth beneath the decimated streets quivering, rising to a terrifying shiver, reminding everyone of the power below the ground. The awful aftershock toppled loose some dangling debris around the perimeters of the rescue center. Then it was over.

nightfall

As things turned out, Tony Qunin found himself in the center of activity, since rescue teams rushed to the CCDC, finding it central to their needs as well. And now Tony was seeing firsthand footage of how the rescuers actually did their death-defying work, as his eyes followed the slow, laborious efforts of the men who called themselves "moles." He watched intently as they tunneled hundreds of feet below the rubble. The two men he was tracking via the monitor at the rescue headquarters were being filmed by an especially small borehole camera mounted on a cable the men carried down with them. Tony was in the enviable position of being able to acquire, for the right price, the exclusive rights to the film, a film that portrayed the movements of a couple of heroes whose story eclipsed Tony's earlier heroic tale of the doctors. One of the new heroes was a Mexican; a small but spunky, brave man named Raphael Naldosa.

Naldosa had earlier rescued a small number of women and children. Qunin had gotten exceptional footage on Naldosa and his partner to the affiliate station in Nevada via a cub plane, paying the pilot with what was left of his bank account and Visa card. One way or another, he promised himself, 3-CTV was going to be involved, even though the chopper and the building housing the station were destroyed, as Jose had reported. It would be Tony's parting shot.

The small *borehole,* a miniature television camera that looked like a snake's head at the end of its five-hundred-foot cable, followed the men who poked through the ruins of the CCDC. The building had housed several thousand patients as well as doctors, nurses and staff, and one particular area was singled out because, if the architect's plans could be believed, the pediatric and geriatric centers ought logically to be located there. Of course, what seemed logical from the surface was an altogether different matter down here.

Ahead of the camera were two moles, as the rescue experts were known. On his hardhat, Raphael Alonzo Naldosa wore a tensor light that penetrated the darkness like a laser in whatever direction he chose to look. Just behind him, his friend and partner, Bjorn Amunsen, also directed a beam from his forehead. Naldosa and Amunsen had worked together before, in Bogata, San Salvador, and in Mexico, where Naldosa got his start. That quake had claimed his own family.

They were at the end of the remote camera's five-hundred-foot cable. The two had penetrated in zigzag fashion down into the mountain of debris, their meandering direction dictated by what those aboveground thought right. They reinforced the walls of debris as they went. Over their faces they wore polyester masks equipped with filters, in order to breathe in the asphalt-choked atmosphere. Every movement sprinkled them with more. Sometimes touching what appeared to be a solid object caused a new groan, always a threatening sound. Sometimes the sounds came not from overhead, but below their feet, where they twisted and crawled over shifting, sharply angled "fallout."

Naldosa said something in Spanish that sounded like a curse. Amunsen irritably replied, "Speak English, Naldo."

"I said this is like walking over the back of the Devil."

"Ahhh, yeah, so comforting."

The men carried one handheld radio between them, which dangled from Naldosa's belt. Although the moles checked in frequently, there had been nothing useful to report for nearly an hour.

Wherever their small beams shone, they saw nothing but another dead end, another stone wall laced with steel. Patiently, they found a new direction which took them crashing through the remains of a cardboardlike sheetrock wall, which was not really a wall, but a floor. They had climbed through holes bored in solid doors, even through metal cabinets. Sections of the tunnel were dotted with desks trapped on all sides, as well as adding machines, copiers, X-ray display panels, telephones, lamps, books, carpeting, tables, and chairs. Crammed into the compacted space they saw paneling, pipes, typewriters, and the always shocking and all too frequent twisted torso, half-buried in the debris. Worst of all, however, were severed body parts, trapped in the walls as the desks had been.

Naldosa had been unable to forget the stomach-turning work earlier that day, when he and Amunsen had had to cut the body of a dead man in half to get to a nurse and six infants, who had miraculously survived.

To have taken time to dig around him could have cost seven lives.

Naldosa held a specially designed, lightweight, hand-held jackhammer. With it the moles dug their tunnels.

He lay prone now, on his stomach, the jackhammer straight ahead, biting and roaring at the concrete blocking his way. As he worked his thoughts returned to the dark-haired nurse and the six *niños* he had helped return to the world. He and Amunsen had sweated for hours in the darkness before they could even hear the woman's cry for help. Naldosa had been the first to hear the woman and to establish communication by a series of knocks. He had told her not to speak or move, since it could bring down more killing debris atop her and the infants. He had feared they would be strangled by the dust.

When the first of the infants came up into Naldosa's protective hug, when he finally got the child into daylight and air, it began to kick and wail as if reborn. When the news got out that seven lives would be saved, everyone cheered.

Once the children and the nurse were freed, Naldosa was cornered by a newsman, who filmed his replies to questions he could not now recall. He had been so nervous it had almost made him ill. All he remembered was the newsman himself, the darkest-skinned Mexican he had ever seen, a man named Tony something or other who had filmed the rescue from beginning to end.

But Naldosa didn't care about the cheers or the TV interview. What mattered was that the children and the nurse were safe now, and resting comfortably. Naldosa's reward would come later, when he would visit them in the hospital.

Right now, a concrete slab was falling in front of him, dusting his thick, black-and-gray mustache, and revealing a glimpse of something red, a sign of some sort. He made out the letter A, then cleared off another section to reveal a large D. In a moment he deciphered the word DANGER, and he let out a tired laugh.

"I don't think the sign worked," he told Amunsen, pointing toward it with his light.

"Maybe it's meant for us, pal. Don't know about you, but I'm exhausted. Must be past midnight."

Naldosa was tired, too, his eyelids dropping and his hands numb from the jackhammer, but he didn't want to quit now, after going so long without a rescue.

"Should have gone with our instincts, my friend," Naldosa replied, and kicked back at the camera eye as if it were a snake about to bite him. "They sent us in the wrong direction. No one's trapped down here."

"Can't blame yourself, Naldo. When you said go right, they said left, and when you said left, they said right. Boys upstairs got the blueprints . . . they're calling the shots."

Naldosa didn't want to give up. He didn't want to find a cot and fall asleep while someone down here, buried alive, was fighting for one last breath. The lucky ones were like the nurse and the infants, but the next luckiest were those instantly killed. Naldosa's worst nightmare was to be buried alive.

"Come on, Naldo, let's hang it up for a while." Amunsen tugged at him from behind.

But Naldosa's ears pricked at a sound just ahead, a moan. Human, he believed.

"Uoo-uuuuuu, wwaaaaaa . . ." it came again.

"Hear that?"

"Just a creaking noise."

"No, no, listen." He flicked on the radio and asked if they were picking up any sounds upstairs.

"None," replied the technician manning the borehole camera from above.

Naldosa held a gloved finger up to Amunsen and listened for a moment. When he heard nothing, he called out. "Hello, *amigo!* Anyone!" He could not give up. Suppose someone were only a few feet away, through the next wall, perhaps only half-conscious from loss of blood or shock? Perhaps unable to answer, or to coherently understand Naldosa's own plea.

"I'm going to keep digging," he told Amunsen.

"But Naldo!"

"What?"

Amunsen's voice soothed suddenly; he understood his partner only too well. "Carefully, okay? Go easy."

Naldosa pumped the jackhammer ahead, *rat-tat-tat* and stop, *rat-tat-tat* and stop.

"Easier, Naldo," warned Amunsen. His job was to build supports and reinforcement around them as they tunneled ahead, and to be an extra pair of eyes for Naldosa. At the moment, too much debris was crumbling around them for his liking.

"We've got somebody here," Naldo was saying over the noise of the jackhammer. "I know it, I can feel it."

But all Amunsen knew was that debris was shifting dangerously overhead, about to collapse on Naldosa. In a sudden lunge, he grabbed both of Naldosa's ankles and tugged viciously moments before the wall in front of him collapsed, sending down iron girders and shattering concrete.

Naldosa didn't know what happened as he was pulled past his partner, but he saw Amunsen ahead of him, suddenly and inexplicably being sucked into a hole. Head first, Bjorn went deeper and deeper into the falling rubble, snagged at one point as if caught on a nail, but then ripped forward, his left arm dangling behind. In the next split second Naldosa saw an enormous pair of dark claws clamp over the bigger man's neck and shoulders. Moments before falling debris buried Amunsen and the claws, Naldosa saw two burning, red eyes against a deformed, blackened face.

Was it illusion? A horrible waking nightmare?

He had seen it and heard its keening noises . . .

. . . he saw it again and again in the recurring, fitful sleep forced on him by a blow taken to the head . . .

. . . he saw himself in the black hole, unconscious, surrounded on all sides . . .

. . . trapped by the collapsed floors, buried . . . buried alive . . .

. . . his worst fear . . .

. . . but there was a worse fear yet . . .

. . . something in the rubble that slithered toward him . . .

. . . something that mimicked human cries in order to lure him and Amunsen here . . .

. . . something scratching at the debris on all sides of him, trying desperately to get at him as it had Amunsen . . .

. . . something that fed on the trapped, on the dying, on the already dead.

three

Lights flooded Dodger Stadium. Vans, ambulances, and a series of Army and Navy helicopters of all sizes came and went, dumping body bags, tons of ice, blankets, tents, clothing, and food. Volunteers arrived from around the country and overseas.

Among the vehicles was the 3-CTV news van, its cargo yet another grotesque collection of corpses, hardly recognizable as such. Jose Ortiz was still working for the doctors rather than for Tony Qunin, but Jose had told Tony of the activity at Dodger Stadium. The newsman was especially glad to hear about the helicopters, some shuttling between Nevada and L.A., bringing in their precious cargoes. Tony had a lot of film to get to Nevada fast, and this seemed the ideal chance to thumb a ride.

Jose and Tony watched a huge craft descending now, large white numbers against its blue sides, a version of the U.S. CH-54A which had seen so much action in Vietnam, capable of carrying loads of up to ten tons. The cargo bay was gone, replaced by dangling, powerful cables on a block and tackle. At the end of the cables was a huge backhoe. From where they stood, it looked like a prehistoric bird with its prey flailing at the end of its talons. The power-driven rotors above the fuselage roared as the propeller slowed, the machine completing its vertical descent, creating a sandstorm in the infield. The outfield was already filling to capacity with row upon row of bodies claimed by the quake.

The grisly business left to the living filled Tony's mind with black thoughts.

> *Take me out to the ballgame.*
> *Take me out to the crowd.*
> *Buy me some peanuts and Cracker Jacks,*
> *I don't care if I never get back.*

Ortiz had caught himself whistling the tune when he had been riding toward the stadium, the dead stacked like two-by-fours behind him, on his sixth ghastly shuttle ride. But nobody was singing on the way to the park tonight.

Jose had also made the mistake of asking someone what all the dry ice was for. Like many volunteers in the park, he was not used to dealing with the dead.

With Tony accompanying him in the van on this latest run, Jose opened up to Tony, telling him of the scenes at the ballpark. He grew angrier as he did so. "I don't like seeing my ballpark turned into the largest morgue in history," he said. "So much death, Tony . . . so *sense-less.*"

"I understand, really, Jose . . . really." Tony knew his friend was deeply affected, and tried to calm him.

"Going to shoot the hell out of the season, huh?" Jose said, attempting a joke, but after it was said, neither man found it funny.

"You okay, Jose?"

"Funny thing, Tony, I'm feeling better now, but, you know, *not* feeling anymore . . . not like at first. Thought I was going to vomit the first run out here. Keep thinking now, I should be feeling just as much, just as bad. Now, it's like I'm just delivering . . . *things.*"

"You're doing real good, *amigo*, real good. There're plenty enough sick and injured. You, you're contributing, doing what you can to help."

That made Jose feel a little better; Tony could see it in his face, his eyes. But he still wasn't himself.

Soon Tony was talking his way aboard a departing helicopter which was headquartered at the naval base at Long Beach. Around Tony and Jose, the young Navy men worked fast and efficiently, long since having put aside the feelings that threatened to overwhelm the others. Now they moved like automatons, as if they had never given any thought to what was being asked of them. They followed orders, having been trained for emergencies.

Dodger Stadium had become a holding place for death; decay would not wait, however, as a terrible odor was filling the stands. Already, people were searching up and down the rows of the dead, thousands of them trampling the grass, checking ID tags, looking for missing loved ones. Tony didn't know what was worse—when someone actually found a husband, wife, child, or relative, or when they could not. It was painful just to look at the silent rows of the dead, inhabiting thick black and green bags.

The pilot of the chopper was not receptive to Tony's pleas until he lied that his mission was at the request of the doctors at the CCDC. "Can't raise anyone to confirm," the pilot complained. "Seems there's some new crisis there—a couple of rescue men are trapped now."

Tony instinctively knew it was Naldosa and Amunsen. He had been watching them for a long time. He knew they were pushing too hard, and had continued even after they were ordered to come up, claiming too much static on the radio to understand. He wondered if the hero of the day before was now dead.

"Ahhh," muttered the pilot, seeing that the digging

machine he had carried was unhooked, "I guess it won't hurt. Come on."

"Thanks, I'll get my camera."

"Camera? It's pitch black."

"It's equipped with infrared."

The look on the pilot's face indicated he was sorry he'd agreed so easily.

When Qunin returned, climbing into a seat beside the pilot, he found it difficult to maneuver with the mini-cam, and the pilot insisted he buckle up. The rotors were put into motion and a vortex of sand swept over the bubble window. Tony fought back a wave of nausea. He didn't like flying, and he hated choppers. Carl Foley had once told him of the astronomical number of moving parts in the rotor shaft, all necessary to the operation of the propeller. Now Foley was dead, his chopper destroyed, not due to any mechanical failure, but due to the quake. Jose had learned that the man had been killed trying too late to get his helicopter off the pad.

Tony took aerial shots of the ballpark as they moved skyward, and he saw Jose's figure grow smaller and smaller until the field itself was too distant to see.

"Keep us kinda low, okay?"

"Hey, I've got to clear the San Gabriels, buddy."

"But we won't reach them for a while. Believe me, these shots are important . . . could get us more help."

The pilot frowned and jerked his bird to tilt opposite of where Tony filmed, sending his camera lens pointing to the empty black sky. Tony cursed and held on tighter, forgetting about any further filming. But he had gotten shots over Downtown L.A., the worst of the destruction, and over Alhambra and San Gabriel. What he had seen made him realize that he and all the other Los Angelenos still alive had survived the worst earthquake in recorded history, and that the 9.4 Richter reading was not rumor but fact. Also, from his new perspective, he knew that Dr. McCain's initial estimate of the number of dead had been conservative, and that property damage was easily in the tens of billions of dollars.

"Wire services are out to and from L.A.," Tony told the pilot.

The younger man pointed to his headphones and then indicated a pair on a hook over Tony's head. Tony put them on and repeated his remark, adding, "That's why the film I have in this camera and in these cans is so important."

"Okay—I understand," the pilot replied. "Same's true of San Diego, San Francisco, the entire seaboard all the way to Portland."

"Anyone hit as hard as L.A.?"

"Not nearly . . . seems we got the brunt of it."

"I couldn't get a flight out of LAX."

"Bet you couldn't!" The pilot laughed. "No one's going in or out for a while. Real mess, like our base. Hell, we lost a couple of planes, a chopper . . . saw LAX right after it happened from the sky. Part of that highway, you know the one curving along the coast in front of the airport?"

"Vista Del Ray, you mean?"

"Not there anymore!" he shouted over the roar of the bird. "Fell into the Pacific along with a good chunk of LAX real estate, including a runway."

Tony slowly nodded in response. He put back his head and tried to relax. He'd been so keyed up for so long now, he hadn't been able to sleep, and now his mind seemed to want to crash. He thought about Jose back on the ground, carrying the dead from the van to designated plots, each given a tag with a number on it and those with identifying papers on them placed on a list. He thought about Doctors Casey Sterns and Michael McCain, about Naldosa and Amunsen. All of these people contributed to the rescue. Most had a remarkable inner calm that allowed them to deal with the grief-stricken and the panicked, the traumatized and those hysterical with pain. The doctors had skills and knowledge and capable hands, hands doing useful work amid the destruction.

He thought about his own work and his own usefulness. The number of poor and homeless in L.A. had always deeply disturbed him and now that number had just multiplied a thousandfold. Would his film footage contribute, help in any way? Or would it simply pander to the morbidly curious in the rest of the nation and the world? So far as he knew, only ham radio reports had gotten beyond the city; no footage had gotten out, unless some relentless, ambitious reporter like himself had managed to get material transported. His own earlier footage, sent out via a courier on a cub plane, may or may not have reached its destination.

His final thoughts before he closed his eyes to sleep were of Raphael Naldosa. Could it be true? Was Naldosa now a victim of the quake?

Dr. Michael McCain was logging his forty-eighth hour at the tent-sheltered emergency center alongside the remains of the CCDC. Ambulances remained a problem. There just weren't enough to go around; six other rescue centers were operating within the devastated city. But rescue help continued to come in through military bases. In addition, an army of volunteers and rescue experts had joined the legion of locals in the often vain attempt to snatch life from the death all around them.

The mayor had summoned federal aid, announcing the official death toll at 25,000 and still climbing. People at the scene estimated almost twice this number, and some believed it would rise to 75,000. At least that many had already lost their homes, and the streets throughout L.A. were lined with blanket-and-tarp tents and makeshift, cardboard shelters. Bread and soup lines had been established at churches and schools, and thousands were sleeping on gymnasium floors and in pews.

Thirty-four square blocks of Downtown L.A. were in ruins, the destruction hopscotching to topple one building and leave another still standing. But some buildings, though still standing, were considered unsafe. They were traps, threatening to collapse with each new wave of small aftershocks.

News broadcasts would later inform the survivors that the quake had caused the earth beneath their feet to shimmy some nine to twelve inches over a period of eighty-two seconds, which in turn whipped tops of tall buildings as much as eight feet. Only hours after the quake some 20,000 bodies filled Dodger Stadium and other mass morgue sites throughout the city.

Great Britain had airlifted fifty engineers from their Central American base in Belize. Japan's contribution came in relief dollars, two million of them. Italy and Mexico had dispatched experts who learned their lessons in the 1984 and 1985 quakes in those countries. Now, as word had it, one of these teams was trapped in a grave of its own.

Time was now the killer. Every minute, every hour that passed meant less chance of finding survivors. The rescue teams were extremely aware of just how the ratio was changing as the clock ticked.

The weariness of two days' work was beginning to show not only in Mike's face, but in his hands. They were cramping up as he worked, crippling knots bunching in the small muscles. He and Casey could not continue much longer, he knew.

Mike remembered only once in his life when he had been nearly as exhausted, and that had been almost ten years ago, during his residency at Cook County Hospital in Chicago, a place that made New York's Bellevue look like Happy Valley General by comparison. As in his resident days, Mike found himself being pulled from

every direction, and, as he did then, he returned to the
cardinal rule of his profession, the one thing that might
allow him to survive: total, professional objectivity.

His goal for the past two days and nights was to
construct around himself an invisible but impenetrable
shield of calm poise. It was like pretending to be
someone else, someone who showed no emotion, safe
within a zone of professional detachment. Impartiality
and good judgment were required to take the blows of
each new horror, each wound that had come from this
new holocaust. Without dispassion, a doctor or a
rescuer could not do the incredible task asked of him or
her: to instantly make life and death decisions.

What was a serious injury in a situation where all the
injuries were serious? Which was most serious, requir-
ing first attention? Which could wait? And for how
long?

What injuries went to what hospitals? Trauma centers
were filled to capacity, but sending certain patients
elsewhere likely meant death within hours, because
most hospitals didn't know how to treat trauma patients. Others required emergency centers with burn
units.

And finally, when was the number of dead piled
nearby no longer acceptable? When did an ambulance
have to be given up to become a hearse?

Mike and Casey had dealt with broken bones, mangled limbs, and bleeding wounds for so long now that
nothing could shock them. Mike was reminded of
something his father had said to him once. As a boy, his
father had driven him past the old Chicago stockyards, a
place where so much slaughter had occurred for so long
that it could be smelled for miles in any direction, the
mind-numbing stench so awful and overpowering it had
forced Mike's face into the car seat. They hadn't even
gotten to within three blocks of the place when Mike
begged to be taken away. When his father complied,

Mike asked him how men could work at such a place day after day, doing the things they did. Mike's father, in his characteristic truck-driver philosophy, had simply replied that men could, *and do,* get used to anything.

Now Mike had seen every degree of bloody injury, shock, and emotional upheaval, and he was getting *used to it* . . . he *had* to in order to survive. But there was so little they could do for the patients here, except prep them for more serious attention somewhere else. They could bandage wounds, temporarily set broken bones. They used gallons of antiseptics and antibiotics, and dispensed comforting assurances much more liberally. With paramedic equipment, they helped those going into seizures and those experiencing heart failure, sometimes saving and sometimes losing a patient.

Meanwhile, wandering survivors assailed the doctors for some news of some lost loved one, until it became impossible to work, and the entire area had to be cordoned off.

Mike wiped his tired eyes and rubbed his aching neck, feeling a stab of pain in his lower back. He knew his time was up, that he would collapse if he didn't rest. Casey, too, must be dead on her feet. He glanced around, searching for her, determined to make sure of her comfort ahead of his own. But suddenly, another patient was brought to him and as coldly objective as he was being, he could not turn his back. The young patient, a wide-eyed boy of perhaps eleven or twelve, was in a stupor, his mind shutting down from the pain and fear, but his eyes clearly registering everything around him. They fastened onto Mike's. His own need to rest would have to wait.

four

It dragged Amunsen's body behind it.

It was difficult work. Amunsen's limbs kept catching on things. He was heavy. One careless tug and the walls could fall in again.

A safe feeding ground was impossible in this unsafe world.

It was hard to think of anything but the pain. The torture all but blotted out its surroundings. Its affliction denied any self-awareness.

It was weak, dizzily weak, and dying. But one thing was certain: hidden inside Amunsen was a great reward.

Instinct told it these things.

Instinct dictated life.

Instinct informed.

It would die without the body below its feet.

It nestled around Amunsen's head. It crawled about the prize, over the wide chest, pressing into the spongy, warm provider. It rested a moment over the bloodied arm socket, licked at the red juices. It needed more fluids.

Abdominal organs pressed for relief the most. They were in control, far more so than its mind. They dictated pain. They made it feel the dry bed of emptiness, the grinding without fluid, the bone screaming on bone. It needed more liquids, and it could find more in the big ones. They alone could save it, nourish it.

Muscles and organs cramped, throbbed, sent searing pain into its head. The least effort—pulling off its prey, even feeding itself—sent fire to every artery, its extremities threatening to burst, its eyes bulging. Its blood vessels were balloons. Its brain was air-locked.

Without nourishment its body parts had become like twisted rope, some organs attacking violently as a result, others becoming useless and numb. Limbs turned sluggish, unresponsive, until it had to drag them along. At its most helpless and vulnerable, one claw had to support the other. The longer it went between feedings, the greater the internal tremors. It dimly recalled the involuntary twitching it experienced before it had ever feasted on the big creature.

It was at the mercy of pain. At times it could only lie in the rubble on its back, rolling, rocking, cutting itself on glass, rock and steel, further ripping its blackened limbs.

Its only recollections were those of pain. Its only desire—ending the pain.

It had known pain that had made death a pleasurable notion. For a time it had lain down and wallowed in the torment. In the grip of the vise, it allowed the sensation to wash over every nerve, every fiber, wishing death to come, to end the pain.

Lying perfectly still, not making a whimper or a noise of any sort, it had been surprised to find itself surrounded by curious little creatures. Strange, hairy things came and sniffed and screeched over it. They prowled about, getting closer and closer. Drawing on a strength it hadn't known it possessed, it instantly and ferociously had snatched one of them, had twisted off its head and fed on it while the others screeched in horror and disappeared into the rubble. It had been these small creatures that had kept it alive till now.

Only the powerful claws could bring down prey. But to use them, it had to move with the killing pain into a position of attack.

Hearing the noise of the creatures with the lights, the ones who somehow ate away at rock, it moved toward them. It had pulled itself along in agony to a position right above them and, at the crucial moment had snared one of them. Its claws had reached through the shifting debris until it had the prize—so fresh that it was still warm.

Even as it scooped out gore-soaked flesh from Amunsen's severed neck, it searched for a delicacy in the tissue.

Then, leaking from wounds inflicted on it by the falling debris, it curiously tasted its own thick fluid, which left a dirty brown trail. It noticed that the dead prize spurted red.

Scraps of elastic skin peeled away from the prize as it began to pound the body with first the right and then the left claw. It lifted each claw with difficulty and allowed them simply to fall, gorilla-fashion. As it fed, every muscle in its twisted torso bulged below the sacklike skin. On its arms and legs it observed red patches of exposed muscle tissue throbbing where parts of its skin had peeled off. In an attempt to think of something other than the pain inside, it flexed these muscles and watched them work like pulleys.

At the moment, the muscles were pumping harder and better than at any time previously, as each mouthful of Amunsen's flesh disappeared into the slobbering mouth.

Deep red, ox-blood pupils offset two black beads which took in everything at a glance, missing no small detail, no slight movement. Its ears missed nothing either, taking in any and all sound, however remote. It was likewise equipped with a powerful sense of smell; a great help in hunting down food, but a terrible handicap when eating. It did not like the stench of its accustomed prey, and the body beneath its clubbed feet and claws gave off a horrible odor that only worsened as it fed.

Its limbs were large, thick branches, covered with layers of rotted, scorched and scaly skin. They moved fluidly as if bone had become latex. The head and eyes, a mass of lumpy flesh, carried two bulging, twisted orbs. The large nostrils formed a snout, recklessly pushed to one side. The torso was that of a hunchback. Skin was the color and consistency of creosote, found inside a well-used chimney. Claws dragged along the ground, too heavy for the weak frame. But they were tough, hard, and metallic.

Its only notion of disease or decay had been what it witnessed in the discarded bodies of the small creatures it had found and fed on. But it was vaguely aware that its skin was remarkably similar to that of the dead things.

Only once had it thought it might survive. That was when it had fed on the first of the large creatures, the ones with heads almost as big as its own.

It had tasted of the big things only once. But that was only a recollection, and it seemed now to have been an eternity ago.

It had moved away from the area of its birth early on, finding only tiny morsels at first: strange, scuttling white beasts with slivers for tails. These offered little in the way of food; they did nothing to end the pain. Larger things then began to make noises, and it had crawled toward them. One with four legs snarled and fought viciously, biting a large chunk of skin from its arm. Even after feeding on this thing the pain returned . . . in fact, it had rarely left. Nothing but the big ones helped, and even then, only temporarily. Still, feeding on the big, two-legged creatures was its only way to stop the excruciating torture.

The noise of the big ones had come just when it was ready to give in to death.

Before the lights came it lay in a cold puddle. It had searched its entire lair. Everywhere it had looked was barren of food. It had given up, given in to the pain. But as it lay still, sounds came to its ears. Where there was noise, there was food; where there was a large noise, there was better food.

It had slithered through the rubble, covering a large distance to answer the deafening, pounding of concrete. It had come far to find the ones with the lights. Maybe this kind were put here especially for it.

It had found some strange allure in the rhythmic *rat-tat-tat, rat-tat-tat-tat* of the newcomers. It had been an entirely new sound, totally alien. Not at all like the moaning, crying, screeching noises it made.

As it now contentedly fed, the pulsating vise of pain deep inside subsided, but did not disappear altogether. A dull ache remained always, a reminder of how horrible the pain could become. The anguish receded only to the edge of its body, waiting . . . waiting to return.

A sound escaped its rubbery lips through teeth that still chewed flesh, "O o o o o o o-u u u u u u u u u-w w w w w w w a a a a a a a a a a."

It lowered its charred face again over Amunsen's, sniffing at his mouth, which was fixed in a scream. Its claws had rent the head from the body, and a little tug separated the two parts. A contented murmur issued over its blistered tongue.

At the same time, its wide nostrils dilated at the stench. Eyes and nose twitching, it began to dig again at Amunsen's neck, searching for something, something it knew must be there.

Then it heard another nearby *rat-tat-tat, rat-tat-tat-tat,* and a gruesome, lopsided look of pleasure twisted its face. It looked off in the direction of the sound, a sound that meant more food.

Raphael Alonzo Naldosa's sweaty, grimy face was covered with a coat of asphalt particles. His mask had been lost in the rubble; his lungs were choked with dust. His lips and tongue were covered in it. Aside from the blood it was all he could smell or taste.

The stocky Mexican came awake, almost by force of will. In a flash of agony he felt pain searing through his body, and a tremendous throbbing in his head, as if it were a spigot left open and spurting. His fingers felt a blood-caked gash at the center of his forehead. His right leg, too, was bleeding freely. He could feel the warmth of it, like tacky gravy. Funny, he thought, how lucid he was despite the pain. The human body was remarkable in that it could endure so much torture. How much of it had Amunsen endured? Was he alive or dead?

"Am-mah-son!" he tried as best he could to shout the name but the effect caused a terrible knifelike stabbing in his head.

It was dark; he couldn't see anything. He may as well be inside a coffin. He coughed, his lungs trying to expel some of the asphalt dust he'd swallowed, and the debris on all sides of him responded with squeaks and groans. It could come crashing down again, to finish him off.

Can't think of it, he told himself. *Got to think of Amunsen, the jackhammer, the radio.* He searched for the tools he needed to survive, and hit something metal that twirled, turtlelike and sent a light into his eyes. His helmet.

He lifted it, finding it twice as heavy as it should be. Unsure whether he was on his back on a floor of debris or backed against a ceiling, Naldosa pulled his head slowly forward and put on the helmet.

The moment he did so, he saw the headless carcass of a German shepherd trapped and dangling over him, the sight making him gasp. It was one of the rescue dogs that had disappeared sometime earlier.

Naldosa shuddered at the sight, and wanted nothing more than to escape it. Pushing back a feeling of claustrophobia, he refused to give in to panic. Again, he searched about the small space for his tools. *Long as you got your tools,* he told himself, *you got a chance.*

Naldosa's mind raced with questions that built one upon the other. How much blood had he lost? Did the numbness in his right leg mean anything especially serious? Could he move? How much time had elapsed since he had lost consciousness? What efforts were being made on the outside to reach him? Had they already tried and failed? Was his worst nightmare coming true? Would he lie here, encased in a tomb of debris and decay and slowly die, buried alive?

He forced back the thought by shouting again. "Amunsen! Amunsen! Where are you, man! Answer me!" His eyes watered from the pain the exertion caused. His body broke out in a cold sweat. Then he recalled the horrible trick his eyes had played on him at the moment of the cave-in, when he had seen his big friend literally sucked into the hole ahead of them by some awful creature of Hell. He'd screamed like a frightened child. But it must have been a trick of his mind, an illusion, or perhaps it was the dog overhead that he had seen. He lifted his eyes to the ugly, mangled body of the German shepherd.

That was it all along, he told himself.

"Amunsen! Do you hear me? Make a noise, anything, man! So I know you're alive."

He was so disoriented he didn't even know which direction Amunsen might be in.

"NaaattttaaaaNzzzNaldosa!" replied a metallic, static-ridden voice.

It was the radio. The voice was Lee Stark's, his boss aboveground. "I'm here! Can you hear me? I'm here!"

"Naldosa, come in, come in."

Naldosa summoned his strength and combed the rubble as best as he could in search of the radio. Finally, he felt it with his outstretched right hand. It lay below his wounded leg, but he hadn't been able to feel the lump below him. He had to free it.

The voice from the small box was going in and out between a beehive of static, but it still felt as if someone had thrown him a rope. He breathed a little easier and coughed out his message.

"I'm here . . . alive . . . hurt pretty bad. Leg seems paralyzed."

"And Amunsen? Is he okay?"

"Don't know."

"Can you get to him?"

"Can't see him. Boxed-in like a cigar down here."

"Hold on, Raphael, we're . . . for you."

Did he say praying or coming, Naldosa wondered.

"Can you get to Amunsen?"

"Maybe, if I can locate my jackhammer."

"See what you can do."

"What about you guys? You going to get us out?"

"Count on it, Raphael."

"How long do I have to count?"

Stark remained silent for a moment. "Not long, if we have any luck."

"You better have enough for all of us."

"Coming in toward you . . . another angle, just to . . . east side of your location, Raphael. Located a tunnel in progress not . . . from you. Can't be more than a hundred . . . ttt."

"Hundred feet, you say? Hundred feet down here is like a mile."

"You're going to come out of this, Raphael! In the mean . . . try . . . contact . . . Amunsen."

"Sure . . . sure."

"Careful though."

"Sure . . ."

"Keep you busy . . ."

"Sure . . ."

"Keep us on target if you make a little noise."

"Yes, I know. Thanks, Lee."

"Be right here if you want to talk."

Naldosa didn't want to give in to the despair that threatened to make his dark little coffin even blacker. Instead, he kicked out his left leg to feel for the jackhammer. Nothing. He could find nothing with his hands or arms either. With great effort and incredible concentration, imagining in his mind's eye the handheld jackhammer along his right leg, he suddenly kicked out his unfeeling leg and struck something hard. The jack- hammer.

He forced his leg and ankle to curl under the hard metal, and through sheer determination brought the leg up a little at a time, carrying the jackhammer with it until he could reach down with his hands.

He announced his small victory to Stark. "And the feeling's coming back into my leg."

"Good, good sign, Raphael."

Naldosa's light hit an enormous black steel girder that lay cross-wise over him. The steel beam was likely all that had stood between him and death. He decided to gauge his work against the sounds and movements he created along the length of that single girder.

He hefted himself up as far as he could on one side and stared at a wall of concrete. His senses told him that it must be the wall that he had been facing when everything fell in. But he saw nothing familiar; it was like looking at a roadmap of Mars. Everything was out of place, turned topsy-turvy.

He climbed around to the other side, hefting the injured leg over himself. It took time and great energy just to accomplish this simple task, but he was rewarded by seeing a small triangular hole, something to suggest another chamber or another way out. It might be the tunnel through which he and Amunsen had come, or it might be the hole through which Amunsen had fallen. He did not know.

He thought for a moment of how Amunsen had suggested they pull back and return to the outside for rest. Amunsen was missing now, perhaps injured far worse than he, or dead. Why hadn't he done as the big Swede had suggested . . . *why?*

"Amunsen, old friend!" he shouted. "I'm coming for you! Stark's coming for you!"

He pressed the jackhammer gently to one side of the small triangle and began working it, slowly and easily as Amunsen always coached. Debris began to fall away from the hole. Overhead, the massive girder made no movement, no sound. He worked another side of the tiny hole, enlarging it again, little by little.

When it was large enough for him to see that there was another pocket of space on the other side, he flashed his light ahead, searching. He saw the red plaid pattern of Amunsen's shirt!

"He's here, Lee! I can see him!" Naldosa announced to Stark.

"Is he alive?"

Naldosa yelled to his partner, but the small patch of shirt did not move. "He must be unconscious, that's all," Naldosa told Stark, trying at the same time to convince himself. "That's all, he's knocked cold."

"Can you get to him, Raphael?"

"Got to dig more."

"Easy, carefully."

"I'm being careful!"

Naldosa continued the slow work, the jackhammer chewing away at concrete and splintering pipe and metal in its way. The hole was enlarging quickly but

Raphael could not wait for it. He put aside the jack and forced his arm through to the shoulder, chattering the entire time to Amunsen, unable to accept the possibility the other man could not hear him.

"You won't believe what I got to tell you, my friend," he began to explain.

Naldosa's arm reached for Amunsen, his hand grappling with and then firmly gripping hold of the plaid shirt. He tugged on the material in an attempt to rouse him, and called his name again.

But the shirt *and Amunsen* lifted with his tug and Naldosa fell back to see his light illuminate what dangled inside the shirt: Amunsen's left arm, attached to nothing.

Naldosa's scream was heard over the radio.

five

Michael McCain's eyes could no longer focus, and his mind rebelled on learning of the fate of Raphael Naldosa and his partner Amunsen. The news had spread a whole new blanket of gloom over the field hospital where he and Casey continued to work nonstop.

More ugly wounds and shattered limbs awaited Mike. A whole line of them needing his attention, Casey's, and the other doctors who'd helped set up the emergency area.

Feeling faint, Mike turned to a young intern on his right and admitted in a dazed tone, "I can't do this anymore." It was as much an admission to himself as anyone else.

The younger man assisting him was named Timmons. He wore a large pair of glasses and looked as if he wasn't old enough to shave. McCain idly wondered how someone so young could stand the horror he had faced.

"I'm afraid I have to agree with you, Dr. McCain," he said calmly.

"Getting sloppy, am I?"

"There are enough hands here now to take over. Get some rest, doctor."

71

McCain studied the sincere eyes behind the thick glasses. "Thanks, doctor."

"If you don't mind my saying so—"

"I know, I look like hell."

"Something like it, yes."

"Appreciate your honesty, Timmons." Mike wandered away, drunkenly searching the area for any sign of Casey. As he did so, he pulled off the grimy white lab coat he wore, so stained with blood that it had turned brown. He became a little tangled in the left sleeve and was hardly aware when someone he didn't know helped him with it.

He found Casey still working over a patient, and he had the sensation that he was approaching her in someone else's body, as if he were to one side, watching a scene in a film unfold. He was overtired, and he knew that she, too, had to be dead on her feet.

Casey stood amid a small army of the white coats of other doctors, paramedics, and nurses. A man lay prone on a table before them, hooked up to a cardiac unit, his heartbeat now a thin, screeching line. Casey was working frantically to revive him, while others were trying to tell her it was useless.

Mike saw his hands, as if from a distance, reach out and take hold of her. From somewhere deep inside himself he found the strength to be firm with her, not allowing her to pull away.

"Please, let me go!" She turned to him. "Mike . . . it's you."

"Casey, I think you and I are just in the way now, and we will be until we get some rest."

"I got a little sleep over there," she said, pointing to a tent that held a handful of cots. Some doctors were resting there now.

He shook his head. "No, I mean real rest. Time someone put you to bed."

"And what about you?" She sounded a little defensive

to him; could a spark of anger remain from their first encounter?

"Me, too, I agree. Only problem is, the Hilton's not receiving guests."

She stretched and tried to feel her neck, which was numb to the touch. "My feet . . . my eyes . . . my brain . . . my every cell is screaming for rest," she finally admitted.

"I know, and people are beginning to take notice of us."

She looked at him quizzically.

"I almost cut a guy over there that didn't need another cut," he explained, pointing in the direction of Timmons.

She glanced at the dead man before her as she was ushered away. "I know what you mean."

"Then no more argument."

"No more, doctor."

"Good, then it's home and bed for you."

She reached out and brushed a lock of hair from his forehead. "And what about you? You're not going to be any good to anyone if you collapse."

"Don't worry about me. I'll find a place to sack out."

"You already have."

"What?"

"I have it on good authority that I have a place to go home to, and there's plenty of room for two."

His lips curled weakly into a smile. "May I take that as an invitation, doctor?"

"You may, and I'll even throw in breakfast—if I'm up first. Otherwise, it's your job. You do know how to operate a Mr. Coffee?"

"Blindfolded."

"Then it's a deal."

Finally allowing a yawn, Casey took off her white coat with Mike's help. He tossed it aside with a weak flourish, a signal to one and all that they would have to find someone else with all the answers, that he was taking Dr. Casey Sterns home for a well-deserved siesta.

Together they made their way up the makeshift stairs that took them to street level, out of the excavation area. Jose Ortiz was just returning from an errand he'd run for another doctor. Ortiz's TV news van had doubled as a hearse, ambulance, and delivery truck.

"Think you can find a taxi for us in this town, Jose?" Mike asked.

Jose stared for a minute and then laughed. "Climb into *my* taxi, doctors. I'll take you wherever you like."

They boarded, and Mike announced he was going to lay down. In the passenger seat, Casey closed her eyes and was near slumber when Jose suddenly said, "You know, Dr. Sterns, I just got to tell you something."

Groggily, Casey replied with a noncommittal, "Uh-huh . . ."

"You two, you and Dr. McCain, you're saints."

This brought a frown to her face, and she looked behind at Mike to see his reaction. He was out cold.

"Saints," repeated Jose, a large smile creasing his big face. "They ought to make you saints, officially, I mean. You ought to get some kinda . . . ah . . . something for all you've done."

"Sleep, Jose, that would be reward enough," Casey said with a halfhearted laugh.

"Naw, I mean something like, you know, the Mayor's Award for bravery or community services or something like that."

"Jose, we're doctors," she replied, as if this summed up the conversation. But he looked at her blankly, making her go on. "It's our job to . . . to tend to the injured, the same as it's Mr. Qunin's job to get out the news, that's all."

"Naw, naw, what Tony does, it's important, sure, but it's not the same, no more than my driving this van is the same. You people help with your hands and your brains. Isn't that right, Dr. McCain?" he asked Mike.

Casey looked back at Mike and laughed. "He's stone-cold asleep, Jose. I think Dr. McCain agrees with me."

"Saints," repeated Ortiz stubbornly.

"Saints don't get tired and irritable and exhausted and frustrated and angry, Jose. Believe me, doctors do!"

"You work so hard!"

"Yes, but—"

"I been watching!"

"Jose." Her tone stopped him. "You know what I was praying for when Dr. McCain pulled me away from there? Do you?"

His mouth hung open and he shook his head to indicate he didn't.

"I was praying that the next quake victim brought to me would already be dead." Her voice broke as if she might begin to cry. "So . . . so I wouldn't have to decide about another life . . . so there would be no reason for a decision . . . so I wouldn't have to think, to come up with emergency treatments." She put her head back and again closed her eyes, trembling. "There's your saint, Mr. Ortiz."

Jose swallowed hard and started to say something, but thought better of it. He returned his attention to his driving, still dangerously hindered by quake debris.

Already the quicksilver of headlights and traffic on Wilshire Boulevard had returned to a steady stream, as if it were a single, winding snake. Casey had long before joined McCain, asleep where she sat.

Jose pulled the van tightly to the curb and jumped it on purpose, to rouse his sleeping passengers. He hated having to wake them. No matter what Dr. Sterns said or felt, she had indeed joined the ranks of the saints in his eyes.

The jolt against the curb woke Casey, who mumbled the word "home," but Mike remained asleep in the back.

"Got to get Dr. McCain up," Jose said, sliding out his side and reaching for the side door. "Tony'll be back by now—he'll be looking for me."

Just as Jose began to wake Mike, the van's radio crackled with static and came alive with Tony Qunin's voice.

"Jose, Jose? Where are you?"

Jose abandoned Mike for the radio and Casey came around to help him out to the curb. He leaned in to her and their eyes met.

"Have I died and gone to heaven?"

"Must be a Chicago line," she replied. "So original."

"Ah, but there's a reason for old lines that never die."

"You mean they work?"

"No, not often, but when your mind isn't functioning so well, they're handy."

She laughed, and he smiled. "Good to be alone," he said, "after all this time."

"We're not entirely alone, my saint."

"What?"

"Jose." She pointed inside the van.

"Oh, yeah, now I remember."

Ortiz came to the curb and raised his shoulders. "Tony wants me back. I'll see you, okay?"

"Does your boss ever sleep?" Mike asked.

"Oh sure, sometimes . . . when nobody's looking." He laughed and nodded at them. "Good-bye."

Mike and Casey heard the squeal of the van's tires on the pavement as Jose circled and shot out onto Wilshire Boulevard. Mike stared up at the apartment complex, and a look of wonder came across his features. He examined the entire length of the block. All the buildings were intact.

"Good to see a whole building again."

"Looks almost invincible, doesn't it?" she asked.

"Think it's safe to go inside?"

"You mean, will the monster return to finish off what it left? I don't think the quake has a mind like Godzilla's, Mike."

"Good. Then you think it's safe." He was pointing to the building.

"Better be, unless you prefer sleeping in the backyard."

He looked at her and nodded. "Give me a sofa or give me death."

He took her hand in his as they approached the enormous oak-and-glass double-doors. They opened on a locked foyer filled with mailboxes and buzzers.

"I don't have my purse. All this time I've been without it."

"No purse, no key. Now we'll have to take the backyard."

"No, I'll ring for Eva."

"Landlady? Housekeeper?"

"Friend and neighbor."

"Oh?"

"I keep a key for her in case of an emergency and she keeps one for me."

"Hope it works. I mean, I hope she didn't lose *her* purse somewhere today."

Casey's face suddenly grew white. "Hope she's home."

He understood the sudden fear that had hit her. "Ring for her. She'll answer."

"Yeah," a gasp of breath escaped her. "You're right."

She rang, and a familiar voice asked her to identify herself. When she did, the woman at the other end began to cry. They entered through the buzzing door and moments later saw Eva running toward them down the hallway, still in tears. She'd had every reason to believe Casey had been killed with the collapse of the CCDC building.

Casey's apartment closed out the world. Ceiling to floor drapes covered the windows. Soft, warm lamps created a mellow, sleep-inducing glow. McCain noted the plush, white carpet, the elegant dining table and teakwood furnishings, and especially the inviting, bear-brown sofa. His mind registered it all, but he was looking at life now through a hazy tea-fog of exhaustion. Colors and moods and thoughts all meshed into one happy, boozey New Year's feeling.

The couch was mammoth and deep, stretching the length of the wall. Mike went straight for it, kicking off his shoes, and collapsed into its warmth.

Casey laughed at his boyish behavior and looked at him for a moment before fetching a blanket and pillow. When she returned, spreading the blanket over him and fluffing up the pillow before putting it beneath his head, she suggested he might like to shower.

"No, no, this is too comfortable. Can't move a muscle. Just fine . . . won-der-ful."

"A shelter from the storm," she said, kissing him on the cheek.

She turned to go, but he took her arm and gently tugged. She sat alongside him and they looked deeply into one another's eyes. He finally said, "This is nice, very nice . . . place."

"It's uniquely mine."

He smiled. "I could see that the moment I came in."

"Meaning?"

"Good taste, nice eye for color, just real warm . . . harmonious."

"Thank you."

"Gives me a feeling of . . . I don't know . . . like it's

all been organized, put together with a master plan in mind."

"Rational coziness, you mean?"

"No, no . . . it's just more safe and sane than any place I've been lately."

"You make me feel safe, Mike . . . almost secure."

He lifted himself to her lips and they kissed.

"When things are more on an even keel, when life's back to normal, we'll have to see if we still feel the way we do." Mike said it as evenly as his sleepy mind would allow, knowing that no matter how Casey felt later, he would still be in love with her.

She felt a warm desire for Mike, a desire to bury herself in him and find in his arms a place to hide from all the horror of the day. To find some semblance of order and sanity, things she had always taken for granted. But in the real world, beyond the door, they did not exist. She wondered if she could find peace and comfort, even if only for a moment, in Mike's embrace.

"If you'd like to shower," she was repeating herself, and felt foolish. But Mike was all but unconscious, unable to fend off sleep a moment longer.

Eva had offered them coffee, but they had declined almost in unison. Perhaps Eva imagined they were anxious to fall into one another's arms. Casey had thought she'd seen that desire in Mike, but maybe she had read him wrong after all. Maybe this *was* just some place to sleep, as far as he was concerned.

Still, she couldn't help but smile at him, and kiss his lips again.

Casey got up and went to the bedroom. She kicked out of the shoes on her swollen feet. Her eyes were bloodshot, her hair tangled, her body aching. Like Mike, she was exhausted. But fear had kept her going for so long now, she wasn't certain she could shut down. Adrenaline seemed to have replaced her blood.

In a moment she had changed out of her clothes. Throwing a thick terrycloth robe over herself, she ventured out into the short hallway and ducked into the bath, where she began to run a hot shower. She knew she would sleep better if she bothered to shower now.

After she toweled off and left the shower, she again passed the sleeping form on her couch. She hesitated over him, studying his fine features, his long, lean body. He was a handsome man, strong and sensitive at the same time. He had made her feel safe when no one could expect to feel that way.

Now, curled up on her couch, he looked like a little boy, hiding from all the pain and horror he had endured throughout the day. But even in his sleep he shuddered and mumbled incoherent but clearly troubled words. Unable to help herself, she went closer to him, letting her robe fall open. She wanted to hold him to her heart, but perhaps it would be a mistake. Perhaps this was like wartime, when men and women fell in love only out of fear of the next day's shelling, the next day's scars.

Bending over him, Casey tenderly pressed her lips to his warm cheek. His only response was a dazed murmur. She stood up, tucking her robe beneath her arms, and slowly walked to her bedroom.

She slipped into a silken nightgown, and then slid into bed. She had slept alone for years now, but she'd never felt lonely or afraid. But tonight, even with Mike so near—perhaps because of his nearness—she felt the bed seemed like a large and lonely sea upon which she drifted.

Casey's mind drifted to thoughts of the sleeping man in the other room. She wondered if Mike and she had any chance at a life together after all this insanity ended, once the upside-down world had again been set right. A troubled image wandered through her mind: L.A. as a fallen Humpty-Dumpty which all the King's men could not put back together again. If the city could not be healed, if the lines of wounded victims never ended, their love could never flower. How could anything grow through stone and blood?

Her mind played over phrases: *rocky relationship, firm ground gone, saved from death, a lot in common, never been saved by a saint before, never been saved by anyone before* . . . *Mike* . . . *Mike* . . . *Michael* . . . *St. Michael* . . .

The phrases floated like waves on the ocean of her now soft, warm bed, his name on her lips as she sank deep into slumber, burrowing into the safe, firm sand on the bottom of her subconscious.

It had fed slowly on Amunsen, savoring those parts it most craved, forcing itself to hold back in order to draw out the feeding. After all, it gained life in the bargain, life free of the pain. Feeding was a balm that coursed through its body to nourish the scarred flesh and twisted limbs. How then could it not help but nuzzle and sniff and lick its prey?

The activity of the hunt and its reward had created in it a sense of peace never before experienced. Silence and darkness were welcome and velvety now; even the puddles of water and filth it roiled in felt warm.

All this the dead prey had brought to it. All this, and even drowsiness, a desire for rest.

It hadn't known sleep before, no more than it had known peace.

But now it had curled about Amunsen's blood-soaked torso where it lay very still, pleased with itself. Soon, it would be unable to sleep, unable even to close its eyes. The torturous pain would see to that. Soon it would have to hunt again, feed again. Soon it would have to go back for the other one.

Casey awoke with a start, screaming, clawing at empty air for something to hold onto as her bed fell away from her into the deep chasm below the ocean, into the jagged mouth of the quake in her dreams.

Casey sat up in bed, trembling in an uncontrollable chill. She wasn't aware of Mike until he grabbed hold of her by both shoulders and pulled her against his bare chest, rocking her gently back and forth.

"Case, Case! I've got you now! Don't cry, it's all right . . . just another of those damned aftershocks."

"Hhhhhhuh . . . M-M-Mike?" She was confused and fought to catch her breath. "H-hold me," she said, and Mike held her tighter.

"For as long as you like."

After a moment, Mike lifted her head, wiping tears from her eyes with the end of the sheet. "You . . . you weren't there this time . . ." she stuttered. "I fell in."

"I'm right here. Was here all along. You just believe that I'll always be here for you." He reached over and switched on a night light which illuminated enough of the room to dispel the inky blackness and give color to Mike's form and features without hurting her eyes. "Maybe you should sleep with a light on," he suggested, his eyes probing hers. "I mean, just until . . . for a while."

"Yeah, maybe. I'm sorry. I feel so foolish—"

"No, don't apologize."

"—for waking you, I mean. You were sleeping so soundly."

"No, the tremor woke me first."

"I still feel . . . foolish." She searched for a handkerchief to wipe away her tears. Mike reached out tenderly and caught one on his finger.

"You're very beautiful, Casey . . . but are you always so hard on yourself?"

She sniffled.

"You go ahead and cry. Let it surface. God knows you've been through a lot."

"But everyone has, and you—"

"I'm fine, really."

She looked into the depths of his eyes, losing herself in their cobalt blue for a moment. He returned her gaze, looking deeply into her honey-brown, topaz eyes. He gently put strands of golden hair into place, looking for a moment as if he were hopelessly lost in her beauty. Then he kissed her tenderly, feeling her trembling change to a passionate quiver. She reached around him, feeling the taut muscles of his back. As they lay in a warm embrace, Casey felt the fear dissipate, magically replaced by desire. Perhaps she *could* find safety in Mike's arms; perhaps it hadn't been a mere fantasy.

Her hands caressed his shoulders, felt the reassuring strength of him. He gently pressed himself against her silk-clad body, his chest heaving a sigh before taking her lips ravenously in his own. Casey returned his feverish kisses with a fire from deep inside her.

Mike enveloped her in his arms, the corded muscles of his stomach and chest crying out for her touch. His mouth explored her long neck, and gently moved downward to find the silk of her nightgown above the nipples of her breasts. His voice filled her ears as his touch filled her being.

"Oh, Casey, Casey . . . from the first I've wanted you."

"Yes . . . yes," she replied, lost in the moment. "I want you . . . too."

She pushed away her nightgown at his insistent touch and his tender lips found her willing breasts, and breathless gasps began to explode from her. Her own touch reassured him, guided his hand to explore her completely, wholly. Her mouth opened to receive him again and again, as his tongue probed deeply, urgently.

In the dim light their hands met, clasped, and opened, flowerlike. Casey felt he knew her every thought, her every action, and he matched her lovemaking measure for measure, kiss for kiss. Warmth and delight filled her

soul and blotted out all the evil in the world so
thoroughly that time itself seemed to stop.

Desire, warmth, and laughter mingled, intertwined
between them like a weaver's threads. Casey's heart
soared as Mike's insistent tenderness sent quiet thunder
through her. Her soul brimming with passion for him,
an electrifying shiver raced through her being, climaxing
in a depth of love and caring she'd never known before.

In Mike's arms, Casey fell once more into the depths
of slumber, their love having melded them. Her fatigue
was different now; fulfilling, *good*. Her helplessness had
turned to faith.

six

On the return flight from Nevada, Tony Qunin had gotten confirmation that the trapped rescue team below the rubble of the CCDC was Naldosa and Amunsen. For Tony, the earthquake was the source of a thousand-and-one stories, representing the best and the worst in human nature. Put on display were the coward and the hero, the suffering and the determined. From Naldosa and Amunsen, the brave moles, who were prepared to exchange places with those poor souls buried alive, to those digging through the ruins of the local K-Marts for bargains—undamaged stereos, TVs, VCRs, all at 100 percent discount.

Grocery stores, savings and loans, taverns, all had been looted. National guardsmen, called out to help in the massive rescue effort, found themselves protecting demolished buildings from vandals and thieves.

But Tony's own on-site filming of Raphael Naldosa emerging from the ruins of a forty-story building with an infant tucked in the crook of his arm had become the big story, the one that gave L.A. a measure of hope and optimism.

Tony had interviewed Naldosa some time after he had come up with the last of the infants. He had talked also with the bright-eyed Swede, Amunsen, who was as shy as a child. Naldosa had a quiet, unassuming manner, and a true dignity that seemed to transcend all the death around him. Tony liked Naldosa and Amunsen, and admired their courage.

"I first start this work in Mexico . . . 1985, terrible earthquake," Naldosa had told the reporter. "I was then only a boy. Stupid maybe . . . young . . . thinking the world is safe place, you know. My whole family, my wife and boy . . . my mother . . . all killed. I worked as volunteer, hoping I, too, would be killed, *take me, take me*, I told the earthquake. I didn't want to live. Now, of course, I want to live, to help others."

Tony, along with the audience that heard Naldosa speak, was touched by the simplicity of his explanation for becoming a mole, a simplicity that was filled with complex emotions. In fact, Naldosa's example had led a whole army of volunteers into the area of Downtown L.A. to do what they could. Everyone wanted to see more of Naldosa and Amunsen, to hear these heroes speak again, to see them at work. And now everyone wanted to know if they were dead or alive. For this reason, Tony purchased, at an inflated price, a copy of tapes created by the borehole camera that had followed Naldosa and Amunsen down the deep, winding passageways. The film was priceless, as far as Tony was concerned. Watching the footage was like breathing the air Naldosa breathed, like being down there with him.

Tony had rushed to the rescue site to claim the tapes from a heavyset, officious technical assistant named Martin Pillsby.

"Everything just went black and they started shouting," was all Pillsby could muster.

"But what happened?" Tony had pressed.

"Don't know. One minute everything was fine, and then nothing. It's dead!"

"And you can't get it back on?"

"Hell no, it's smashed." Pillsby shrugged his massive shoulders, his stomach hanging down in rolls beneath his Bureau of U.S. Mines uniform. "Going to cost a fortune. All we're getting now is audio—"

"Audio?"

"Naldosa's alive down there. We've had communication with him, but nothing from Amunsen yet."

Now Tony was waiting for the film to be shown in his own apartment. He'd located all the help he needed.

All of Los Angeles's television and radio broadcasts remained severely handicapped in one fashion or another. For a time, any reports coming out of L.A. had to be routed to an affiliate station, as Tony had done. Whole sections of the city were still without electricity or telephone service. And without running water the city was a civilized man's nightmare. The few areas that continued to enjoy such amenities became targets for vandals, who felt everyone should share the misery.

Tony had taken the precaution of hiring personal guards to protect his building, a remodeled warehouse with an elevator that opened onto his apartment. His place was in a dimly lit section of the city, in back of the wharves; it was probably safer from the roving bands of vandals than most. But he couldn't take chances, since he had made up his mind to turn it into a new base of operations for 3-CTV.

Nevada, Arizona, and Texas affiliates of Tony Qunin's TV station had come to the aid of 3-CTV News, seeing that Tony was determined that the fledgling "City Television News" would continue operations. With the good graces of these other stations, he had actually gotten help and equipment.

Tony's own fatigue was beginning to wear him down, but he now found himself in charge of a skeleton crew working late into the night and early morning. Men and women began to drop off from exhaustion; crushed cans and discarded boxes and wrappers were everywhere amid the smoke-filled rooms.

In a back bedroom which had never been fully stocked with furniture, they had set up a developing studio where the film could be edited as quickly as possible. Here, Les Code, a gangly black man who was one of the city's best film editors, monitored the footage he had just copied and developed from the cassette given him by Tony Qunin. He was running it through an editor's viewer, an instrument meant for one pair of eyes, but over his shoulder Tony breathed down his neck. Behind Tony was Ortiz, pacing now.

"Can't believe how much you paid for this stuff, man," moaned Les. "How much this turkey skin you for, Qunin?" A grin spread over Les's face. It wasn't often Tony made a mistake; he should have his face rubbed in it good, to remember.

"I think Les is right, Tony," said Jose. "Except for the dead woman they found, there's nothing here, and that's too gruesome to pass for news. Let's close up."

"If that's all we got, it'll pass," Tony said irritably, his own dark features set in what had become a perpetual frown.

"Boring shit, Tony. Chalk it up, man. Nothing here like when these dudes saved those babies. Now *that* was good."

"Keep rolling." Tony stared at the grainy film as each frame passed the light in the square below Les's hands. He saw only a pair of near indistinguishable forms in the film, Naldosa and Amunsen, crowding out everything else with their own bodies.

Suddenly, the moles' voices were cut short by the roar of the cave-in, and the last of the film slipped through the viewer, the screen going completely white with light.

"Replay that," Tony said to Les.

"Now there's something at the end you might use," replied Les. "Not much, maybe, but dramatic."

"Play it again."

"Coming around."

Jose inched closer and tried to see.

The room was dark around the tiny square of light at the monitor as Tony watched the celluloid figures reenact the final moments before the cave-in. The young, strong hero, Naldosa, and his strapping sidekick, Amunsen, performed their parts again.

Naldosa hears something, responds, calls out, digs. Amunsen tries to dissuade him, urges him to come away for a much needed rest. The big Swede suddenly pulls Naldosa to safety, risking his own life, then disappears amid cascading debris that blots out everything but Naldosa's screams.

It all had the feel of contrivance, the look of a hoax film, like the first pictures that purported to come out of Russia as actual footage of the Chernobyl incident.

The film itself was blurred, nearly indistinguishable. Despite that fact, however, this film was real; Naldosa and Amunsen were real men, not actors in a low-budget movie. Tony wondered if it would play that way on the A.M. news. He wondered if the film was worthless, or if it could be salvaged. He wondered all this as he watched the inevitable unfold again, wishing it could be rewritten, torn out of the script.

Amunsen's frame seemed propelled forward in a bizarre, unacceptable way, as if he leaped into a typhoon's eye. It was as if he were dragged through the hole like a rag doll.

Again the rumbling of the cave-in was pierced by Naldosa's screaming.

"My God," said Les.

Jose crossed himself.

"What exactly happened?" asked Tony.

"You saw what happened."

"No, I don't think so. I want to see it again, Les."

"Here, you do it," replied the black man, getting up and stretching. "I'm getting some sleep."

Tony waved him off and sat down before the small monitor, and began to run the film again. The quality of the picture was awful. In the falling debris, images of all sorts might be seen, but Tony was nagged by one in particular. He took the frames slowly now, eyes glued to each. His concentration caused Les to delay his exit, to turn and look over his shoulder at the small monitor screen.

"I can't believe Stark missed all this, you know . . ." muttered Tony. "Missed the whole damned thing."

"How could he?" Jose wondered aloud.

"Easy enough," replied Les. "Sip your coffee, take a drag on a cigarette and you miss it. Happened so fast."

"There's something else *in* there!" shouted Tony, pointing. "See it?"

"What?"

"No, I don't see nothing, man."

"In the mess, in the junk, on Amunsen's shoulder."

Les and Jose stared, exchanged a confused look. "Don't see it, Tony."

"How soon can you get this blown up, Les?"

"Whoa, man, I'm out of here."

"This could be important! It could mean the difference whether those two men live or die!"

"Yeah, sure, and whether your career goes up or down the tubes, I know, but—"

"Triple-time-and-a-half!"

"You can't authorize payroll, Tony, come on."

"Then, goddamn it, I'll pay it out of my own pocket! How long?"

Les frowned and looked down at the film and then yawned at the darkened ceiling. "Take a day, at least."

"A day! I want it for the A.M. telecast."

"That's crazy, Tony. We don't have the equipment here!"

"I'll set it up!"

"Where?"

"Leave that to me."

"Where?"

"UCLA!"

"UCLA?"

"They've got a great lab."

"Yeah, fine, but how do we get in?"

"Time to call in a favor."

"You know somebody there?"

"Just the guy who runs the place."

"And he's going to open it up for you at—" Les glanced at his watch, "—three A.M.?"

"When else you figure the place is free? Bill Scanlan told me anytime. *Now's* the time. So, how long for this to be blown up, sharpened, given some contrast?"

"More time than we got before the morning broadcast."

Jose stood nearby, staring at the two men. "Tony," he said, his eyes boring into Qunin, "you aren't going to really use this on the air, are you?"

"Only if we can pull a decent copy off this." He held up the film.

"But suppose . . . I mean, maybe . . ."

"What is it, Jose?"

"It just don't seem right somehow."

"It's news, Jose. Time to go wake up Scanlan. Meet you two at the van."

Raphael Naldosa was alone. For three days he'd been alone. Despite the radio, despite all of Stark's reassurances, he was alone. Like the fading light on his helmet, he felt his spirits weakening.

Raphael had followed Amunsen's bloody trail. He had broken through to the chamber where the man's arm lay amid the rubble like another portion of garbage, trying to avert his eyes the whole time. He had reported finding Amunsen's severed limb once he regained control of himself. He had reported his belief that Amunsen was beyond suffering.

"Crazy, Stark . . . crazy," he mumbled into the radio.

"Take it easy, Naldosa. It's not your fault."

"I've seen something, Stark, just before I blacked out, and now I know what it was. Back home, in Mexico, we got a god, you know, an ancient Aztec god, with a name you couldn't pronounce. He's got an ugly face and huge arms and giant fingers."

"Keep a grip on yourself, kid."

"I seen him, down here, Mr. Stark, really. Like he's coming for me."

"Naldosa!"

"Blood sacrifices, you know, that's what the old gods wanted . . ."

Stark's conversation now had long stretches of silence. Raphael knew those on the outside thought he was cracking up. "Keep the jackhammer going, Naldosa."

"Sure . . . sure . . ."

"Fight back."

He locked in on Stark's words, and fought for calm, for resolve, for clear-headedness, all as important as his tools if he were to beat the odds. "Can't make sense of this . . . what happened," he mumbled.

He went over a mental list, possibilities for all that he had seen or thought he had seen. He tried to place the headless dog into a scenario that didn't fit. He tried to imagine what in the debris could have wrenched Amunsen's arm from its socket. He tried to imagine where the rest of Amunsen could be.

Had he been buried below? Was Naldosa atop his grave this very moment? His flesh crawled at the thought.

"I saw Amunsen's arm ripped away," he muttered. "I saw something alive take hold of him and drag him through the falling concrete."

"Say again, Naldosa," asked Stark from above. "Can't hear you."

Naldosa repeated himself, clearly and emphatically.

Stark didn't reply.

"Think I'm crazy, don't you?"

"Naldosa, we're getting closer all the time."

Naldosa didn't speak. Instead he began to remember. Was what he saw a nightmare that came when he blacked out, or was it part of a real nightmare?

"Can't be," he told himself aloud. If it were true, if he had seen claws take hold of Amunsen and drag him down into that hole, then something more horrible than the Aztec gods of his childhood was crawling around down here.

Then he noticed a strange discoloration against his asphalt dusted skin. Beneath the white, his skin was mottled with strange little rings, darker patches of skin. His eyes had to squint in the dim light to make it out, but there was no doubt . . . unless it was another hallucination.

But Naldosa was hurled from his thoughts by a sound, a sound both strange and familiar, a kind of cry.

"Oooooooooowwwwwwwwwaaattttaaa . . ."

It came from all around him. It sounded like the pained cry of a wounded animal. It sounded like the noise he had heard when he had argued with Amunsen, moments before Amunsen disappeared.

Naldosa lay silent, silent and paralyzed.

Stark's voice crackled on the radio. Naldosa cut it off. His light blinked once, and went out.

seven

It was confused by the sounds coming from two separate directions. One seemed steadier, louder, demanding. The other sounded faint, hesitant, but closer. It had gone in the direction of the first noise only to turn for the second, then changed direction again.

It was feeling stronger by steady degrees. It had found and consumed the special delicacy inside the big dead carcass, and had discarded the remainder. It was looking for more.

Suddenly, the loud buzzing and drilling noises made by the concrete chewers told it that there were a lot of them. Searching for the missing one? In a sudden lull of noise, a light flooded into the chamber where Amunsen's body lay amid a puddle of blood and sewage, and it darted under stones and concrete slabs.

There it lay, believing the light-eyes had seen and followed it, that they would come and force their concrete-eating limbs into its face. They could hear its labored, frightened breathing, couldn't they? They had enormous eyes that blinded it, flooding the blackness of its lair, turning its world into theirs. They could smell it, couldn't they? And they had the evidence of the carcass to know it was near. They would surround the hiding place, jab with their noisy, deadly arms and destroy it.

As it lay silent, trying desperately to remain still, it watched them, watched the way they moved, their clumsiness.

It took them a long time to find the body.

Even with their eyes of light they were blind. Some put aside their chewing arms. They seemed dangerous, but stupid. And within each one was sustenance, a chance to end the pain.

It thought of feeding.

Gratification came only after feeding. It did not know taste, or the joy of appetite. It didn't feed for those reasons. There hadn't been any taste to the carcass; there had only been *need*, an insatiable need, and, *as it fed*, a lessening of the torturing pain. It felt good when it fed on them.

It whimpered softly as the light-eyes came to claim the carcass. Fear of losing the dead one and having no replacement sent shivers through its gnarled body. What should it do?

Attack? Or wait?

Hatred ignited every nerve. Frustration filled its thoughts. There were too many of them.

Again the pain was mounting in its gut, threatening to bring on a wail. Instead, a low keening sound escaped from it.

But the light-eyes were deaf, too. They made noises of their own, far louder. They cried out and cupped hands around their mouths to increase the noise. They began chewing away another wall while others in their number pulled at the carcass which was still filled with morsels that it wished to suck out.

While the light-eyes were busy, it darted to a new position. The light burned and pained its eyes so that it could not look straight at them. It wanted to tear off their eyes as it had the other one.

Then they took hold of the dead one and started away with it. One searched deeper into the chamber; perhaps looking for the hidden head?

It darted closer to this one. Like the others, this one seemed blind.

It wondered if it could entice this one closer by keening a little louder. But before it could do so the others broke down a wall, shouting and screaming as they dragged another one, one without a light at the center of its head, into the chamber. This drew the closest one away, toward the others.

They took the carcass. They took the other one, the one without the eye, and began to file out. It darted after, trying to get nearer, when the lightless one screamed and pointed, having caught a glimpse of it. It vanished below the stones into its original hiding place.

The others turned and stared, the bright light cutting into its lair. But there was no reaction. They looked but did not see.

How to lure one closer, away from the others . . . how to get hold of just one?

But they were gone, and already the suffocating pain was coming on again.

It must feed again. All it knew for certain was that it must feed . . . feed on them . . . on them.

Outside, Tony Qunin and Jose Ortiz had found their way to Stark's assistant, Pillsby, and heard the cheers come over Pillsby's receiver. News of Naldosa's rescue flashed across the crowd and everyone shouted in celebration. Jose grabbed Tony in a powerful bearhug. Whistles and hurrahs filled the air. For a few seconds, Tony allowed himself to believe that everything was going to be all right. Les Code would finish up at UCLA in time and the tragic scenes Tony planned on airing would have a happy ending. Then he heard Naldosa's screams, his madman's voice.

"Never mind me! Look! Look, you fools, behind you!" The crowd became hushed. "Flash your light over there! There! Did you see it? Did you? A demon! A demon of Hell! It killed Amunsen! *It killed Amunsen!*"

"Been talking crazy now for hours," Pillsby said in Tony's ear. "Looks like your hero cracked under pressure."

The rescue crew was coming out, carrying Amunsen's mangled body ahead of Naldosa, who was on a stretcher. "Give me that camera, Jose," Tony ordered, hefting the mini-cam to take shots of the dramatic moment.

"Got some fascinating audio material for you, Mr. Qunin," Pillsby whispered in Tony's ear.

"What's that?"

"Naldosa, your hero. Got him ranting on about some Mexican devil or something. He got to believing there was something down there with him, maybe Amunsen's ghost, coming after him. Said he heard it coming for him."

Tony kept shooting. Naldosa was shouting, fighting until anesthesia was administered, silencing him. Others carried Naldosa to a waiting ambulance, while Amunsen's body was covered and carried away, bound for Dodger Stadium.

Everyone involved in the rescue attempt stood silent and stunned. Tony cursed under his breath.

"What about it, Qunin? How much for the audio tape?" Pillsby asked.

"You keep 'em, Pillsby. Play them for yourself at bedtime."

Pillsby stared, sneering. "Okay, I'll sell 'em elsewhere. Some hero."

"Why don't you get lost, before I drop this camera on you," Tony threatened.

Pillsby moved off, seeing the menace in the reporter's glare.

Tony went straight to Stark, who put up a large hand to stop him.

"I want to talk to Naldosa."

"What's it to you, Qunin? Ratings? A promotion? Christ, you bloodsuckers are all alike." He started off.

Tony grabbed him by the arm and turned him around. "I like to think I do what I do for good reasons, Stark. I liked—*like* Raphael Naldosa—I care about what happens to him."

"Sure . . . sure you care about Raphael."

Tony looked into Stark's deep-set eyes, and realized that the man's mind was made up. And perhaps he had a right to feel as he did. "I admit, it has been a long time since I felt . . . personally involved in a story."

"Raphael's not a story, Qunin . . . he's a man."

Stark walked off, his gait heavy, as if weighted down. Tony watched him go, wondering if he were right. Perhaps he had forgotten that Naldosa's life meant more than just a headline.

Just then, several screeching, racing lab monkeys plunged through the tunnel created by the rescuers. The animals were panicked, splitting the air with fearful cries. Confused, they jumped from place to place with no direction, falling over one another.

Several of the doctors began a roundup attempt, using cardboard boxes, and surgical gowns as nets, and anything else they could find for the task. With the aid of paramedics and nurses, the doctors began cornering the terrified creatures.

Tony began filming instinctively. A doctor Tony knew as Timmons got hold of the largest animal, and had him in what appeared to be a safe, firm hold when suddenly the beast broke loose, leaving the doctor with a vicious bite to the forearm.

A gunshot exploded, and the monkey fell at Timmons's feet, its body curled into a mound. Doctors began screaming at the baby-faced young officer who had shot the primate.

"There was no reason to destroy that animal! We have them under control!" Even Timmons, nursing his swelling arm, shouted at the young policeman.

Like everyone at the site, the cop had been there too long, and his exhaustion had made him dangerous.

The rest of the monkeys were rounded up with less commotion. Timmons was surrounded by concerned people as he began to turn white and dizzy-eyed. He complained of a buzzing inside his head and a lack of feeling in his arm.

"Couldn't have severed nerves . . . I mean it was only one bite . . ." There was clear concern in his voice.

Other doctors were asking him questions, but he seemed tranquilized, unable to hear.

"Better get that sterilized and bandaged," said a nurse, guiding him away.

Tony motioned for Jose, who had remained near the perimeter, near Pillsby's little table. "Want me to take the cam?" he asked when he reached Tony.

"No, Jose, take this." He stuffed money into Jose's hands.

"What's this for?"

"The Pill."

"Pillsby?"

"Get the radio communications tapes he has on Naldosa. Pay him what he wants."

"But Tony, you said—"

"Never mind what I said."

"But Tony—"

"Damn it, Jose!"

"Tony, think about this one. You could hurt that boy, Naldosa. You want to drag him down?"

Tony glared at his friend. "Who works for whom here, Jose?"

Jose stared back, a shadow of hurt in his eyes. "Sure, we know who works for who." He ambled off to find Pillsby.

Tony stood, surrounded but alone. He was aware of the suffering and death, of the need for an end to it all. But the quake was still very much in evidence amid the ruins.

Despite Naldosa, despite the doctors, all attempts to create some semblance of order seemed pitifully small. The quake mocked all of them.

To fight back, Tony knew he must film, he must edit, write and rewrite, to reorder the chaos into his stories. Otherwise he was no different than the forlorn army of people still roaming the streets, minds numbed from pain and loss, unable to speak, wandering without aim or purpose.

The quake had caused great suffering, but some bastards didn't suffer. Leo G. Copellmier had lost his precious center, but where was he? Had he escaped harm while hundreds lay dead below the floors of a building Tony was certain had been built to substandard specifications? The center had fallen like a house of cards when the quake hit, while other towers sustained less damage. It wasn't just coincidence. But now this Naldosa thing nagged him almost to distraction. Raphael Naldosa did not strike him as the kind of man who would give in to madness, not even temporarily.

One of the doctors nearby was examining the carcass of the dead monkey, and Tony heard him remark about a strange splotch of rust-red color on the animal's cheek.

"Saw something like that on one of the others," replied another.

"No telling what they got into underneath all that rubbish," said the first doctor.

"This isn't just some chemical or paint. Its face is burned, some facial hair and skin are gone."

"Excuse me," said Tony, "but is it possible that Naldosa could have seen this animal down in that hole?"

"Very likely."

"Would scare the hell out of me."

The doctors laughed.

"It's dark, you're buried alive, you see this thing and it looks like some kind of horror movie, right?"

"It would explain a lot, yes."

Tony gave the doctors a half-smile and nodded before joining Jose. It was pure conjecture, but it made sense. It had to be the answer.

Perhaps, armed with the truth, he could do something for Raphael Naldosa, give something in return to the man who had earlier given all of them so much to cheer about.

Two nights and three days of intensive rescue efforts at the CCDC site had taken Mike McCain and Casey Sterns through a kind of living hell. The only peace they knew was in each other's arms, and now Mike reached out his hand to her, finding her mouth a willing receptacle for his fingers as she sleepily nibbled them. Morning light had penetrated the drapes like a beacon, telling them it was time to prepare once more for a grueling day of emergency medicine. As fantastic as it seemed, quake victims were still being found alive out there.

Mike reached across Casey in an effort to see the clock. It was 9 A.M. Beneath him Casey gently rose, her body meeting his, eyes blinking wearily, a provocative smile on her face.

Her yellow hair was spread beneath her like sunlight, and when her eyes came fully open they contemplated him gently, a deep joy reflected in their glow. She raised her head to kiss him lightly. He returned the kiss passionately, taking time to savor her, parting with a loss of breath.

"Oh, Mike . . ."

"You know, I could get used to this."

She snuggled up to him, unsure of how to say what she wanted to say.

"There'll be time," he whispered.

"Can I take that to mean you'll be staying over again?"

"Any time you'll have me, doctor."

She kissed him again, by far the best reply.

"You're my every fantasy come true, do you know that?"

She laughed lightly. "Nice of you to say so, especially since I was more than half asleep when we made love."

"If that was sleeping, I may die of passion when you're awake."

"You wouldn't be one of those types who always says just the right thing because it's too painful to tell the truth, would you?"

"Now, Casey, tell me, have you ever met a man who could fool you?"

She thought for a painful moment of Leo Copellmier, whom she had at one time admired. She would never have allowed him to maneuver her into bed, but he had most certainly used her to maintain his reputation.

"What is it?" Mike asked, seeing the frown.

"Oh, nothing . . . just a thought."

"About me?"

"Leo, if you must know."

"Ahh, worried about Leo, huh? So am I, but there's still some hope he escaped the quake."

"I don't want to talk about Leo. I want to talk about your fantasies."

"Oh, you do, do you?"

"Yes, for instance, you ever have one about a blonde who's wide awake when she makes love to you?"

"Hmm," he feigned difficult thought. "I think she's always just half-conscious."

"So, you fantasize about taking advantage of groggy women, huh?"

He laughed lightly. "To be perfectly honest with you, Case, I was half-asleep last night, too!"

"Not true, not true, unless my mind has played a very cruel trick on me."

"Well, what do you say we find out what was real and what was a dream?" He moved closer, the passion suddenly returned, his kiss demanding but gentle.

She reached around his body and drew him to her. After a moment's caress, she rolled him over, pulling the sheets to cover them. "Whatever you say." Her words came out in a breathless voice.

Mike shivered at the touch of her tongue against his bare chest. She pursued him as he turned onto his stomach, lowering herself over him, her tongue sending darts of lightning into him, causing him to tremble beneath her. Her hands caressed, explored, magically bringing forth shivers of delight that rose and rippled through his muscular frame. She felt his excitement and this delighted her.

Casey turned him over, smothering him with her own demands, her darting tongue, her anxious hands. He lifted off the bed, lifted into her lovemaking.

Suddenly he felt the urge of passion and rolled her gently away, matching her hunger with his own, creating the same desperate responses in her that she had created in him. Time and again their passion rose and swelled as if they had become swept away by the same tide. Emotions swirled dizzily in a steamy vapor that formed into one single urge between them.

The alchemy left their bodies suddenly still, Mike feeling himself deep within her. But it was more than that; they had both merged into a warmth that was *their* special lovemaking, that had evaporated into love itself.

Her hunger for him seemed so fully sated that she thought she could remain content forever. Her imagination flew.

"Like . . . like me awake?" she breathed.

"I like . . . love you *both* ways."

Mike felt whole, his mind and body at peace, fulfilled. He now luxuriated in a hot shower, and not even the horrors of the quake seemed able to touch him. He had a feeling, too, that his nights would no longer be taken up with insomnia and mindless late night TV shows.

As he lathered, the stream of water washing over his body, he could not hear Casey calling to him with the news that breakfast was ready. She came in and knocked on the shower door. He suggested she join him.

"Save that fantasy for another time. Right now I want you in the kitchen! Hungry?"

"Starved."

She threw him a towel and he switched off the water and climbed out.

He *was* starving. More than his work, more than anything, sex aroused his appetite. It had always seemed a strange aberration, but he had the notion that a lot of men suffered from it. "Someone ought to do a study," he said to himself as he dressed, the shower steam smell already being replaced with the aroma of fresh coffee wafting in from the kitchen.

He found that Casey had set a complete breakfast of scrambled eggs, toast, coffee, and juice.

"Hey, this is wonderful . . . *you're* wonderful."

"So long as I have you fooled!" She poured hot coffee for them both and sat across from him.

"I wish I could take you out for breakfast. I didn't know you were going to so much trouble."

"We'd have more trouble eating out. Do you have any idea how many people must be eating out this morning?

Besides, I did promise you a place to sleep *with* breakfast."

"I thought *I* promised to make breakfast?"

"Eat, enjoy! It's been a long time since I cooked for anyone other than myself."

He smiled. "Is that a fact? Good. Guess I should shut up and eat."

"Before it gets cold, yes."

The coffee was rich and strong, the way he liked it. For a time their eyes did more talking than they did.

"If you'd like to, Mike . . ." she began hesitantly. "I mean, if you want—"

"Just until I can relocate." He tried to help her out. "Can I stay?"

She bit her lower lip and moved her hand across to his, her touch warm. "You're welcome here for as long as . . . as you like."

"You're sure?"

"Yes, I'm sure."

"I tend to leave things a mess."

"I know, I've been following you around. The couch, the bath!"

"I snore at times."

"I know."

"I'm not much good in the kitchen. Can't heat soup without scalding it, or myself, or both."

"That's not a problem."

"I can do dishes, but I drop them from time to time."

She laughed.

"And my garbage-bagging took last place in the Hefty semi-finals."

Her smile was radiant.

"And as for toothpaste—"

"Mike, having you here with me will get me through the effects of the quake, and that will more than make up for *all* your shortcomings."

He gave her a mock frown. "Is that a compliment?"

"Don't think I have no faults, please."

"I've seen none."

"I tend to ignore people when I'm involved in my work. Hadn't written or called my father in months, until this morning."

"Is he in the city? What about other family?"

"Dad's in New York; he's a professor in biophysics. Mom, well, I didn't know her too well when she left us. I was an infant. Rest of my family, aunts and uncles, are all in and around New York."

"You got a call out to New York? When?"

"Before you woke up. I got out of bed, made the call, and returned before you missed me. Dad had heard about the quake and the CCDC going down. He was frantic, of course, packing and trying to book a flight. I calmed him down, thank God." She looked across at him. "What about you? Want to try Chicago?"

"Nah, no one there is worried about me."

"Don't pretend such modesty, Dr. McCain."

"I mean, I have no family."

"Oh, sorry . . . I was thinking of friends at your last job, U of C, all that. People around the CCDC have been buzzing about you since Leo brought you in."

"Acquired me, you mean?"

"We've all been acquired, Mike. Leo likes to surround himself with talented people."

"He recognizes good work. That's why you're here. I understand you had a hand in finding a vaccine for chicken pox, along with Weintraub. Due out on the market this year, isn't it?"

She nodded. "That's what Leo likes best; results he can turn to profits."

" 'Course, at the time, I thought you were a man."

She stared into her coffee, not hearing his last remark, asking, "What now, Mike? You can't sit around L.A.

waiting for Leo to rebuild his empire. Of course, you probably have a job to go home to."

He looked thoughtfully at her. "I don't know exactly. I mean, I really haven't allowed it to sink in yet. When I first came here I couldn't believe my luck, you know? I mean, for the first time in my career I was given everything, *carte blanche,* and the idea that someone was willing to pay me to go in any direction my mind wished to go, and maybe help people in the process . . . well, you know the feeling."

She sipped the last of her coffee. "I did . . . once."

"Can't believe I didn't run into you sooner."

"Carefully orchestrated."

"Oh, yeah."

"I'll confess it all one day. Give me time."

"Sure . . . no rush."

The door buzzer pierced the silence between them, and Casey went to the door, speaking into a panel on the wall. "Yes? Who is it?"

"Dr. Sterns, it's me, Jose . . . Jose Ortiz. I'm here to take you—" His words were cut off; he had let go of the intercom button too soon.

"How nice, Mike, our chauffeur awaits us."

eight

"I was there, Dr. McCain," Ortiz said, his voice cracking. "A horrible thing, I tell you . . . horrible. Amunsen's head ripped from his body, his arm gone . . . Naldosa out of his mind, and then Dr. Timmons getting bitten. I tell you—"

"Timmons? Dr. Thad Timmons?"

"Yes, sir. Those monkeys, doctor, acted crazy. Like they were mad."

"Animals are as prone to panic as people; fright's not just a human reaction," said Casey. "I mean, monkeys are likely to bite people when ill, or afraid."

"Those monkeys, doctors, they *were* afraid . . . the way they ran out squealing like pigs! I could see that," Jose said.

"Do you know Dr. Timmons well?" Casey asked Mike.

"Yes, he's a good man . . . good doctor."

"So terrible about Amunsen and Naldosa," Casey said.

"Where'd you say Naldosa is now?" Mike had turned back to Jose.

"Isolation ward, UCLA Hospital, or so Tony says.

Tony tried to get in, but they wouldn't let him. He got some pictures, though, and some film."

"I'm sure he did," Mike said sarcastically.

"Wonder if any of those monkeys were ours?" Casey said, thoughtfully.

"*Yours,* doctor?" Ortiz smiled for the first time that morning.

"Experimentals, Jose. AIDS virus."

"Holy Mother! I mean, the men handling the monkeys, won't they get it?"

Casey smiled and shook her head where she sat between the two men. "Not a chance. But monkeys with AIDS aren't aggressive, so I don't think—"

"They are saying Naldosa's rantings frightened the animals," said Jose, "but Tony, he's got his own ideas."

"Which way are we going, Jose?" Casey asked suddenly. "This isn't the right way."

But Mike was asking at the same time, "What ideas does Qunin have?"

"Oh, he thinks the monkeys frightened Naldosa, made Naldosa think there was some kind of . . . I don't know . . . horrible monster down there with him."

"I see."

"Jose," Casey broke in, "this is not the way to the CCDC."

"I know," replied Ortiz, looking guilty. "It's the way to UCLA."

"What?"

"Why are you taking us to the university?"

"Tony . . . he wants to see you . . . has something he wants to show you."

"Show us?" In spite of her anger, Casey was curious.

"Something about Naldosa . . . the monkeys. He insisted I bring you. Please—"

"We're needed elsewhere, Jose," Mike said firmly. "And frankly, I'm not interested in Tony Qunin's next news story."

"But it's important . . . important you come, important to you both."

"There's important work waiting at the CCDC," replied Casey. "Now, please, Jose, turn this truck around."

"What Tony's got to show you is about the CCDC, and it's important. I know Tony, he wouldn't pull you away from your work if it wasn't important." The doctors could see that Ortiz's pleading was sincere.

Casey exchanged a look with Mike, and he saw in her eyes that she had already relented. "All right, Jose, but this better not take too long."

"It won't, I promise. I promise, doctor."

"In the meantime, tell us what you know, Jose." Mike pressed for an answer. "What's Qunin up to now?"

"Tony, he don't always tell me what he's thinking . . . but it's got something to do with the film."

"Film?" asked Casey.

Jose described the film he'd watched in the early morning hours with Tony and Les Code. "Les's probably enlarged it by now," Jose finished.

"I don't get it," said Mike. "Why does a TV newscaster want a couple of doctors to view a film?"

"That's the part I don't know," Jose said.

Mike and Casey followed Jose Ortiz down a series of brightly lit corridors. Casey looked overhead and had to shade her eyes from the sun shining through the many skylight panels that fed the plants and trees which lined the walkway. The school atmosphere reminded her of a painting by Rembrandt—or was it Titian?—a painting of Socrates and his students in a great hall of learning with light streaming down.

The university building had been untouched by the quake, and Casey felt a strange but warm feeling of being in a sanctuary, as if the gods of the quake did not dare enter here. The campus recalled a wonderful time in her life, when she was a student with her whole future ahead of her. Although UCLA was not Stanford, stepping into the bright corridors here was like basking in a fond memory, as if stepping back in time. The light all around her felt like the light of knowledge, and she had her entire life been a faithful believer in the rational and intellectual.

But outside, in Leo G. Copellmier's world of finance medicine, she had been always ill-at-ease, as if she had lost something of herself, something valuable and irreplaceable.

Suddenly, a door with a small porthole window in it swung open and Tony Qunin rushed out to them, breaking Casey's reverie. "Doctors, you've finally come! Please, come in, come in."

"What kind of a game are you playing, Qunin?" asked Mike.

"No games." He met Mike's stare, and then looked at Casey. "Something you must see to believe."

"A film, I understand, of the death of Amunsen. I'm not sure we really need to be subjected to—"

"I need expert advice, expert eyes," Tony cut in. "I need you both."

"And so we're supposed to drop everything and come running?"

"Please," he appealed to them. "Bear with me . . . this could be vitally important to the health and well-being of the entire population of the city, doctors."

"Your investigative reporting is now public-service oriented, Mr. Qunin?" Mike asked acidly.

"It is being pushed in that direction, yes."

Mike looked into the darkened screening room and then at Casey. "Looks like we go to the movies, if you have no objections, Dr. Sterns."

"If it's as important as these gentlemen seem to think."

"It is, it is," Tony assured them.

Inside, they took seats in the front row of an empty viewing room. Qunin shouted to the projection booth for the tape to begin. He then sat beside Casey. Jose disappeared somewhere in the gloom behind them.

"I've got two short tapes I'd like you to examine."

"You keep saying 'examine' instead of 'watch,' Mr. Qunin, why is that?" asked Casey.

"I want you to look closely, very closely and critically at what you are about to see."

"We're not film critics, Mr. Qunin; we're doctors."

"I know, but you must see . . . every detail."

The film was rolling, and they watched the celluloid replay of Naldosa's rescue. First the emergence of Amunsen's corpse on a stretcher, the camera zooming in.

"Christ, I hope you're not planning on using this on the air."

"Look closely, doctor, please! There, see the arm?"

"Yes," said Mike. "What the hell's the point?"

"Stop, Les, run it back frame by frame," Tony ordered.

It was done quickly and efficiently.

"There! See that, McCain?"

Mike stared at the unusual markings on Amunsen's arm. Aside from the grease, asphalt dust and grime, there was clearly an odd pattern of dark patches on the skin.

Casey stared at the screen, eyes wide.

"Run ahead, Les!"

The film moved smoothly onward to reveal the first glimpse of Naldosa, who was fighting with his rescuers. The film zoomed in tight to catch the action but did not come as close as it had to Amunsen.

"We have Naldosa on the tapes complaining of some kind of skin rash that was burning and irritating him. If you look closely, you might see it had spread from his hands to his face. I saw the same markings on the monkey that bit Timmons, and filmed a closeup of the animal. Here it comes."

The screen was filled with the face of a dead rhesus monkey, its hair stripped away. Large, dark, oval patches, some solid, others like rings, discolored the animal's features. Then the film came to an abrupt end.

"Okay, Mr. Qunin," began Mike, clearly irritated, "so, you want us to make some kind of medical judgment based on this?"

"As to the lesions on the animal, on the men, yes! Can you give me any clue as to how they got there? What they mean?"

Mike and Casey exchanged a look. "They appear to be some sort of burns," Casey remarked. "From the coloration, I mean . . . but . . ."

"But what?" Tony pressed.

"Too symmetrical, too patterned to be ordinary burns," replied Mike, studying Casey's eyes.

"Toxic chemical?" Casey wondered aloud.

"What kind of toxic chemical?"

Mike put Tony off with an upturned hand. "You thinking of a leak?" he asked Casey.

"Possible, isn't it?"

"Sure, in fact it's likely in some areas down below the quake debris."

"What kind of leak, doctor?" Tony asked doggedly. "Radiation?"

Mike folded his arms against his wide chest and released a great pent-up breath of air. "Don't go off half-cocked, Qunin!"

"Hey, I get a little shaky when I hear the words toxic and leak used together. Can you blame me?"

"We're talking about a toxic gas, Mr. Qunin, used to . . . to sterilize instruments in routine operations and procedures," said Casey.

Tony looked at her and frowned. Her calmness might have enraged him, but for the sincerity in her voice. "Routine, huh? All just routine. Copellmier put me off all the time with words like that when I interviewed him about the CCDC."

"As I recall it, Dr. Copellmier gave you a complete tour and answered all your questions," countered Mike.

"No, not all of them," Tony replied, his eyes narrowing. "And now you two are trying to dismiss this 'routine' toxic leak that disfigures people."

"We're not dismissing it, Mr. Qunin!" Casey glared at the reporter. "It happens."

"It happens, it happens."

"It has been known to happen in hospitals before. Yes, even hospitals that have not undergone the radical damage brought about by an earthquake!"

Tony looked from her to Mike, and Mike nodded. "Not routinely, but she's right."

"Then these marks, it's nothing dangerous? No deadly Bhopal kind of incident that might occur here if they lift off one too many concrete slabs?"

"No, none."

"No need to alert the public?"

"None."

"I hope you're right, Dr. McCain . . . but what about the animals, the monkeys?"

"What about them?"

"They're all dying in hideous pain, and they all have the lesions."

"Oh, my God," Casey whispered, her eyes finding Mike's. "This might be much more serious than we thought."

"Where are the animals now?"

"Isolated."

"Where?"

"Here, on campus, in a germ-free environment."

"The new medical complex?" asked Casey.

"Yes, but—"

"And Naldosa? And Amunsen's body?" asked Mike.

"Naldosa's being transported here now. As for Amunsen, his body is lost."

"Lost?"

"We think it's at Dodger Stadium, but so are thousands of others."

"Who's searching?"

"Stark's men are working in conjunction with the paramedics. They have a line on the guys who were driving the ambulance that took him away. The cops are involved. Can you imagine, an APB on a dead man?"

"Who ordered the isolation and search?"

"The coroner's office was contacted by Dr. Albert Tobler."

"Who's Tobler?"

"A doctor here at the university," replied Casey. "Something of a genius in medical technology, and the only man I know who ever turned Leo G. Copellmier down."

"Come on, let's go talk to Dr. Tobler and see if there has been any determination of what this thing is."

"Wait, doctors," said Tony, blocking their way at the door.

"We don't have any pat answers for the noon report, Qunin," said Mike derisively.

"There's one more film you must see."

"Oh, for Pete's sake, we don't have time for—"

"It's the cave-in, the final moments before we lost visual contact with Naldosa and when Amunsen was . . . disappeared."

Casey put a hand against Mike's chest and said, "It could be useful."

"It's not long," added Tony. He didn't give Mike another chance to disagree. "Roll number two, Les."

"All carefully orchestrated," mumbled Mike into Casey's ear. But immediately both doctors' eyes were glued to the screen, mesmerized by the film of Amunsen's final moments on Earth. They listened to the chatting of the men, the noise of their movements, their eyes registering the odds and ends of trash that made up the moles' dungeon.

"Had this film computer-enhanced," Tony spoke softly from behind them. "This resolution is good compared to what we had originally. It's taken us all night and most of this morning to clear up the graininess."

"Stop it there, Les!" Tony suddenly ordered at the instant of the cave-in. "Back a frame, one more, there!" Tony rushed to the screen, pointing to Amunsen's shoulder. "Look closely here, doctors. Tell me, in your opinion, is that a human hand? Is that Amunsen's left hand on his left shoulder? No, it's not. And what are these? Fingers? Or claws?"

Mike got up slowly and moved between the screen and the projector, briefly blocking the light. Casey followed. Together they stared for a moment at what Qunin was pointing to. On Amunsen's left shoulder and around his neck there appeared, amazing as it seemed, a full set of massive claws, as if he had been grabbed by some mad prankster wearing a werewolf Halloween costume.

"Some kind of metal . . ." Casey said. "Just pieces of metal falling down with the rest of the debris over the man . . . that's all."

"And you, Dr. McCain?"

"I admit, it looks strange, like something out of the Twilight Zone, but Dr. Sterns is right. There's got to be a simple . . . explanation."

"Stand back a little and watch," said Tony.

Les advanced the film. The claws, while at first appearing stiff and metallic, moved with life. They were not inanimate. They squeezed and ripped in one blinding second, and the screen was suddenly glaring white, the end of the film snapping in the screening room.

Les had played the film in slow motion at the end, and still everything seemed to happen in the blink of an eye. Casey wasn't sure what she saw.

"So, what the devil was that?" Qunin said as he flicked on the light.

"I couldn't tell you," said Mike. "I don't know."

"Really? Who would? Copellmier?"

"Mr. Qunin," began Casey, "you're going to have to accept the fact we're just doctors, researchers . . . we're not quake experts or monster hunters, and—"

"Would you care to see the film again?"

"We haven't time," Mike said emphatically, "not if there really is an epidemic of some sort spreading."

"I think a lot more was going on at your research center than anyone let on, doctors. I think this film may prove me right."

"That's ridiculous!" Mike's tone held more sarcasm than anger. "You're reading too much into this."

"Was there anyone in the center working in the field of cybernetics?"

"Yes," replied Casey, "but—"

"The claws on Amunsen's neck were not animal claws."

"Mr. Qunin, really, you don't believe that . . . that some sort of robot—"

"Cyborg, perhaps?"

"—is . . . is crawling about the rubble killing people?" Casey finished.

"Can we go now, Mr. Qunin?" Mike asked.

They started to leave, when Mike stopped halfway through the door and said to Tony, "Oh, by the way, I hope you have the good sense to keep this film buried. If you try to tell the public what you just told us, they'll put you away."

*   *   *

The monkeys lay on their backs, transformed into something akin to sloths, hairy little lumps of flesh and bones, eyes rolled up into sockets as if they had been drugged. Mike and Casey had no trouble locating the white-haired, bow-tied professor of medicine, Dr. Albert Tobler. They now stood over the small animals, each monkey encased in separate bubbles, small life-support systems normally used for premature babies.

"They look drugged," Casey noted.

"They aren't," said Dr. Tobler. "We were contacted by doctors working at your CCDC facility, who stressed that the animals may be carrying something contagious. We isolated them carefully and here they have remained. Are you here to take them away?"

"We're here to examine them," Casey replied.

"I see."

Mike had been studying the animals keenly as they talked and now he said, "I do hope your people took all precautions in handling them, doctor."

"Of course we did! I was told about the unfortunate Dr. Timmons, who, by the way, is also isolated down the hall, as is this fellow Naldosa. Are you here to examine these men as well?"

Mike looked at Casey, and she said, "I think we should."

He nodded. "These creatures are suffering, but not all of them are our AIDS animals, and yet, the symptoms are quite similar."

Casey studied the monkeys one by one, each uglier than the poor creature before it. One blinked uncontrollably, its pupils dark, the whites of its eyes turned a dull shade of brown. Another had tremors, but most lay about as if they had no spines. She saw clearly the rust-colored, circular marks all over the little animals.

Any vet would have destroyed them by now, but if they were carrying a contagious disease, these little animals could help to answer the hundreds of questions their present state raised.

"What do you think, Case?" Mike whispered in her ear.

"I . . . have no idea."

"Qunin must be right."

"Huh?"

"Toxic leak, maybe something more deadly than the gas we use to sterilize instruments. Maybe Leo did have some kind of research going on that we didn't know about, something lethal."

"Leo's no saint. I wonder if anyone's located him? Maybe he can tell us what it is we're supposed to be treating before it spreads much further."

"Better keep this between us, Case."

She looked at him and slowly nodded. "Of course."

"No sense panicking everyone. At least, not yet."

"We better have a look at the men. Hope they're better off than these poor devils." She gave a final glance to the monkeys. One turned its head to her, bared its teeth and screeched with a madness born of pain.

They followed Dr. Tobler toward the isolation rooms where Naldosa and Timmons were being kept. Tobler was proud of his facilities and praised them as they walked.

"We have the best and the most modern equipment in the city, a state-of-the art surgical center, as germ-free as anyone is capable of making a hospital."

Albert Tobler, as tall as Mike and just as vital, was an intense man with a contagious smile. His beard was thick and gray, and a pair of tinted glasses completed the image of a genius, or a mad scientist. The doctor wore a bow-tie, old sneakers, ill-fitting horn-rim glasses, and a lab coat which was in dire need of laundering. He seemed out of place amid a "Star-Wars" collection of gadgetry, giving the impression he could not possibly know what to do with all his high-tech labs and operating theaters.

Tobler's tour of the facilities took them past glass-walled labs framed with stainless steel. "This area," he told them, "includes rooms where the temperature remains a constant thirty-seven degrees centigrade, so that human cells taken from the body—"

"—will not spoil," finished Mike.

"—will feel at home," the old man countered. "In incubation chambers where the atmosphere is a special mix of nitrogen, carbon dioxide and oxygen—"

"—cells are exposed to the same environment that is found inside the body," Casey completed the explanation.

"We're not unfamiliar with such facilities, Dr. Tobler; you see, we worked under similar guidelines at the CCDC."

"I see. And did you have chambers, Dr. McCain, where temperature is kept at minus-eighty degrees centigrade, such as these?" Dr. Tobler pointed to tables lined with serum chambers.

Casey's smile registered a fondness for the old man; she appreciated the pride he had in his research facilities. "Cold enough to preserve cell-lines and proteins," she said matter-of-factly.

"And samples of sera for extended purposes," added Mike.

"Yes, but also to keep our beer cold!" He laughed lightly. Tobler then pointed to the conduit pipes that glistened like ribbons of silver up and down the corridors overhead. "Special plumbing for carbon dioxide and vacuum lines, doctors. I'm sure you can appreciate that. Everything necessary to your work is right at hand! We have ovens to bake and cleanse glassware, and plenty of staff and technical assistance."

"How many autoclaves do you have, doctor?" asked Mike.

"A full dozen."

"Centrifuges?"

"More than fifty. No waiting in line."

"I can see," said Casey, "that ventilation and air-conditioning's no problem."

"In fact, my dear, we have laminar airflow lab benches to protect experiments from any environmental contamination, as well as high intensity, untraviolet lights to protect—"

"—us from our own experiments!" finished Mike, making Tobler laugh again.

"That's one way to put it, yes."

Mike could not hide his admiration of Tobler's labs. They rivaled the CCDC's in quality. There were positive pressure labs, airflow always outward, guaranteeing atmospheric sterility. There were controlled access rooms, backup systems for every contingency.

"You ain't seen nothing yet," said Tobler, a grin swelling his beard. "Come! You must see the operating theaters."

As they moved on, Tobler said, "If my facilities can help, treat them as your own for the time being, doctors. From what I have seen, I fear we do indeed have a contagious disease of some sort on our hands."

He opened a door to a room featuring a view that dazzled Mike and Casey. They stepped into an overhead viewing room that looked down on an operating area that impressed them both. Surgeons were at work, but they wore, as a matter of course, protective suits with air supplies, suits that minimized the risk of infection via virus or germ.

Long, tubular hoses moved back and forth between the spacesuited men and women. Faces were hidden behind helmet visors rather than surgical masks. Surrounding the surgeons was an enormous plastic bubble. They operated on a young woman, perhaps sixteen, in the center of the room.

"They're working on her hip," said Tobler. "Crushed beyond repair."

"A quake victim?"

"A fortunate quake victim, one we have a replacement hip for. It's plastic, but it will serve her for the rest of her life."

"Incredible," said Casey.

Mike watched the skilled physicians work. He heard Tobler tell Casey that the patient might also require a prosthetic knee.

The spacesuited doctors looked like benevolent aliens come to save mankind, Mike thought. The bubble, too, was remarkable. Inside its protective walls the girl was shielded from any invasion of bacteria to the open wound. Any such invasion would quickly destroy an otherwise successful operation, making such implants dangerous by virtue of any number of complications that might begin at the microcosmic level. If the implant could be done without interference from bacteria, the new hip would work in every way like the real thing.

"A fan blows filtered air in from the top of the bubble," Tobler explained. "It goes out the bottom, and during the operation the airflow is kept constant. Meanwhile, the doctor's own breath is kept within the confines of his own unit."

"It's all amazing," Mike commented.

Casey nodded her agreement.

"Thanks to our advanced methods and equipment, our teams of specialists can repair brain arteries to *prevent* strokes, dissolve spinal tumors with soundwaves, open clogged arteries with balloons and simultaneously transplant livers, pancreases, and kidneys—and in some cases, hearts and lungs."

"Sounds like the real fountain of youth," said Casey.

"Perhaps." Tobler beamed. "We are going to be among the first to be involved in surgical repair of bones and joints—my particular specialty. The important thing is that our infection rate has been cut by more than two-thirds, and it's getting better all the time."

"Look, Mike, the surgeon's using a light-ray scalpel," said Casey.

"The ultimate scalpel," Tobler said. "It is clean, precise, and leaves minimal scar tissue."

Casey craned her neck to watch the incision.

"If you're interested in trying one, it can be arranged."

"Think I can learn to use it, doctor?" Casey asked.

"Of course you can, though I never thought I would see the day when a million-dollar piece of equipment would be used to perform an autopsy on a monkey. I'll have to explain it to the dean, but it shouldn't be a problem."

"What about getting us a room like that one?" asked Mike, pointing. "If there is something contagious, I don't want either of us contracting it."

"Oh, I quite agree. I have just such a room reserved for you."

Mike looked at him in confusion. "Then you knew we were coming?"

"As far as I know, doctors, you two are L.A.'s leading immunologists. After conferring with the coroner's office, I hoped you would consent to help us."

"No wonder we get the grand tour of the million-dollar laser and the billion-dollar lab."

"You, Dr. McCain, Dr. Sterns, are our best hope right now."

Casey looked back at the operating room and turned to say, "I want to help, Mike."

He nodded. "I do, too."

"Good, good!" said Tobler. "Now, I will see to it you are fitted for one of those suits, and then you can see your patients, doctors."

"Where do we scrub?" Mike asked. "Or do you just run us through a de-con chamber?"

Tobler chuckled and then said, "Oh, Dr. McCain, I'm sure you've heard about Fels naphtha soap. That's all I ever use."

nine

The noise of the big ones with the light-eyes moving all about the ruins now caused it great concern. It was certain they had seen it and were returning, their numbers doubled, to kill it. A hiding place must be found.

Explosive noises drove it deep into the ruins, back and back until it came upon a large, wide-mouthed pipe. The pipe was dark and forbidding, but so much pain racked its body now that death would be welcomed as a friend. It pulled itself over the lip of the pipe and slid in, its body curling to the contour of the metal. The descent was slow and gradual at first, until it allowed gravity to take it down, deep into the darkness where a continual *thrumming* noise offered some small measure of comfort.

The pain was growing like a separate life within its body. It bellowed out when a flood of sewage fell over its head, only to have its lungs fill with the filthy water.

The current was powerful, a thousand times more powerful than it. In its weakened state, it was swept and flushed out onto an unknown course.

Then it was jolted hard into a concrete slab and it lay against it, pained and exhausted. All around it were concrete gray walls and twisted pipes, which spewed forth more water.

Was this the place to die? There was no food, and the torturous, rolling pain inside was overtaking it again.

Its limbs were soft, too soft. It could not have been flushed through the pipe if they hadn't gone soft. Feet and legs, once enlarged after feeding, had become shriveled again, near useless. How long could it survive the pain? How long could it go without feeding again?

Withered arms reached for the top of the slab it was plastered against and it somehow pulled itself over. It lay panting, fighting for air, but knowing better, knowing only one thing could ease the pain. On its back, it watched as its claw-hands hovered overhead, as if they had a life of their own. If it dropped them hard on its own throat, it would be ended, the pain, the agony, the emptiness. Instead, one claw rested beside its elongated, misshapen jaw. The other touched the blackened tissue that hung loosely over its left eye, blurring its vision, carefully peeling it off and dropping it into its mouth so it could be chewed into a ball and spit away. Its claw tips touched a nose, sunken and buried in flesh. Its nose twitched, but not as a result of its touch. There was an odor on the air. Something was near, and creeping nearer.

It could hear it. Nails softly scratching over rock on the right, over its shoulder.

With its last reserve of strength, it raised its right claw high above it, and let its arm suddenly collapse. Its claw had pinned a cat-sized rat that had creeped to within inches of it, examining what it took for a mound of sewage. The second claw ripped off the rat's head, and it sucked at the small creature's neck for what it wanted, and tossed away the empty shell.

It wasn't much, but it was something.

Even as it fed on the near useless morsel, it knew that it was going to die—to die in horrible pain.

"*Aaaaaaaaaaaaa—waaaaaaaaaaaaa,*" it moaned softly.

"I need help in here stat!" Mike McCain shouted over the intercom and several physicians rushed immediately to assist him. Mike had been alerted when Naldosa's monitor suddenly went dead, only to find the patient had torn away from the tubes and wires connected to him and was crawling across the floor toward Timmons in the next bed, the look of a mad dog in his bulging eyes.

"Where is he? Where's Naldosa?" the others wanted to know.

"Under the bed," replied Mike, pointing.

"He's frightened," said Casey, who had entered behind the others. The now blackened, deformed man was in an uncontrollable fit, his body twitching beneath the bed in tormented spasms. It took every available hand to retrieve the patient, the task made more difficult by their protective suits.

"The sedation isn't working on these men any longer," Mike told Tobler when he rushed in. "Look at Timmons."

"*Help me, Dr. MaaaaaCaaaaannnn,*" Timmons moaned.

"If normal sedation doesn't work, we have to try using electrodes to the nerves," replied Tobler.

"Get him back onto the bed," Casey told the other men, going over to Naldosa and looking out at him through the visor of her suit. "He's clearly out of coma, but he's in horrendous pain," she said, her eyes searching for what was left of him inside his eyes. "Poor man."

"He's dangerous, Casey; take care."

Naldosa's body had gone mad with gyrations and spasms. To protect himself and those around him, he had to be strapped down.

This done, Tobler went to his side and immediately

hooked him up to what looked like a car battery.
Electrodes were placed at key points on his body. "The
same as acupuncture points, actually. The mild current
is not electricity but soundwaves."

"Soundwaves?" Mike asked, never having seen this
procedure before.

"The waves sent into the nerves act as a triggering
mechanism to release endorphins from his own brain,
natural painkillers."

"Any treatment in a storm," said Casey. "God, these
men look horrid."

Naldosa was literally turning black as each of the
lesions metastasized.

"If this works on Naldosa, we'll switch Timmons over
to your soundwave machine, too."

Tobler nodded. "I have a spare. I'll see that it's
nearby."

Naldosa seemed the opposite of Timmons. Where
Timmons was bloated and swollen, the Mexican was
shriveled and sunken. Was it due to some difference in
metabolism, diet, or environment . . . or was it a matter
of time? Was Timmons soon going to go the way of
Naldosa?

Mike put out a gloved hand to his dying colleague.

"What's hap'ning to . . . me . . . doctors?" pleaded
Timmons. "Tell me . . . what . . . is . . . it?"

Mike saw Timmons was staring down at his arms and
chest, covered now with copper rings.

"We're onto it, Timmons," Mike lied, swallowing the
truth hard.

"Promise me," he pleaded, staring across at Naldosa,
"before I be . . . be-come . . . him, you will let
me . . . die? Won't you?"

"I don't want to hear any talk like that!" said Casey,
calling up her bravest smile. "Give us a chance, we'll lick
this yet," she tried to reassure him.

Tobler returned with the second soundwave unit and

Mike decided to go ahead and hook Timmons up. Already, Naldosa was lying calm and still, his eyes only half open now.

Timmons, too, responded well to the oscillating soundwaves wafting through his nerve cells. The doctors were glad that their patients could rest in relative comfort, but it reminded them how futile their attempts to treat the disease had been thus far. They went back to work.

Mike McCain monitored vital signs on a green screen where a series of bright white lines and bleeping noises told him that Raphael Naldosa still held onto life. With chart in hand, wearing a light blue protective suit and helmet, he felt like an astronaut in space watching a comrade slip away into the vast unknown. The fact that he had been unable to do anything to keep Naldosa from drifting away before his eyes made Mike feel more than helpless, it brought on a sense of utter depression.

Naldosa was a brave man, a good man. *Why him?* he wondered. But he hadn't time for such questions, he must concentrate on medicine. What was killing this man, and how? When a man died of injuries visible and definable, from a diseased pancreas, a faulty heart— even a sudden aneurism—at least there was some way to rationalize it, something to hold up to the light. But Naldosa's condition remained a mystery.

Mike felt a well of frustration bubbling within himself. He'd been unable to pinpoint the terrible cause of the distress, and he'd begun to internalize the guilt, blaming himself for not solving the mystery. He knew it was irrational behavior, and that it made for bad medicine. But the facts did little to dispel his gloom, or the glacial feeling at the pit of his stomach.

Although lab work was hard, Mike preferred it to treating patients, and now he knew why.

It wasn't so much because he dreamed of helping

large numbers of people with great discoveries, but because of the more selfish reason he'd learned as an intern: it was much easier to face a diseased chick embryo than a man for whom you had no answers.

Mike now stared through a glass partition at Naldosa and Timmons, considering their chances. Naldosa had slipped into a complete coma, perhaps the mind's way of combating the disease. Odds against both men grew astronomical with each passing hour, complicated by the fact that their doctors had no idea what was killing them.

All that seemed certain was that the disease, possibly bacterial, possibly a virus, affected the nervous system. Neither patient had had control, or proper use of, his nervous system. Mike was hard at work trying to determine if it were indeed a bacterial infection of some sort or a virus. To do so, he was nurturing cultures. Bacteria proliferated under any circumstances, while a virus could only survive within host cells.

Young, innocent-looking Dr. Timmons lay asleep at present, his body having been duped into believing there was no pain. But how long could he be kept under?

In another room, Mike had worked with tissue samples from both Naldosa and Timmons—minuscule scrapings from the lesions formed on their skin. These were now "brewing" as tissue cultures and it was waiting time . . . the hardest time for Mike.

At one time Timmons had been almost lucid, and had said something to one of the doctors. Mike thought it might be a clue. Attempting to understand his own condition, Timmons had said the pain was concentrated in his muscles and organs, that he could feel the outlines of his kidneys, lungs, stomach, heart, and the musculature throughout his body, that it all seemed both swollen and dehydrated.

Mike returned to his microscope where he stared at the strange life swimming in the first culture he had prepared. The light of the comparison microscope showed a teeming, energetic life force, feeding on everything in its environment. Mike checked the slide against a boxful of generic slides, looking for any similarities, any clues to the killer. He was coming up empty.

When he met with Casey, his mind was a receptacle of questions. "Did you have any more luck than me?"

"Something peculiar came up, but I don't know what to make of it."

"Tell me about it."

They were in the outer room, where, after sterilization, they could take off their helmets and speak to one another directly.

"It was the blood."

"Go on."

She pushed her hair from her eyes, having now discarded the gloves. She poured herself coffee. "Lots of drugs, Mike."

Mike wondered why she was stalling. "Okay, like what kind of drugs?"

"Drugs that shouldn't have been present . . . unless—"

"Unless what?"

"Unless someone at the CCDC was playing with steroids, doing some kind of experimentation I've never heard about."

"Steroids? Not so far as I was led to believe."

"You saw the size of that rhesus, didn't you? Arms, legs ballooned out to here. All his internal organs were misshapen, almost as if—"

"Misshapen? You mean enlarged?"

"Enlarged in a horrible way, not just larger, but as if each were put on a rack and . . . and stretched."

"And the muscle tissue?"

"The same! Elongated, enlarged, stretched, misshapen."

"Could such a metamorphosis occur in a fully grown man?"

"It appears to have happened in a fully grown monkey. I mean that was not a young specimen. He'd been around for years."

"Doesn't make any goddamned sense . . . steroids, enlarged musculature, misshapen organs."

"That monkey's almost as big as an orangutan, Mike, and I don't know what could cause that. Some kind of instant gigantism, maybe acromegaly?"

"But that's impossible."

"What then? You tell me, was someone playing with adrenalin, somatotropin, what?"

Mike went over to the window that separated him from the patients. "Look at Naldosa's hands, his feet, the lower half of his face." Mike had indeed observed signs of acromegaly in Naldosa, a chronic disease marked by overgrowth of the extremities and the lower portion of the face. "Case, you think the AIDS virus could have joined with something *else* to cause all this? I mean, so far as we know, all that monkey had was AIDS. No steroids, just AIDS."

"There's something else, Mike," she replied, indicating a slide. "Have a look."

Mike took it and slipped it under the microscope. He stared in silence for a time before he said, "Is this from the monkey?"

"Yes."

"Is it what I think it is?"

"Growth hormone GH. GH, the hormone that prompts growth in early life, continues growth through adolescence—"

"—to enlarge and develop all body tissues," he finished.

"As well as growth in the number and size of body cells, Mike."

"I know, I know, but it makes no sense. How? Where did it come from?"

"I had the same reaction, especially since the wounds on the animal refused to heal. Naturally, if you could control your own GH-factor, you could heal yourself by regenerating new tissue, new cells."

"But it's against nature," Mike protested, "against all known biological facts and—"

"From what I saw of the animal's brain, biological facts don't amount to much in this case."

"Meaning?"

"I wish there *were* some meaning in all this, but . . . I only know that there was some sort of hormonal-steroid-chemical war going on inside the animal's nervous system. Frankly, if I had to give an opinion immediately, I'd have to say that all the stops were let out, all the safety checks and balances in the system, the secretions, the glands . . . they were all drained and only the strongest organs and tissues in the animal's body could survive much beyond the point when it was shot."

"You looked at the adrenal gland then? A breakdown there?"

"Enlarged, probably pumping out twice the normal adrenaline."

"The pituitary?"

"Every gland regulated by the brain, Mike, was functioning out of control, so far as I could see."

"I took a blood sample on this monkey not twenty-four hours ago, Casey, *the same animal.* I tell you there were no steroids in its bloodstream."

"What we've got to look for is a disease that can cause rapid breakdown of vital autonomous systems that regulate the flow of natural steroids." Casey looked thoughtful as she continued, "At least that rules out some disorders, but still, it doesn't add up, Mike.

Acromegaly doesn't come on overnight, nor does Addison's disease. But we're seeing symptoms *like* Addison's."

"In both Naldosa and Timmons, yes. Weakness, fatigue, weight loss, low blood sugar, low blood pressure, increased skin pigmentation beyond just the lesions, right?"

She nodded. "Pernicious anemia, gastrointestinal disturbances, yes, but—"

"Cortisone has had no effect whatever, nor has hydrocortisone," Mike interrupted. "I've tried giving those men steroids, and now you're telling me that perhaps they're being pumped full of steroids by their own out-of-control glands? Damn, I knew I should have waited."

"This isn't Addison's, Mike. Addison's isn't infectious and—"

"I know." He sounded angry, and calmed himself, placing his hands on her shoulders. "But it resembles Addison's, and time's running out for those two in there."

"Drawing at straws, Mike, isn't going to save them. I agree, the symptoms are akin to Addison's, but we can't treat with steroids."

"What about vitamins and salt? Should we continue those? A million unanswered questions, Case, and you just dropped a million more onto the table."

Mike knew he was tired and upset with himself and the situation. "You're right, Case, I know that . . . drawing at straws is not what we specialists are trained to do."

"Let's try for the brass ring instead."

He smiled and nodded. "If we only had more time."

"I need Amunsen to work on," she said, taking in a long breath of air. "I just know he could tell us a lot more than all of our monkey friends put together. It was clumsy and stupid to have lost him out there some-where. I need a look at the effect on human brain tissue. As it is, all I've got is an infected monkey. I've got assistants doing cross-sections of its brain now."

He kissed her quickly before they parted. Mike watched her go for a moment before returning to his own detective work. Beside him lay a slide that was marked "Addison's." It had been the closest thing to the virus he'd seen, but he had been kidding himself all along. The lesions that covered Naldosa and Timmons were skin lesions, albeit curiously congealed around the nervous tissue, while the Addison's slide was from a cross-section of brain tissue.

Mike's hope of helping Naldosa and Timmons con-tinued to battle the quicksand of inadequacy, threaten-ing to engulf them all despite their combined knowledge and all of Dr. Tobler's technological wonders.

There was more space here, less steel and stone and glass. All around was the soft sound of the water. It liked the liquid. It liked to lay in it, to submerge itself. It had even wiggled down off the slab and back into the swift current, allowing it to take control.

It found itself in a new place, one that was calmer and more to its liking.

For a time it considered its own body through its pain. It knew that deep within itself a battle raged, and the only peace came from feeding on the big creatures. Perhaps it had been foolish to have left the spawning ground. Perhaps it should have remained and fed on them until they overpowered it and sent it beyond the reach of pain.

It floated to the surface, the attacking pain following it no matter where it went.

In the distance, a noise and a light.

Toward the light . . . toward the light, it told itself.

The memory of the light-eyes was indelibly imprinted on its brain. As it approached, the light grew larger, more intense. A high-pitched whistle hurt its ears.

One of them was coming, coming straight toward it.

How best to attack? From the rock wall which it could cling to and drop from? Through the water itself, to take hold of the light-eyed thing from below? Surprise was on its side. A sense of excitement eased back its pain enough for it to carry out its design.

It swam salamander-fashion for the legs, curling around them and locking on, dragging down the heavy weight, paying no attention to the screams which replaced the whistle. In an instant it had engulfed the big thing and was stabbing its claws into the throat to sever the head as quickly as its instincts told it was possible. Its speed was not out of concern for the prey, but to get at the raw material of survival hidden deep within these strange creatures who seemed destined to sustain its life.

It ripped at the head and began its search, devouring the first of the magical gray-brown stuff that converted its pain into power.

On feeding, it felt the twisted muscles in its torso relent, it felt the easing of the pain. A climactic, arousing feeling. For the first time it felt hope, hope of ending the torture altogether, forever. For the first time it realized that with each feeding, it was healing itself, growing stronger. With each feeding reflexes were sharper and instinct grew into thought. It began to imagine a time when it could feed at will.

In fact, as it finished the slippery meal caught between its claws, it began to wonder where this creature had come from? Which direction? Perhaps there were more.

Allowing the ravaged torso to float off in the murky water, it looked down the black caverns and went in search of another, perhaps a larger one.

Moments later it was looking up at a pale, blue light

flooding in from overhead, at a tubular ladder reaching down to the water. From the opening came sounds, both strange and familiar. It knew what the sounds meant. Overhead, not far off, there were more of them, perhaps an endless supply. It knew that to survive, it must explore the possibilities.

ten

Sleep had eluded Tony Qunin since the first destructive eruption of the quake. His nights had been busy, grueling in fact, and he should have been able to fall asleep through sheer exhaustion. But whenever he tried to sleep he was disturbed by images. Images of Naldosa and Amunsen, of the twisted grimacing monkeys, of the claws around Amunsen's shoulder, tightening and tightening until they pulled him away, wrenching his arm from his body. Tony could almost smell the blood, could almost feel the pain. Then he saw the menacing eyes of his alcoholic father leering at him, prepared to beat him. They became the cold gray eyes of Leo Copellmier, staring at him, a contented smile on his face.

In these waking nightmares, Tony saw the faint lines of the blueprints of the CCDC building which Stark had been using at the rescue headquarters. The lines crisscrossed behind the images like the ghost lines on a poorly tuned TV. They wouldn't go away. They stood as a backdrop to all else.

A sudden clattering thundered in Tony's ears and he instinctively covered his face and head with his hands, certain the quake had returned. He sat bolt upright, his eyes and ears registering the sight of Jose Ortiz cursing him.

"Dammit, Tony! Shiiiiiiiiit! Look at this mess!"

Eggs, toast, and juice were splattered across the table and on Tony.

"Is this how you say good morning?"

"Tony, you told me to wake you at seven! I didn't expect to see you nodding off over breakfast."

"I couldn't sleep, so I made myself something. Next thing I knew, I was drowning in nightmares."

"No wonder; you've been running like a top. You should take things easier and—"

"Jose, you'll make somebody a fine wife someday!"

Jose frowned at this and began cleaning up the mess while Tony went to the bathroom to shave.

"The way you live, Tony, you're going to have a heart attack someday, and where will that leave me?"

Tony looked in from the other room and managed a smile. "You've been picking up ideas from those doctors."

"That's got nothing to do with it."

"Did you have any luck getting the blueprints?"

"Got a copy. Les took photos; he has them ready for you."

"Great," Tony said, pulling together a suit of clothes as they made their way to the crowded main room in the studio apartment. Reporters pecked at typewriters like so many chickens over their feed, complaining continually over the Royals, IBMs and Smith Coronas Jose had been able to scrounge up.

The moment Tony stepped into the "newsroom" a reporter named Jill Amper rushed up to him.

"Tony, you've got to do something about the number of people around here! This is crazy. We've only got one camera, and somebody's got to make some decisions as to how it's going to be used! Wally's priorities are asinine. Important stories are being dumped and waysided for idiotic public-safety tips. I mean—"

"Jill, please," Tony slowed her down. She was short and perky, with a beautiful head of red hair and dazzling eyes.

He put her at arm's distance. "I don't know anything about scheduling; that's Hal James's job. I don't make those kinds of decisions."

"Hal's dead, Tony."

He dropped his gaze. "Yeah, right."

"Nobody's taking me seriously. I tried."

"Try harder! Make 'em listen. Or Tom, what about him? I saw him here somewhere."

"Tom's on Wally's side. They've caved-in on hard news and are taping public-service announcements all day."

"I'll talk to them, but I'm not administration, Jill."

"It's your goddamned house, isn't it?"

"Mack Dawson's the boss. I'm just letting out space."

"Dawson's out of it. His wife and children are missing. Tony, face it, for now you're the senior here, and word has it that the big shots back East will be looking for you to take over when the dust settles."

He stared at her for a moment, hearing the rumors for the first time. "Hell of a way to build a career."

"Got to start somewhere. What about my problem?"

"All right, Jill, for now you're our new program manager—you make the decisions on scheduling. Tom goes back to copyediting and Wally turns back into a technician assistant."

"What? Wait a minute!" She stopped him as he tried to retreat for the door. "I'm not program manager, I'm a reporter."

"You want to report stories, do it on your own time. As for now, you're our new manager."

"But Tony . . . Tony!"

He'd already disappeared with Ortiz, entering the elevator and closing the door on her complaints.

At UCLA Tony and Jose located Les in a small room filled with plastic chairs and tables, one wall lined with vending machines. Les was drinking steaming black coffee from a Styrofoam cup, bitching about how weak it was. Les had radioed Tony and Jose while they were in transit, telling them to meet him in this room. He had found an expert to read the mysterious blueprints. The expert sat across from Les; a boy in a Levi's jacket whose sandy curls fell across his sleepy, blue eyes. A backpack loosely dangled from one shoulder. Like Les, he had a cup in his hand, but his A.M. wake-me-up was Sprite.

"So, where is this expert on prints, Les?" Tony asked on entering.

"Right here, boss," Les said. "I told you the man with the bread would show," he said to the boy. "Want you to meet Mr. Aaron Willis, Tony. He knows prints."

Tony was less than thrilled, and his face showed his displeasure, but young Willis stood and shoved his hand at Tony enthusiastically. "Pleased to meet you, Mr. Qunin," he said. "I've seen you on TV, lots of times." Willis put on a thick pair of wire-rimmed glasses that lay on the table.

"Mr. Willis, no offense," began Tony, "but we have to know precisely what this set of blueprints is saying to us. You understand? There's no room for error. I mean, Jose, Les and me, we just see lines, rectangles, and—"

"Yeah, that's what my girl says." He laughed. "I'm studying architecture. Blueprints, hey, Mr. Qunin, that's like child's play to me. I've already looked at these prints, and I can answer any question you like."

"All right, Mr. Willis—"

"Aaron, you can call me Aaron."

"All right, Aaron, tell me, did you see anything unusual in the prints, anything at all?"

"Depends."

"Depends? Depends on what?"

"He wants to know if you're really going to pay him, Tony," said Les.

"Oh, no, I didn't mean that . . . but I am wondering how much . . . but no, I didn't mean that . . ."

Tony gave Les a look and asked again, "Depends on what, Aaron?"

"What you'd consider unusual."

Tony looked blankly at the young man. "Unusual as in deceptive," said Tony, "intentionally so."

"Deceptive?"

"As in a secret door, a panel, a false wall with a room behind it, anything."

"Hmm. Prints show a normal structure and all the necessary supports. Even if there were, say, a room or a wing kept out of the overall plan, that place would have to have an access, and it would have to be taken into consideration in the building. Especially if you're talking about a sub-basement section, you know, where extra supports would be required. Are you looking for something belowground?"

"Did you see anything to indicate there was something under the basement?" Tony asked, now hanging on the young man's every word.

"I didn't really know what you were looking for."

Tony felt suddenly deflated. "*I* didn't say there was a sub-basement, *you* did."

"No, I didn't say that, Mr. Qunin, but—"

"What did you say then?"

"I saw an elevator shaft—"

"Elevator shaft?"

"An additional one, yes, with only two entrances and exits, one at each end. One at the suite at the top, and one at the bottom. But I didn't look carefully at it on account of the fact I didn't know what exactly I was looking for."

"Then come upstairs with us and look again," Tony said.

"I don't have the time."

"Look, Aaron, this is important."

"So's my time. I've got a lot to do, what with the earthquake and all. But . . . I mean, however . . ."

"All right, I'll pay fifty bucks."

"Now you're talking, Mr. Qunin. Together, maybe we'll burn the sucker who built this place, huh? I wasn't lying when I said I watch your newscasts all the time. I love to see you get the bad guys."

"Any number of sub-levels could've been placed below the superstructure," Willis was telling them moments later, "without causing any undue stress, and without too much more labor. Depends totally on what the owners wanted. But this shaft, here, ends at this level, and I don't see any stairwells below the basement level, so my guess is that there was only one sub-level and it was confined to a relatively small space in the southeast corner."

"Corresponds closely to the area where Naldosa and Amunsen were working," mumbled Tony. "And the shaft opens on Leo Copellmier's suite. Interesting."

"Copellmier?" asked Willis, confused. "You telling me these are prints from the CCDC? Holy shit."

"Hey, Aaron, Aaron." Tony put an arm around the young man's shoulder and pulled out the bills to pay him. "You keep this under wraps. No one's supposed to know, and if it stays our little secret until I'm ready to do something with it, I'll send Jose here around with double that when the story breaks, okay? Deal?"

"You got it. Deal."

"Thanks and good-bye, Aaron."

Willis hefted his backpack. "It's been a pleasure, Mr. Qunin," he said. And he was gone.

"What's all this mean, Tony?" asked Jose.

"Something was going on below the research center, maybe some secret project only Copellmier knew about. I can feel it."

"But maybe this place was just for storing chemical waste, like a temporary dump, and when the quake hit, it was like the doctors said, it leaked."

"Maybe, my friend . . . only Copellmier can say for sure, and so far he's nowhere to be found."

"You think he may be dead, Tony?"

"Be a shame to nail him now, after all this time, and not have him to kick around."

"I was thinking of the sick men, Naldosa and Dr. Timmons. If Copellmier's dead, and if he's the only one who knows what's causing their disease . . . they're dead, too."

Tony nodded, feeling guilty for thinking of the consequences of Copellmier's death in such selfish terms. But he had suspected the man of every kind of fraud, from building-code violations to embezzling government grants. He'd slowly and painstakingly stalked his prey for so long, it had seemed more important than anything else.

"Yeah, Jose, you're right."

"I know, Tony."

"Guess that's why I like having you around. You're a humanist, Jose, a natural humanist."

The biopsy on the penny-shaped lesions all over Raphael Naldosa proved them to be a symptom of a disease bacterium, not unlike a fungus in the plant world. Whole forests of flourishing trees might slowly begin to show dark spots, until the leaves were covered with a crusty, scaly fungus. Such diseases didn't kill the trees immediately, but fed on them like leeches. The fungus allowed sunlight to filter through itself to get at the leaf below, and it allowed the system by which the leaf gained moisture to continue, until, after years of torture, the tree died.

In the case of this biochemical fungus which Mike and Casey were desperately trying to understand, people were killed quickly but with no less torture, it seemed. All but two of the monkeys that had emerged from the CCDC ruins lay dead now. Their skin had been eaten away, the nerves beneath covered in a thick pus, an oozing fungus. This fungus remained geletinous with a layer of ulceration that acted as a kind of defense mechanism. It fed on bacteria and filled the cavities it had created for itself in the tissues of the skin, surviving on the host organism.

Casey had confirmed Mike's biopsy and the open diagnosis, still something of a mystery, stared them both in the face. The few hours of sleep they had gotten had helped, but only a little. The sole good news had come when they learned that Amunsen's remains had been found and were awaiting their attention. Casey, with Mike assisting, now worked over Amunsen's gruesome body.

Casey had learned her lessons on the laser knife with the monkeys, and now she parted the human tissue with ease and precision. Both doctors had become, if not comfortable, inured to the bulky spacewear, and worked within the self-contained units.

To guard against the disease as much as possible, they also stood inside one of the large protective bubbles. There was a cordless mike recording the autopsy, and Casey spoke casually into the system as she worked.

"Going through the upper chest now . . .

"As in case of monkeys already dissected, evidence of massive discoloration . . .

"Lesions, organ enlargement . . .

"Swollen muscles . . ."

The laser silently seared through the tissue as Casey made a clean incision downward, opening Amunsen wide. Everywhere was evidence of massive disease attack. The killing disease fed even more comfortably on the dead than on the living, unencumbered, it seemed, by the bloodstream that pumped relief to the affected areas.

"Christ," moaned Mike on seeing the brown ooze congealed over the organs, making them all look like the liver.

"My God, Mike," said Casey, her gloved hand inside Amunsen now.

"What is it?"

"This man has no spinal cord."

"What?"

"It's gone, gone! Only the backbone remains."

"How can that be?"

"I don't know."

"Nothing like this in the monkeys?"

"No, no, of course not. I would have said something."

"Well, we know this thing likes nerve tissue, but how could it have so completely devoured the spinal cord?"

"I want another look at the first monkey's brain."

She started away, Mike following. In an outer room they stood beneath high-intensity radiation lamps and waited for the door to open automatically once the soaping was done.

"If this thing goes right for the brain," Casey remarked as she approached the lab table, "then it is conceivable it also goes for the spinal cord. I thought several things were odd when I opened that monkey's cranium."

"Like what, precisely?"

"Lack of moisture, inflammation."

"Encephalitis?"

"It would be nice to give it a name, but I can't, not yet. I hate being in the dark as much as you, but . . ."

"It's definitely in the brain-disorder category, some sort of brain disfunction, similar to . . . to what? Addison's, Alzheimer's, encephalitis? All three?"

"It has developed too quickly to be any of those, and it's certainly not hereditary."

"Damned bizarre."

"I think, Mike, we've got to accept the fact that we know of no disease that could do to Amunsen's corpse what this disease has done."

"Back to Qunin's theory of a deadly, unknown toxic chemical?" His voice was shrill with irritation.

She put a hand on his arm. "Some unknown virus, Mike. I'm almost certain now it's a virus, some new strain, perhaps manufactured by accident, perhaps not. But one thing's for sure; it could destroy this city, or worse."

Where the light was brightest, the noise was loudest, and a clattering, squeaking noise preceded the biggest, roundest prey it had ever seen. There was another, smaller one with it. They pushed and shoved one another. One was light-haired, slight of build by comparison to the dark-haired one. Neither had a light at the forehead, and it wondered if this meant anything. It didn't like the lights; they hurt its eyes. It knew it must try to get one of these. If at all possible, the large one.

They shouted and hit one another.

"You fat cow! Pig meat!"

"Stink breath! Ass wipe!"

They staggered, colliding.

The small one pushed the large one away. The light-haired one was coming directly in its path, straight down the dark lane lined with high fences.

"Carol! Carol! Where are ya? Bitch."

The small one slowed, stopped, stared right at it but did not see it; then began to coo and whisper.

"Candy? Is that you, honey? Com-ah, com-ah, come on to momma, baby." The small one stepped closer. It waited patiently, watching. Far in the distance, the other one was shouting; but the small one paid no attention.

"Candy . . . come on kitty-kitty . . . told you to stay outta the garbage . . . come with momma. Got nobody left but you . . . Harry's a toilet."

It had climbed to the pale blue light and had come out of its dark cave into another world, a world filled with big creatures. Its sensitive ears had heard these two staggering along the street. Its eyes had watched the small one groggily approach. How much nourishment it would provide, it thought. Perhaps enough to end the pain.

The smaller one rattled into the cans where it hid in the shadows, beneath the steps.

"Keep it down, out there!"

"It's that damned woman again!" another creature shouted from up above.

Yet another knocked open a door and came out with several black bags, and stuffed them into cans. The light-haired one spoke. "When we going to get it on, Charlie? Huh, huh? Stinkin' lousy old man of mine can't even find it anymore," it said to the empty alley. Then, "Candy, Candy, don't play games."

Suddenly, it leaped on the small one's face, and it screamed and toppled, striking out madly. None of the others had fought with such ferocity. It raised one claw overhead and brought it down, spiking its victim's forehead, drawing a stream of blood. The blow split the cranium, instantly silencing the creature.

It looked up. The large one stood nearby, face white,

eyes bulging. It had come in answer to the first one's cries.

It pulled away its claws, the weight of the bloody victim dropping beneath it. Slowly, it moved on the new one, who stood stone still, unable to move. This was odd behavior, perhaps a trick. But still the large one stood there, without a light, without a concrete chewing appendage on his arm. It seemed too simple, too easy. The large one mouthed something, *"Ogod."*

The enormous claws sliced through the air with a *whoosh* and severed this one's head between them. It then dragged the body into the darkness and fed, saving the small one for the safety of its subterranean home.

It fed long and well on the big one.

Then something awful happened. A giant light-eyes abruptly filled the alley, blinding it while racing right at it. The small one lay in its path. The enormous creature would gain possession.

It reached out and latched onto the body by the still-intact head, snatching it into the dark beneath the stairs moments before the big thing would have reached it. In fright, it dragged its prize quickly to the grate it had come out of.

Climbing down, descending into the welcomed darkness, it dragged its victim with it, realizing that this time, it was not so hard a task. It *was* becoming stronger and stronger. But then it was abruptly stopped. It couldn't pull its prize any further. The hole overhead was too small to accommodate the body, only the head, its loose hair dangling in its eyes and face now.

Feed here . . . now . . . hurry.

It carved away at the flesh and began to take its fill. It parted head from neck as was its custom, split the head with a crashing blow and searched the cranium for the expected morsel. There must be more in the body, it thought, digging through the morass of tissue for what it seeked, having already devoured the slimy gray matter. It now hooked onto and pulled slowly forth the spinal cord which came out like the roots of a tree.

Disappointment again filled it; although the pain was greatly diminished with the double feeding, a small twinge could still be felt.

eleven

Casey Sterns worked late into the night over the many cross-sections taken of the first monkey's brain, in the hope that it would reveal something she did not already know. She was so fatigued when she looked through the microscope lens that the image there seemed like a weird mirage.

Again and again she found the dark, ulcerated areas on the cerebral cortex. Valleys and plains of the brain were battlefield sites upon which were left bruises and scars, twisted and destroyed neurons. The black centers of destruction were covered with the thick, syrupy congealed substance found on the other organs.

Slides were done of a younger monkey, a three-year-old female in perfect health, a specimen that had nothing to do with the AIDS experiments at the CCDC. Comparisons had confirmed that the infected monkeys had been unable to put up any sort of fight against the alien disease.

"Mike," Casey called through the intercom. "Can you come in here a moment?"

"Right there." His voice was a reassuring sound after so many hours in silence.

When Mike came in she pointed to the comparison

microscope at her lab table, telling him what he was looking at. "Brain disfunction, clearly," he said, "but it still doesn't make sense. I don't know of anything that attacks the brain so quickly and so viciously."

"There's nothing to compare it with," she agreed, her voice giving away the fact she was near exhaustion. "And right now, Mike, it's spreading through Naldosa's brain and Timmons's. If we only had Amunsen's brain, we might learn something more definitive."

"No such luck, Dr. Sterns," came a voice over the open PA system. Mike and Casey looked up to the overhead viewing room to find Tony Qunin there.

"Mr. Qunin?" replied Casey.

"Amunsen's head was found, cracked open like a coconut, minus one brain."

Casey dropped her gaze. "How awful."

"Nothing you two have any reason to feel responsible for," Tony replied. "I mean, *you* didn't know what old Copellmier was doing, right?" Tony's words dripped with sarcasm.

"What do you want, Mr. Qunin?"

Tony shrugged. "A progress report. How's Naldosa? Timmons? I know about the monkeys."

"Mr. Qunin, we'd very much appreciate it if you would not use the PA to interrupt us," Mike said firmly. "We've got enough to worry about without having to wonder if you're sneaking about."

"Please, don't let my presence slow you down." Tony turned his back on the doctors, and left the room.

"Mike," began Casey, shaken, "what the hell is going on? First the body is missing a spinal cord; now it's the brain. What does it mean?"

"It means that Amunsen not only contracted a strange disease, but was also the victim of a freakish accident as a result of the earthquake, that's all."

"Tobler's got an electron microscope down the hall.

Let's take a look at these cross-sections under it," she said, trying to get back to the business she knew best.

"I think we're going to have to send samples out, Case, maybe to Atlanta. We need help. Someone, somewhere has got to recognize this."

"I'm way ahead of you," she replied.

"Oh?"

"I know a good man at the National Institute of Neurological Diseases and Blindness. It's going to take time, but I'm preparing samples for Dr. Nathan Wexler."

"I've heard of him; he's supposed to be the best."

"Let's get a change of scenery and a cup of coffee. There's a pot near the electron microscope, or so Tobler told me."

Mike and Casey were soon out of their bulky protective wear, the samples safely under glass and being slid automatically into the electron microscope. It was an enormous gray metal tube that looked like a torpedo turned on its nose, ending in a small viewing screen that fit snugly over both eyes at once.

Casey focused the mammoth machine, which photographed the samples by bombarding them with electrons to give a subatomic impression of the cross-sections. In a short while, the first of the impressions was finished, and the two doctors stood over it, astounded at what they saw.

"Look at the nerve cells."

"Like black holes in space," said Casey.

The nerve cells had been destroyed by what looked like long, thick asteroids. The animal's brain had become a bizarre environment where deformities flourished.

What she stared at unnerved Casey, and she fought to calm herself. She had spent years studying diseased

organisms, tracing the pathways of various illnesses as
they left their slug-trails in the brain. But nothing in her
experience had prepared her for this.

"Whatever this thing is," she said, "it likes nerve
cells." In spite of her efforts at self-control, Mike saw
she was trembling.

"Come on," he said abruptly. "I'm taking you out of
here."

"But we've got so much to do. . . ."

"You need something to eat. You can't keep going this
way."

She nodded. "On one condition."

"A woman's prerogative."

"You bring me up-to-date on your progress trying to
reproduce this thing in a sterile environment."

"I'll be only too happy to, now come on."

A short walk away they found a small restaurant that
was open for business. The walk and the restaurant
almost made Casey forget the lab, and the awful
possibilities that lay ahead for Naldosa and Timmons.
Under other circumstances it would have been a roman-
tic evening.

After they ordered, Mike launched into a description
of his work so far, and for the first time Casey realized
that despite the circumstances, Mike was working with
enthusiasm born of the love of his work.

"I've begun a painstaking effort to uncover any viral
links whatsoever. We'll see if this thing can be repro-
duced in a sterile environment. Not that I'm overlooking
other possibilities. I have a bacteriologist on loan from
Tobler looking into the other possibility."

From his description of the procedure and the care
he'd taken, Casey understood why Copellmier had hired
Mike. He was an expert at the delicate art of tissue
culture.

"Working in that damned spacesuit was bothersome," he said. "Still, if any bacteria were introduced into the experiment, we'd have nothing."

He told her what antibiotics he'd used in the sterile *soup* into which he had placed the tissue samples.

"A million things could go wrong," he was saying when the waiter came with their food. "Even if everything goes smooth as ice, and I successfully clone the virus, it'll take days. By then . . . who knows."

Casey was aware that the tissue sample Mike was speaking of was from Naldosa's fingertip; a second one had come from Timmons's. If it were a virus, it was hiding deep inside the cell walls of the tissue. From what they had recently seen through the electron microscope, Casey guessed it was located deep inside the nerve-cell walls.

"Of course, working blind like I am, I can't be sure all the conditions for cloning and isolating the damned thing are right. I mean, I'm trying to use the right conditions, but the right conditions for what? If it is a virus, as I'm assuming it must be, it's got to be something pretty damned exotic, some new strain. Your cross-sections show that."

"Amen," she agreed.

"I mean, was thirty-seven centigrade the correct temperature? Should I give it a day, or two, or a week? Should I wrap it in tinfoil and keep the lid on the flask, or leave it to breathe? At what point do I put it through the centrifuge? When do I transfer it to another flask with a fresh medium to grow in, and start the attempt all over again?"

"Well, we know it proliferates internally so your temperature seems okay, but maybe your medium should be nerve cells, maybe taken from monkeys."

"This time, I'm ahead of you. One of my cultures is precisely that."

"Then I'd say we seem to be doing all the right things."

"If it is a virus, Case, a serum will have to be found to inoculate against it. Best way I know to find a serum is through tissue-culturing. Only trouble is, it could take time, lots of time . . . time we don't have."

"I've been hearing this enormous clock ticking in my ears since I saw the monkeys; I know what you mean." She met his eyes.

"But culturing's the only way I know of getting from nowhere with a virus to learning to control it."

"You be careful with that stuff. I don't want to lose you," Casey said, reaching across the table for his hand.

"Don't worry, Case, I'm taking every precaution! But if anything should happen to *you* now I . . . well, I'd be lost."

Her eyes misted, and Casey finally allowed herself to say what she was feeling. "I love you, Mike . . . I don't know precisely when I discovered it, but I do."

His own eyes were trapped by hers. "I love you, Casey."

For a short time, they let all else be forgotten.

The last two meals it had taken had been good . . . but they hadn't been enough. For a time it had forgotten the pain. It had good balance, sufficient strength. It was not afraid.

For a brief time.

But its insides began to rebel again, the torture began again. It knew now there was a place where there were enough of them to feed on. But it must venture out, be more aggressive.

During the day it had located holes through which it could crawl to the surface. From any one of these, it could strike, and bring home its prey.

When darkness came, it climbed out again.

This time it found trees and grass instead of concrete and metal cans. Through the green here ran a moonlit thread of water. In the distance were the unmistakable noises *they* made. But the sounds were muffled, not at all threatening.

It remained close to the earth, darting from one patch of darkness to the next, cautious, fearful. It knew instinctively that they'd kill it if they were given the chance. It knew instinctively that they hated it. Fear of them made it careful, kept it alert and alive. Slowly, it approached the source of the noise.

Out in the open air, its large claws and feet felt heavy. It dimly recognized that it was out of its element. It preferred the constricted world of tunnels and water, belowground. It listened to the sound of its own labored breathing. It wasn't as strong as it had been after feeding the night before.

Its knotty eyes bulged at movement ahead. Strange, little versions of *them*, running, jumping, sliding in dirt. It hadn't known about small ones.

It watched from the black bushes until they suddenly began to leave.

One was straggling behind, mumbling to himself.

The others yelled back at him as they sped away on wheel machines. The straggler went about picking up things from the dirt when suddenly he looked up and stared right at the bush where it hid. So often the big ones had done this and had seen nothing, so it didn't bother to hide, instead holding perfectly still.

"Whoooo . . . who's there?"

It was silent.

"Wait up, you guys!" the little one called, carrying things to his wheel machine. He hurriedly straddled it but fell over.

This was the moment.

It raced across the ground separating it from the small one. A screech escaped its lungs.

From beneath his bike, Jeff Hanna, who would be nine years old next month, saw it coming. His pant leg was caught in the ten-speed chain. In the distance were all his friends, angry with him for having to break up the game. His parents had insisted he be home before twilight. Now it was after dark, and he was paying for his disobedience. He'd had nightmares brought on by guilt, had expected to be struck by lightning for lying, or the time he stole a candy bar from Mr. Motto's corner store . . . but this! Nobody deserved a monster, not in real life, no matter what they'd done.

It was coming!

It moved faster than he could think. Every nerve screamed *run,* pushing his body to move and quickly.

He yanked and kicked at the chain.

It was coming.

He grabbed for the penknife his dad had given him for Christmas, but he knew the blade would take forever to go through the denim cloth. He tugged at the stubborn cuff but it was hopeless. There wasn't time!

It was closer.

All around Jeff was his scattered baseball equipment. His left-handed fielder's mitt, his official Reggie Jackson baseball, and his Louisville slugger. His mind wanted to scream that it was all a horrible dream. But the ugly, black hunchback coming for him was real!

It wanted to eat him up!

He forced the bike frame up with effort born of fear, just enough to get to one knee. He used his remaining strength to grab for the bat. He clutched the bat tightly and righted the bike, straddling it anew.

It was leaping!

Enormous claws lifted like spears as the monster sailed through the air. Jeff purposely dropped the bike and himself at the last instant, and the awful creature landed with a powerful thud a few yards behind him.

Jeff still couldn't get his pant leg loose. Again, he scrambled to one knee, the bike so much dead weight on him.

It was up again . . . coming!

Jeff had held onto the bat. It was his only hope, but his back was to the creature.

He braced himself, planting both feet on the ground, and jerked the bike around to face his worst nightmare come true. He almost toppled over in the effort, but somehow he got the bike turned, and with the attempt he felt his pant leg slip from the teeth of the chain.

It crouched, ready to spring.

Shakily, Jeff lifted the bat.

It jumped!

Miraculously, Jeff's swing caught the creature full in its face. At the instant of impact, Jeff heard a terrible crunch, and caught a glimpse of the monster's terrible red eyes.

But he hadn't time to waste. Instead, he dropped the bat, which had momentarily stunned the creature. He pedaled furiously, racing away in first gear, second, fifth.

Shaking, his insides tight with cramps, Jeff's mind was numb with fear. Later, his parents would punish him for leaving over a hundred dollars worth of equipment in the middle of Griffith Park. How could he explain it? No one would believe him, least of all his parents.

It wandered toward a lighted structure, squinting at the harsh light and watching the creatures unload the bodies of their fellows. It couldn't believe what its eyes registered. Row upon row of dead ones, who could not put up any resistance. More coming all the time. Mountains of them.

It was angry with the little one, and had hoped for a second chance at it, but this . . . this was infinitely better. The little one had led it to paradise, a feeding ground, littered with the food it required.

It remained there for most of the long night. Hiding. Watching. Waiting. Preparing for its chance.

Finally, the park grew silent. The number of live ones dwindled to one. It saw the lights go out, and inched forward.

It went about the periphery of the herd of dead ones, dragging off those on the ends of rows. Here was a garden to provide it with all its needs; a garden ripe for harvest. It soon would feast.

Its work was difficult, however. It took precious time and energy. After it had pulled off five bodies, it was exhausted. Pain was causing periodic spasms. It settled in to feed beneath the deep cover it had found.

But the savoring was short-lived.

Feeding on the first, flesh peeling away like dry dough, it found the gray organ and shapely chord it desired, but the feeding hadn't had the desired effect. The pain *hadn't* lessened. In fact, it continued to grow. The second was the same, as was the third. It felt gorged when it should feel sated. Then the horror of the moment closed in on its mind: the fourth and fifth would not help.

Still, it split the fourth skull with powerful claws, tore out the gray matter, devoured it over floppy lips, only to confirm what it already knew.

Why? Its mind reeled with confusion, and then it understood. Dead ones were no good. It required the living, the fresh flesh, the still throbbing food.

Lolling its head to one side, its eyes registered movement. Something walking. Making a low sound like *hummmmmm* that rose and dipped.

It was one of *them*. Walking about the rows of the dead, the only living thing in the night.

Besides *it*.

Refreshed, it returned to the concrete tunnels. Feeding had gone easier with the big live one. The big one had stood still, frozen, and invited attack.

Now it slept in something near peace, on a ledge.

Rushing water was a soothing sound now.

It knew the sounds here . . . understood them.

Then it heard a steady, deliberate noise in the water. A sloshing sound, coming closer.

The overhead pipes made a good hiding place. It squeezed between, listening, waiting. In moments it smelled *them*. Had they followed? How many were there?

Two of the creatures advanced in the bleakness with weak lights held out. No noise of the concrete chewing machines, just the *slosh, drip-drip, slosh*.

It slithered from behind the pipes to the wall, and dropped into the water.

"Did you hear something?"

"Hear lots of things down here. You'll get used to it, kid."

"Not sure I want to."

Slosh, drip-drip, slosh, drip-drip, slosh . . .

"I tried to tell you to buy through the company. Those damned boots you got aren't going to keep much water out. You need the hip boots down here."

It heard the murmur of their conversation from where it lay in the water. It stared at their enormous legs, moving with difficulty through the filthy liquid.

It darted and wiggled between the four legs, causing one to stumble. It wrapped itself, tight and snakelike, around the legs of the standing one. He went down.

It clawed its way across the length of this one's firm body.

Screams filled its ears. Instantly the right claw clamped its victim's throat. More screams came from behind, where the other one watched for a moment, then began to run and stumble.

Slush-slosh, slush-slosh, slush-slosh . . .

Its left claw rose from the water, hesitated for a

moment, then dove into the victim's forehead. The prey
went limp, and floated on the heavy water. But the other
was escaping.

It skimmed over the surface of the water, drawing a
bead on the second prey. It dove, went eel-like for the
legs again, knowing what to do.

This one had found a ladder and was halfway up but
his wet clothes slowed him down. At the exit hole they
met, it clinging to the ceiling. The sight of it made the
prey lose control, screaming wildly and falling from the
ladder.

In an instant it pounced, trapping its victim.

The creature wheeled away, but it had anticipated
that, its claw grazing the metal hat worn by its prey. The
metal on metal sound reverberated the length of the
tunnels. A second blow split the helmet. Below the eyes
were bulging, registering the state of death.

It quickly dragged him below the water and locked an
arm in the ladder, storing its food. It must go back to the
first kill, partake of its nourishing parts as fast as
possible, then return to this one.

It returned to feed on the one left dangling on the
ladder, to partake leisurely of this one. But the body was
gone.

Had he not been dead after all? Had the water pulled
the lifeless form from the ladder?

It must follow the wash of the current, it told itself. In
order to find either carcass or living thing. Ahead it
heard the wash of falling water. It sought out the source
of the noise, not at all like *their* noises. A pale, gray-blue
light ahead showed there was an opening at the end of
the tunnel. The current was swift, the water flushing
straight out into the outside world.

It came to the opening and peered out over a vast
concrete valley. A row of dark buildings loomed along
one side of the street, towers of steel, pipe, and concrete

on the other. Both sides were partitioned off by wire fences. Not far away, it saw the cringing figure of the one that had escaped, clawing his way up the concrete incline.

The water spewed out into the aqueduct, three feet below. It was preparing to jump when the carcass of the other man, riding on the water, suddenly hit it and sent it splashing into the aqueduct, alerting its prey.

The water in the moat was only a half-foot deep, and when its victim's carcass crashed over its head, this hurt it more than anything the same creature had done to it when it was alive.

Struggling, it found a foothold and scrambled now for the one who was escaping.

The man hit the fence with a crash, clinging to it as if it meant the difference between life and death. He raggedly climbed over the top, cutting himself when he leaped down.

But it had him by the neck as he jumped.

The scream turned into a gurgle as his air was cut off by the enormous claws. He was lifted back, up and over, his neck broken.

"Hey! Hey! What's going on over there?"

It looked up to see another one of them approaching, pointing a finger. It was already feeding, savoring the last little strips of this one's spinal cord.

Having had so much food in so short a time filled it with a new sensation: a feeling of great strength and elation. For once it enjoyed a sense of being in control.

It disappeared behind a nearby bush to allow this new one closer, to let it stare at the carcass. It remained cautious, as before, but now with a sense of purpose. Where it hid it could reach out and touch the fence. It began shearing the wire squares with its claws.

The entire length of the fence shook in response. From where it hid, it could see the white-faced one looking in horror at the carcass, falling to his knees and spilling out a thick vomit from the mouth. On seeing the fence shaken by invisible hands it began to back away, then ran to one of the wheeled machines. Inside, another of his kind called out, "What's the matter, Phil? You sick? Phil?"

It darted through the hole it had made, tearing its own flesh in the bargain. Slipping beneath the car, with one claw it grabbed hold of Phil's ankle, yanking hard. And down Phil came, his skull making a cracking noise on the pavement.

It pulled Phil toward it. But seeing the other run away shouting for help, it dragged Phil back, pulling him against the fence that caught at him, tearing his clothing and skin.

It ripped and tugged, but finally got Phil through the fence. It dragged Phil down to the water, into the moat and to the tunnel mouth, lifting him with newfound energy and power, tossing him into the sewer. It then climbed down and fought the current with Phil safely across its back.

twelve

Policemen were everywhere, both plainclothes detectives and uniforms, some arguing precinct boundaries and responsibilities. It seemed to Tony Qunin as he made his way through the cordoned-off area that the cops from Burbank and Hollywood might come to blows on just whose case this was. Not that either group wanted it.

The boundary line between the two precincts was the viaduct. Hollywood argued that because the body was on the grass on the Burbank side, it was a Burbank police matter.

Some plainclothesmen had a little old man surrounded, asking him questions. He was the one who had reported Phil's murder.

"No, no, we weren't in no fight!" said the little man, his beard straight out from agitation. "We had differences of opinion, but we were friends. Phil and me liked to argue politics and—" he stopped himself. "I didn't have nothing to do with this other guy, and I don't know what happened to Phil!"

Tony Qunin and Jose Ortiz were driving in the van when they heard on the police band that a body was discovered, the head gruesomely twisted off. Police reported a second man missing from the scene and suspected a bar brawl; it had happened just outside the "Lazy Susann." The news of a homicide, however, seemed pale by comparison to the on-going stories surrounding the earthquake. Amazingly, rescuers were still finding living people under the debris, in pockets of safety where, by the sheer luck of the fall, they had come out with hardly a scratch.

Still, a homicide was always important news, and so the two men listened to the reports. But not until they heard a near breathless police officer report that the corpse found was missing his brain, that his head and throat had been split open, did Tony respond. By the time they arrived, police had found the telltale hole in the fence through which, as the coroner had discovered, a body had been forced. The coroner, a keen-eyed medical investigator named Herman Grogan, also pointed out that the body found on the other side of the fence was probably not the same body as the one which had left skin and blood on the prongs of the fence.

"Down here! I've found him!" cried one of the policemen searching the moat. Spotlights hit the area, revealing a prone figure, wafting on the water face-down. The officer grabbed the floater by his belt buckle and yanked him toward the concrete shore.

"Looks like a sewer worker by his clothes," the cop added, then suddenly realized the body under his hands had nothing but a ragged hole where his head ought to be. "Christ, Captain! His head's gone! Ohhhh, Lord . . . Lord . . ." He backed away from his find, as other officers made their way to him. Grogan, whose open trenchcoat looked like a cape riding up behind him, precariously moved closer.

Tony, meanwhile, jumped the fence with one bound. He tried to look nonchalant, as if he belonged. But a uniformed officer put a hand on his chest and backed him away.

"Where's Phil? Where's Phil?" the bearded, old man kept shouting.

Cameras were flashing, and policemen shouted at the small group of newsmen. Already, a reporter in the crowd had named the killer the Brain Snatcher.

"Look," Tony pleaded with the policeman holding him back, "I have to talk with Grogan. It's important."

"Dr. Grogan don't like to be disturbed when he's on a case, Qunin, you know that. Now, let's see you jump back over that fence in your best Olympic-form."

Tony stared down at the moat. He wanted to be down there, listening to the discussion, but it appeared hopeless, unless he could divert the cop's attention.

"You going back, or do I have to call for help and haul your ass over?"

"Okay, okay . . . but give me just one look at this guy."

Tony dropped to his knees and pulled back the white sheet covering the youngish body and face of the sewer worker. The young man's head was halved, as if split by an axe, but conspicuously empty of any contents. Even the eyes were gone, leaving only empty, black sockets staring up at Tony. The body seemed like a wax dummy in a horror show, not yet completely put together. The sight was enough to turn Tony's stomach.

"Seen enough, hot shot?" barked the policeman. "Now, get outta here. Go on."

The second body was being hauled up the wash. Like the one Tony saw, it was covered with a sheet; body bags were still at a premium in the city. Tony knew that both Grogan and the captain would say as little as possible to the press here and now, that a low profile would be kept. Far below, flashlights created an eerie glow in the darkness, as men searched the open tunnel at the end of the aqueduct for any sign of the killer.

Tony was forced to vault back over the fence and wait for the police captain in charge to give out his formal statement. But Tony knew Grogan well, and decided to get the unofficial statement from him as well. After the captain's short speech, Tony pushed through the crowd, found Jose, and indicated the van.

"Where to now, Tony?" Jose asked as they got into the van.

"The morgue."

"Awww, Tony—"

"That's the place to be right now."

"I've seen enough of morgues to last me a lifetime!"

"I've got to talk with Grogan."

"I hate that place. Besides, they're yelling for you to get back to your apartment."

"Jose . . ."

"You've got to check on Jill, make sure she hasn't killed somebody, or that somebody hasn't killed her, and—"

"Jose, you can wait outside but—"

"I plan to!"

"—but I have to talk with Herman Grogan."

"I'll wait in the van."

The L.A.P.D. morgue was housed in the bottom-most floor of the modern facility for Criminal Medical Investigation and Forensic Medicine. Any clue taken from the scene of a crime would find its way here.

Tony had waited until he saw Grogan's car go down into the reserved parking area before he entered. He quickly found a well-used stairwell that would take him to Grogan's area, the morgue itself. Tony was no more fond of the place than Jose, but he had gotten some of his best leads from Grogan in the past, and he knew the man could be trusted. He was a man of integrity, and had never sent Tony off on a wild-goose chase.

The walls in the corridors were lined with stretchers; bodies were everywhere. Even a small lounge and conference room was packed. The quake had effectively filled every inch of the morgue. But the offices were bright enough to almost make up for the bleakness, and inside one, Tony saw Grogan taking a moment to look over messages left on his desk.

Herman Grogan certainly was not what most people expected a coroner to be. At a party once, Tony recalled seeing people laugh out loud when he told them what he did for a living; they were sure he was joking. He was healthy-looking, well-tanned, with 20/20 vision, lacking the stereotyped characteristics of paleness, weakness, and near-sightedness. Herman was big and muscular, a former basketball star with UC at Berkeley.

There had always been a move afoot to replace Herman Grogan with a more "acceptable" man, someone straight-laced and rule-conscious, who looked the part of coroner. But Tony Qunin knew Grogan was very good at what he did, and couldn't be so easily dismissed.

Tony rapped on the windowed door and entered. Grogan's smile was both natural and weary at once. "Tony, I've missed you! I wondered if this case might catch your notice."

"It has, all right."

"Been boring around here," Grogan began sarcastically, "what with all the bodies I've had to do since the quake. You'd be surprised at the number of bodies brought in that looked like quake victims who weren't at all. Some were victims of murder made to look like casualties of the quake. Had a real interesting one come in this A.M., two in fact—"

"You know why I'm here, Herman," Tony interrupted.

"Yeah, I caught a glimpse of you at the scene."

Grogan was clearly tired and now he collapsed into an office chair that offered no comfort. Behind him, on the shelves, medical books and case studies shared space with a human skull, books on basketball, and a beautiful scale-model of the "Star Trek" starship *Enterprise*.

Nestled among the paraphernalia were pictures of his wife and three children.

"I suppose you want me to tell you off the record that the three men brought in tonight were victims of the L.A. Brain Snatcher, the guy that's been hacking up people since the quake, right?" As Grogan spoke, he rubbed his tired, red eyes with balled-up fists.

"Three guys?" Tony was taken aback.

"You didn't hear?"

"No."

"A third body was found inside the tunnel, not far from the opening."

"The old man's friend?"

Grogan nodded and yawned simultaneously.

"In the same condition?" Tony asked.

"Head skewered, and minus one brain. Work of the unknown Brain Snatcher, or at least that's the rumor."

"Look, I know you haven't had time to really look these bodies over, but—"

"Police want answers, too, Tony. They'd like to label this as the work of some mad axe-murderer which is what the captain told the press . . . but it was no axe that cut open these men at the throat and skull. Certainly nothing you'd pick up at the local hardware store."

"What then?"

"So far as I can surmise, the damage was done in a quick, neat fashion which might otherwise point to the sudden swing of a heavy axe. But there are problems with that theory."

"What kind of problems, Herman?" Tony sat down in a chair opposite Grogan.

"Axes are messy, especially when used against bone. They leave shards, like broken glass. The three men I saw tonight had nearly identical wounds to two other bodies that came in this morning. We at first thought these two were victims of a falling axe. But I had time to look them over very closely, and besides the fact that their brains were neatly scooped out, as if taken in large sections—"

"You say you saw *two others* this morning?"

"A husband and wife, last seen leaving a bar near Second and—"

"What kind of madman rips out the brains of his victims?" Tony thought of Amunsen's headless body.

Grogan sat shaking his head. "The world's full of maniacs, Tony. You, above all, ought to know that." Grogan hesitated before going on. "Anything I might say about the psychology of such a killer would be pure speculation, but I have some literature on serial killers you could have a look at. Since this guy has taken out five people that we know of, we can safely say we're dealing with a killer who will most likely strike again. Who knows, maybe the quake set him off."

"Anything else you can tell me?"

"Off the record?"

"Off the record, yes."

"With the two I examined earlier today, I discovered two additional interesting facts."

"Yes?"

"Tony, you give me your word? Off the record?"

"Yes, yes."

"I don't want to cause panic, but the two bodies I saw this morning were sent over to UCLA, to Dr. McCain and Dr. Sterns."

"What? I don't understand."

"They showed signs of a disease the doctors are researching. The bodies were speckled with it, and like the body of that rescuer, Amunsen, neither body had a spinal cord *or* a brain."

Tony looked at his longtime friend with astonishment, wondering if he could possibly be putting him on. "Then, if this is true, they're all connected?"

"Right . . . if it pans out to be the same thing."

"And there's a carrier out there somewhere?"

Grogan nodded.

"A carrier *and* a killer?"

"Perhaps driven to kill because he is a carrier of this rare, unknown disease. The way it's shaping up at UCLA, the disease seems to effect the mind."

Tony was stunned at this latest development and he sat in silence, not knowing what to say. He was dimly aware of the decay and formaldehyde odors that permeated the office, threatening to make him ill.

"Tony, we were getting all kinds of quake victims, but I soon realized that some were being molested *after death* by this sicko. I mean, their heads were ripped apart and brains taken out. Someone's been going through the wreckage, collecting gray matter like you or I might collect deposit bottles. God, can you imagine it?"

"Where did these bodies come from? The CCDC building?"

"Hell no, Tony. You haven't been listening. The one woman was found with her head stuffed down a manhole, while the rest of her was in an alley off Sanchez, near Second Avenue. She wasn't even a quake victim! You've got a real hang-up about Copellmier's place."

"But the quake victims themselves. Where did they come from, exactly?"

"Who knows, for Chrissake? You see how many are lining the walls outside. You been to the ballpark lately?"

"But all of them had the signs of the disease, those brown circles?"

"Yeah, all of 'em. Damned strange . . . whole business is damned strange."

"Grogan, you've got clout, right?"

"Some, maybe . . . what do you want?"

"I'd stake my reputation on some important clues

being unearthed in the very area McCain and Sterns have placed a quarantine on."

"At the CCDC building?"

"Right . . . think you could get past the ban? We could go in protective gear, the whole nine yards. What do you say?"

"What do you hope to find?"

"Answers."

"Let me think about it. I'll let you know."

They parted quickly, but Tony knew he had planted a seed in Grogan's mind. The coroner was like him in at least one way. He didn't like a lot of loose ends and unanswered questions.

It became too dangerous to remain in the tunnels. *They* were everywhere, too numerous to fight. Safer to find shelter here, in the dark stone room, where it rested and waited for nightfall.

Once darkness fell, it ventured out, skirting from the shadows to the undersides of stairwells, making its way down the alleyway. It saw a dark field, and recalled the little ones it had once seen in a similar place. Was this the *same* place?

It ran toward the park, but a wheeled machine suddenly came from nowhere, its lights blinding it.

Machine and monster collided, and the latter hit the pavement, stunned.

The machine stopped with a screech. One of *them* got out and raced toward it cautiously, then stopped cold, staring and gasping.

It lurched up and was on the human instantly, rolling her over into the blackness beyond the bushes.

The feeding was quick, feverish, but even before finishing it knew that one meal wasn't enough. To recover from the crash, it needed more, as when it had gorged on three in one night. It must search out more.

It went spiderlike into the darkness of the park, its keen eyes accustomed to blackness, searching.

Then it saw them: four-legged, snarling creatures, their teeth bared, racing directly at it. Behind these creatures were men with lights held in their hands. They'd seen it. They were after it!

It turned away, but the lead animal leaped onto its back, ripping away skin. They'd taken it by surprise, a sure sign of its weakened condition.

One tore into its right leg, sinking teeth deep and pulling viciously outward. Another had it by the right arm, its jaw locked like a vise. It tried to fight back, shaking its entire body wildly, trying to bring its one free claw to bear. It struck the one at its ankle, sending the animal bounding away and yelping. It pinched the throat of the one snapping at its back with the claw and brought it over the shoulder, blood spurting geyserlike from the beast's throat. Then the third was cut down like a flea by the claw. But a fourth animal had it again by the ankle, when there was a sudden, deafening explosion that shook the earth all around. Dirt and grass flew into its eyes. It felt a second such explosion at its back.

The big ones with lights were causing the deadly explosions, and it felt stinging pain in several locations. Its neck, arms and legs were torn ragged from bites the animals had inflicted.

With a burst of energy born of fear, it slammed both claws down on the fourth animal, which dropped like a stone, its head severed. Bright light hit its eyes, making it screech. It expected the next explosion to blast open its stomach, but when nothing came it dove from the light and into the surrounding bushes.

A third explosion shook the bushes near where it had scrambled. A tree close to its eyes absorbed the next explosion. Another ripped through leaves.

Then it saw the water, a ribbon of safety in this

strange world. It slinked from the bushes and into the water, diving below the surface, escaping from them. But the fear was so great it could not remain under, gasping as it swam, swallowing water in the process. As it rose for air, it could hear them. They were searching the shore.

It lifted first its eyes and then its head, taking in more air, preparing to dive again. But then it saw they were all gone, all except one, who was left behind on the bridge.

Carefully, silently, it moved through the water to the base of the bridge. It climbed onto the rock, clinging to the side of the bridge. It hung there for long moments, taking time, giving this last one time to think all was safe. It had come to the park to find the place the little one had led it to . . . not to feed on the dead ones, but to feed on the live ones guarding them, as before. It had had a plan. *But this would do.*

The stones were hobbled and cold to the touch, reminding it of its birthplace. It had been safer there . . . but had it remained, it would now be dead. It knew these things now.

It inched straight up, slowly. Senses alert, catlike, it climbed closer to its prey, freezing its own motion at the slightest sound. The prey on which it fed were stupid creatures, and this one looked right at it and saw nothing.

It inched closer when the light moved farther away. Closer, closer, it wanted to make a cooing, contented sound at the thought of feeding again, but did not dare to . . . *not yet.*

These creatures could be dangerous despite their stupidity, using the four-legged ones to pin it down, then sending explosives into it. Blood dripped from the several wounds, streaking the stones.

Two, it thought. How much better it would be if there were two of them on the bridge instead of one. Should it wait? Or take this one now. Suppose they all returned?

It was at the top now, an inch from the rim.

It waited for the right moment.

The creature's light came nearer. Metal scraped against the stone bridge. Fat white hands were pressed on the stone and the pale eyes scanned the trees and bushes along the brook. It knew the time was right to strike.

The right claw shot up like a rocket, spearing the pale-eyed one in the throat, soaking the claw in blood. Even with a crushed voice box the creature managed a mangled cry, however, and it heard the others racing back. Another blow reduced the cry to a pitiful wheeze.

Now hurrying to claim its prize, it grabbed its prey by the hair, then lifted the second claw in an arc, coming down guillotinelike, snapping off the head. This done, it kicked off the side of the bridge in one fluid motion, disappearing into the water with its bounty.

It regretted leaving the morsel of the cord, but feared the explosive machines and the four-legged creatures too much.

Below the water, it took what it wanted from the head. The men on the bridge, horrified at the sight they had returned to, searched the water with their lights. Soon they spotted what remained of their friend's head bobbing on the still water like an empty jack-o'-lantern.

thirteen

Deputy Medical Examiner Herman Grogan had difficulty pulling his long, lanky frame out of the city coroner's car, a Datsun. He had parked as close as possible to the CCDC, where he had agreed to meet with Tony Qunin. He had bad news for Tony; there was no way anyone was gaining entrance to the restricted area. Grogan had personally spoken over the phone with Mike McCain and Casey Sterns, and they were both of the opinion the disease was caused by a virus that they had not as yet identified.

Grogan picked his way past scattered rubble which reminded him of the disarray of the morgue from which he had come. Just ahead he could see the mobile hospital units that had converged on this centrally located area of the city. Inside them, life and death struggles continued. He recognized the Channel 3-CTV news van, and he marveled at Ortiz's ability to get such a rhinoceros past such calamity. Beyond the police and paramedic vehicles he saw the lights and tents where doctors continued the rescue effort. But everything had slowed considerably. Fewer and fewer survivors were being located in the rubble.

"Dr. Grogan! Over here!" It was Tony Qunin's voice,

but the man coming at Grogan was a fully suited-up spaceman. Alongside him stood a second man in full protective wear.

"Is that you inside there, Tony?"

"Want you to meet Lee Stark. He's in charge of rescue efforts in this sector."

Grogan nodded to the other man, then took Tony aside. "Look, Tony, I know you think there's some kind of clue inside there, but I've just spoken with Doctors Sterns and McCain, and I'm afraid any search is going to be put off. You see—"

"Oh, no, Herman. I don't want to hear this."

"Tony, we may well be dealing with a virus here. You go in and you're very likely to come in contact with it. That means placing a lot of people at risk, not just yourself."

Ortiz and Stark both inched forward to hear what Grogan had to say.

"I'm going in, Herman."

"Ortiz." Grogan turned to Jose. "Will you talk some sense into your friend? Please."

Jose nodded and said, "Tony, maybe this time you should listen. If it is a virus—"

"Stay out of this, Jose."

Stark pulled off his headgear and said, "If the doctors think this thing is life-threatening, we'd best do as they say."

"A good, healthy thought, Mr. Stark," agreed Grogan. "Hold onto it firmly."

But Jose had learned to read Tony's features like a book, and he knew Tony would not be dissuaded easily. "Tony, this is wrong, what you're thinking," he told him.

"Wrong, hell. It's madness," added Grogan. "I've got more bad news, Tony."

"What's that?"

"Naldosa . . . he's dead."

Tony was visibly stunned, even through the bulky protective suit. "No . . . I . . . can't believe it."

"Believe it, and you'll be just as dead if you act stupidly now."

Tony looked from Grogan to Jose and back again before saying, "I guess you're both right."

But the moment Grogan turned to speak with Stark, Tony suddenly dashed for the entrance of the cordoned-off area.

"Stop him, Jose!" cried Grogan, racing in pursuit.

Jose caught Tony moments before he disappeared into the tunnel Naldosa's rescue had made. "No way, Tony. No way I'm going to let you do this!"

Grogan caught up to them, his eyes registering his anger. "You expect us to stand idly by and watch you commit suicide?"

Tony didn't answer; instead he pulled off his protective gloves, holding out his arms and hands to display discolored patches of skin everywhere.

Grogan recognized the now familiar lesions and groaned pityingly.

Jose's eyes bulged in fear and concern. "Oh, God, no, Tony!"

"Look at them. Look at my hands," Tony said. "Now, you tell me, what do I have to lose? I'm going to wind up like Naldosa anyway!"

Both Grogan and Jose were too stunned to stop Tony, as he disappeared into the debris-lined tunnel ahead, hauling a mini-cam and a light. As if waking from a dream, Grogan rushed back to Stark, demanding his protective suit.

"But you just said . . ."

"I know what I said! Help me into this suit!"

"I don't know, doc." Stark was shaking his head as he spoke.

"*I* should go in after him," said Jose, confronting Grogan.

The coroner saw the concern in Ortiz's eyes, but he said firmly, "If we're going to play out Tony's game, Jose, I can help him down there far better than you."

Jose started to object, then nodded. "I guess you're right, doctor."

Grogan wondered momentarily if he were right at all, but he didn't allow the thought to linger. Worse than the fear of this disease was the thought of Tony, down there by himself, carrying death in the form of coppery, circular lesions. He simply couldn't allow Tony to think that he was truly alone.

A last-minute notion on Grogan's part sent Stark for a flame-thrower. "In case there's anything down there that should be destroyed," he told the others moments before disappearing into the black tunnel.

In its mind was a picture, a picture of a place.

The image wouldn't go away.

It kept picturing the birthing place. So vivid was the image that it smelled the odors, heard the sounds.

It had been safer there, darker . . . with countless hiding places. It smelled good. It wanted to return.

It wanted to go home.

The thought blotted out the stinging pain where pellets had been buried deep in its flesh. This single desire drove it back along the concrete tunnels, over rock and fallen pipe in search of the way it had come. It sought out the odors and telltale signs it had unwittingly left behind to mark its passing.

It didn't know why, but it seemed important that it return. There was something desperate about the act. Something was waiting for it there. Something it must see . . . long forgotten, but nonetheless important.

At times on all-fours, sometimes upright, sometimes swimming, it fought the water to return.

* * *

The concrete tunnels had become congested with the man-things. They knew it was here. It had to hide.

It kept picturing the darker, safer place in its mind. It had had the advantage there.

It now climbed completely out of the water, along the stone wall. Everything looked different, and with deeper water entering from somewhere ahead, the scent trail it was following was nowhere to be found.

The search was taking too long. It felt a renewed sense of urgency.

The insistent need was more gripping, more powerful than the awful pain had ever been. Somehow it knew that something worse than death would result if it did not find its way back.

The feedings had filled it, sated it, only to drive its body on to some new need. As the feeding had progressed, the image of home grew in its mind. Now, it appeared it would never find home.

Then it smelled something familiar and went toward a black-sided, wide-mouthed pipe.

It had to squeeze into the pipe, which led upward. It ascended, strong claws clanging against the metal, powerful feet pushing against the sides. With each new feeding it had become steadily stronger. It recalled a time when it would not have had the strength to scale such a height.

It brought its eyes over the lip of the pipe first. When they registered nothing, when its ears perceived no threatening sound, the thick cranium came over, followed by the elongated, balloon jaw. Next, it pushed one claw out and over, followed by the second, causing some clattering. Once free of the pipe it gazed about, and knew it had come the right way after all.

Growling, rumbling noises rolled up from its abdomen, sounds that had once meant terror, that had signaled the return of the awful cramps. But now the pain was different, cushioned.

Back, it thought, it was back at last.

It now started ahead, but suddenly went toppling over, face forward, hitting the rock-strewn earth with a thud. Something had caught it by the ankle. Looking down, it saw a thick gray creature that was so long it disappeared in two directions. That was what had grabbed it.

A single, swift strike of its right claw spliced the thick cable, sending electric sparks flying, and shocking it into a stunned withdrawal. Shaken, it rushed to a nearby boulder, found room between it and a wall, and slid out of sight, not wishing to battle with the fire snake, now lying in two enormous sections.

"I've lost all visual contact, Tony," came Stark's voice over the radio. "Will keep this line open. Do you read, Dr. Grogan?"

Both men responded, Grogan still behind Tony, still searching in the oppressive darkness. Each step took him into still smaller pockets of space, dug out earlier by the moles, or created haphazardly by the quake itself.

"Tony," he called out again, "wait up, will you?" Grogan had hurried to find Tony, passing a radio set to him. But once more the reporter had gotten ahead of him.

"Why'd you come down here, Herman?" Tony's voice came over.

"Couldn't miss the opening of the crypt."

"Crypts carry diseases."

"I've seen disease before."

"Just got your curiosity up, huh?"

"Yeah, you could say that," replied Grogan. "Am I getting any closer to your position, Tony?"

"Hard to say. Keep coming. Oh, no, Jesus God!"

Grogan heard falling debris ahead. "Tony! Tony! What is it?"

There was no immediate answer, and Grogan rushed ahead, discarding the flamethrower in order to move faster.

Tony was almost buried in the debris and chalky powder that had come careening down on him when he backed into a pile of rubble he thought was a wall. The sight he had moved away from was still there, just beyond the beam of his light.

It was more than a simple dead body. The dead man or woman was hanging upside down, feet jammed in overhead debris, as if suspended in ice. The body was without a head, but that fact had not caused Tony so much alarm as had the condition of the carcass. His light had revealed movement, something crawling across the body. He'd gone closer, trying to determine what it was he was looking at, when he realized the victim's entire body was covered in a substance that looked for all the world like a brown mass of living organisms banded together and sustaining their funguslike growth by feeding on the cadaver. The brown soup covered every inch of the torso, and it teemed with movement.

It was this that had made Tony lurch back and almost bury himself. Fortunately, his hands and arms were free. Now he extricated himself and backed off, steeling himself for another look at the body.

"Tony! Answer me!" Grogan called from behind him.

"It's okay . . . I'm all right."

"What happened?" Grogan entered the chamber.

"A little start, that's all, but I found something you'll want to have a look at."

"You look like a ghost, Tony," said Grogan as he came toward him.

"I'm going to have a look this way." Tony pointed toward a narrow hole. He started ahead, and whistled into his microphone.

"What is it?"

"The place is one-hundred percent demolished, but I think I found my hidden chamber."

Grogan joined him, pulling himself carefully through the small opening. On the other side he saw a man-made cavern, furnished with the remnants of crushed machinery. It had been a high-tech lab before the quake. Tony's hunch had proved right. Grogan circled the room, and spied an adjoining area, little more than a cell. Amid the crushed furniture, toilet, sink and fallen concrete lay scattered papers and an empty cassette player. He began to assemble as many papers as he could pull from beneath the rock and concrete. He was glancing over handwritten notes and formulas when Tony shouted for him.

The newsman had gone straight toward a twisted black metal beam which was part of a pattern of such beams around a concrete base; the remnants, it appeared, of a special chamber. Tony was staring at the interior, pointing.

"What do you make of this, Herman? I found an identical one back there when I nearly caved-in the place."

Grogan stared at a second brown corpse lying near the back wall of the chamber, its head torn away, the flesh distorted by the brown-to-gray mass moving over it in an obscene dance of life.

At first Grogan didn't know what he was seeing. The brown gel was swirling, moving over the corpse, causing the color to change to a pink-brown, then gray-brown, then deep brown. It moved with such singlemindedness that at first he thought he was imagining it. But most certainly the stuff was animated.

"Never . . . seen anything like . . . like this, Tony."

At the center of the room, sticking straight up from behind the blackened steel counter, was a metallic claw and arm, covered with a crusty, scaly brown substance.

Grogan guessed it was the same substance on the body, but that on the metallic arm it had been unable to survive, creating instead dried pustules.

"We've got to torch this guy's remains," Grogan said, regaining his voice.

"You got any matches?"

"Better than that, I brought a flamethrower. Left it just beyond the next chamber."

"I'll get it."

"I'll check for any tapes that may've been left undamaged."

"Forget it," said Tony. "No such luck . . . I checked."

"Then I'll see if I can dig out more of those papers. They could be vital."

While Tony was gone, Grogan explored another section of the room, and saw amid the debris another metallic claw, like the one inside the chamber, only larger, bigger than a man's hand. He reached between some rocks for it and found it attached to a sleeve made of soft, synthetic material, a protective suit of much finer quality than the one he wore. Grogan tugged hard, working it loose enough to see that straps, buttons and zippers held it to the completely trapped sleeve. He continued to work, feeling the hair bristle on the back of his neck, as if he were being watched. He chalked up the feeling to the horrible sight lying inside the chamber not ten feet away. Nothing brought on paranoia like the thought of being trapped alive with a cadaver as your only company, and a hideously diseased one at that.

Something moved behind him. He saw a shadow, felt a presence. He whirled and directed his light. Nothing there. *Foolish*, he thought, and went back to releasing the metal glove from the trapped suit. Finally, it came undone.

"Whataya want with that?" asked Tony, startling him from behind.

Grogan breathed deeply, a hand on his pumping heart, trying to calm himself. "Following a hunch of my own."

"Oh? Anything I should know about?"

"I'll let you know if anything comes of it. But before you start playing with fire, I do want to look for more of these scattered notes."

"I have to figure this thing out anyway," replied Tony. "Go right ahead."

Grogan began pulling sheets from the rubble. After examining them, he shouted, "Arthur Robel! Dr. Arthur Robel! I thought he was in D.C."

Tony looked across at Grogan, who was still studying the papers. "You know this guy, Robel?"

"Sure, he's internationally known."

"For what?"

"Developing CBWs."

"CB-whats?"

"Chemical-biological weapons."

Tony said nothing, but a look of smug pride came over him. "I knew Copellmier was up to no good. Now we've got a story."

"According to this, his wife was with him. It's a combination of notes and records on the project they were involved in."

"Yeah, think I found his wife earlier. She was covered with that brown . . . shit . . . too."

"We'll have to torch them both . . . and pray these notes give the doctors at UCLA something to go on. At the same time, *you're* going over there, protective suit and all. Once you leave here, Tony, you're a patient, under quarantine, got that?"

"Only on certain conditions, doc."

"I might have guessed there'd be conditions."

"Nothing too stiff." Tony moved the flamethrower to within range of the corpse in the chamber.

"Don't linger, Tony. Touch off the torso and move.

That stuff may just convert to an airborne virus once the smoke surges. Set it ablaze and back off. Then we'll do the other body and get the hell out of here."

It had found the deep recesses of the secret place when odors of *them* told it it was not alone.

It listened for their sounds, stalked their shadows, saw their hated lights. It saw they were bigger and baggier, their strange skin marking them as a different breed.

Angry and frustrated, it was filled with hate for them. Unable to control a low, spiteful snarl, it wished to kill them *now,* then scatter their remains. So repulsed was it by the intruders, that the thought of feeding on them did not occur to it. They'd violated the most secret place, and for the first time it wanted to kill out of sheer hatred for what they were.

But it couldn't risk an attack. A struggle might mean that others would return in larger numbers. The secret must be kept . . . at all costs. These creatures always came searching for their dead brethren. To kill these two here, now, would lead others back, and in time they would find the secret.

It had returned to spawn the secret.

Its body, especially its lower abdomen rippled with spasms and cramps now. It must find the fertile ground, return to the place it had unknowingly prepared. It crawled below girders, searching instinctively for the exact spot, while something deep inside was pressing, pressing on it to turn inside out.

The pressing at its lower abdomen came in rhythmic throbs now. The throbbing increased to a spasm, that in turn created a shiver running the length of its body. The feeling was one of a foot being forced down its throat, but it was different from the unbearable torture that had made it wish to die. This was more a feeling of painful growth from within. Feverish and chilled at once, it tried to understand these new sensations, but all its mind was filled with the remembered sight of the fertile ground. It must find that place . . . *now*.

Hardened and dried lesions and scales on its outer skin began to split and break off. Blackened skin, brittle and tough, cracked off at its touch. Some pitted holes remained, while in other patches where skin fell away, it was replaced by a less scaly, supple substitute.

The pressure against its internal organs was tremendous now, threatening to burst from within.

It must hurry and locate the secret place. Then it saw the fertile ground: dangling by its heels, one of *them,* a *special* one of them which it had hidden here, especially for this reunion. It realized for the first time how inextricably linked its own fate was with the creatures it so despised, the creatures it fed upon.

It crawled up past the gaping hole at the neck and curled about the chest, covered now in the brown life, its own residue, which had transformed the useless corpse into a fertilizing earth. The small mucous sacs began dripping from it, attaching themselves to the man-thing and the velvety brown "earth." Here the sacs would dry, burst and mix with the fertile ground to become embryos. They would develop, hundreds of them, taking their first sustenance in the soil of the cadaver. As each embryo enlarged it would go in search of *food,* to carry on the species, each a clone of the one who spawned it . . .

It wanted only rest now, now that its work was complete. It yearned for peace and death to wash over it, silently and without pain. For the first time in its memory, it felt hopeful of sleeping forever, imagining that its fevered brain could be allowed to go numb, its racked body and contorted limbs finally at rest.

Then it heard the frightening, terrible *whoooooosh!* A noise like nothing in its experience, a noise it did not understand. But somehow it knew the noise was brought on by *them.*

Another *whoooooooosh,* and another. Then came a scent like nothing it had ever smelled before. Crackling noises made it move stealthily away to explore the source of the strange sound. It searched serpentlike for the disturbance, slithering about its former den, sensing this could mean danger to its young. In a moment it gazed into the large open area to see the thick, black smoke billowing from the chamber at the center.

They'd found the other fertile ground and they had destroyed it. Panic gripped its senses now as it realized its young were left helpless. But the moment it turned back, it heard another series of horrible sounds: *whoosh, whoosh, whoosh!*

"Aaaaaawwwwwwwwaaaaaaaaatttttaaaa!" It pierced the air with a terrible scream that blended with the fiery explosion. It lifted back head and throat and teeth in anguish, repeating the cry.

Tony Qunin hadn't seen the frothy, translucent bubbles on the corpse until he'd ignited the second body, and then it was too late. Like lightbulbs they exploded, bursting away like corn in the searing heat, roasted into oblivion. Then the dark, syrupy, earth-and-gray color seeped out and melted down as the corpse itself caught the flame. The entire process was awful.

The diseased corpse had reminded Tony of a dog he'd had once as a child, a mutt by the name of Pal. Pal had contracted a disease that had covered his face so badly that the animal could no longer open its eyes. No amount of attention had helped the dog, and he was suffering. Tony watched his foster father destroy the dog, and Tony was given the unappealing duty of burying Pal in the backyard. His last thoughts, as he covered the dog with earth, was that the animal had done absolutely nothing to bring such horror onto itself.

Tony's heart went out to the person whose remains were now blazing before him. No one deserved such a death.

Just then Tony and Grogan heard the strange noise emanating from the chamber they had left moments before.

"*Aaaaaaaawwaaaaaattttaaaaa!*"

"What in hell do you suppose that was?"

Herman pulled Tony on. "We haven't time to discuss it! Come on!"

As they hurried back through the tunnel, Tony pressed Grogan for an answer. "What do you think that noise was?"

"Loose material giving way? Maybe the heat caused a cave-in."

"Sounded like a trapped animal to me . . . sounded almost . . . human."

Stark's voice came through their headphones. "Got the explosives wired like you wanted, Dr. Grogan. Soon as you two are outta there . . ."

"Explosives?" asked Tony.

"You don't think I'm taking any more chances with anyone else coming down here, or anything else coming *out,* do you?" Grogan carried the papers he'd gathered and the large glove he'd dislodged from the suit he had found.

"What are you going to do with all that stuff now?"

"The glove goes back to my lab with me. You and the papers will go to UCLA to be turned over to Sterns and McCain. Don't even bother climbing out of that suit, unless you want to infect Ortiz and Stark and anyone else you come into contact with. You understand, Tony?"

"I don't know how good a patient I'll be."

"You're the most *im*patient person I know! But you've got to follow orders this time around. You have to respect the quarantine . . . and if you do, Tony, I'll give you everything I come up with on the Brain Snatcher case, I promise you."

"I like the way you sweeten a deal, Herman. All right, I'll behave . . . for now."

When they saw the light of the outside world filtering toward them, both men felt a great sense of relief. But behind them they heard the echoing, haunting wail of a creature in horrid, tortured pain. No amount of rationalizing could keep both men from wondering if, somehow, the awful cries were emanating from the cadavers so recently put to flames.

"Awwwwggggaaaaaa . . . aaaaawwwwaatttaaaaa . . ."

fourteen

Chief Medical Examiner Elmore Brooks was building a fire inside his gut waiting for Herman Grogan to return from his unauthorized disappearance. Like everyone else, Brooks had been working round the clock at the city morgue, for the first time in years rolling up his sleeves and getting his hands dirty. Truth be known, he was glad to be a doctor again, and at least for a time forget about the headaches and problems of his administrative duties. But Grogan was flaunting a red flag in front of him again, and ulcer or no ulcer, he was fuming. When Grogan came into the lab, Brooks was in his face immediately, ignoring the younger man's smile and his *now Elmo, now Elmo* crap. The chief M.E. ignored the curious metal box Grogan thumped down on a lab table.

"Where the hell have you been? Where, Grogan? This place is a madhouse! Corpses backed out the door, piled to the goddamned ceiling!"

"I left you a message, Elmo! I tried to get hold of you." As Grogan spoke, he went to a shelf and picked up a human skull, Elmo following. Then he returned to the steel box.

"Really? You mustn't have tried very hard because I

was right here the whole time, Herman, all one hundred and forty-one minutes! Now, you want to try again?"

Grogan didn't slow down. He headed for an isolation chamber with the metal box and the skull. "Guess I shouldn't try to fool you, Elmo. But this *was* important. It may prove vital."

"Important, vital—your two favorite adjectives!"

"This could help the effort at UCLA with the disease they're working on, Elmo." The chief M.E. stopped his ravings, but was still suspicious. He followed the younger man into the chamber. But Grogan stopped his superior at the door with a look. "You don't want to be in here with this, Elmo. Could be contagious."

"What is it?"

Grogan stepped out. "Close the door. I have work to do; you can chew me out later."

Brooks gritted his teeth and backed off, allowing the door to seal. Grogan went to the window and put his hands and arms into long latex gloves that reached into the chamber.

Brooks was a nervous, round-headed, bald man with large oval eyes outlined by horn-rimmed glasses. At his neck, a bow-tie bobbed on his protruding Adam's apple.

For all his faults, Grogan respected Brooks. He had learned a lot from the older man over the years. What's more, Brooks had proved a valuable ally in many situations. He had gone to bat for Grogan on many occasions over the years, putting his own reputation on the line in some cases, often absorbing a lot of political heat in the process.

For this reason Brooks shared "an image problem" as L.A.'s medical examiner with Grogan. While Elmo looked the part of a "team player," he maintained a sense of justice at all times and kept his integrity intact against overwhelming odds. Grogan knew that if it were not for Brooks's cushioning him from attacks coming down through the system, he wouldn't be working in what he considered the most fascinating field of medi-cine.

Grogan had lifted the metallic glove out of the box and began taking measurements of the palm and the sharply contoured fingers. He wished to examine the material itself, to determine what it was made of. A number of ideas were running through his mind when he realized Elmore Brooks was shouting at him again.

"Are you going to bother with an explanation for your behavior or not, Herman? You realize, don't you, how much work we have to do?"

"It'll keep."

"It'll keep! Herman, we've got work to do, and you're playing with . . . what is that damned thing?" It looked to Brooks like a metallic monkey's claw.

Grogan said firmly, "Elmo, I may have found the weapon being used by the Brain Snatcher."

Elmo said nothing for a moment, then shook his head doubtfully and replied, "You have good reason to believe this, I assume?"

"You know I have."

"Frankly, it doesn't look like a very powerful tool. Are you sure?"

"Take a look. You tell me," said Grogan, shoving his latex-covered hand into the giant, metal-plated glove. He lifted it over the skull, and with a grunt, slammed it into the bone. The force drove a sharp, clean cut down the length of the cranium, cracking it on both sides. Brooks was impressed.

"This skull's old and brittle, but I have a hunch that with a living man, there would be a clean, wide hole made in the head. Imagine one of these damned things clutching a man's throat," Herman said, his eyes still pinned on the shattered skull.

Elmo nodded. "I know you're good at your work, Herman. That's why I put up with you. Okay, take what time is necessary. This *is* important and vital. I'll try to get along without you for now."

"Thanks, Elmo . . . really."

"Yeah, yeah . . . just get me some results."

The Robel papers Qunin and Grogan had unearthed at the CCDC site, as disjointed as they were, provided Mike McCain and Casey Sterns with a mixture of amazement, horror and hope. Hope because, for the first time, they could draw a bead on the central causative agent in the disease, the little known, little understood Kuru virus. To make things more difficult, however, the rare Kuru virus had been altered into something the Robels referred to as XK2, a gene-spliced, sinister cousin to an already deadly virus which Mike knew as the most extreme form of parasite on Earth. The new man-made viral *double* occupied a strange netherworld between the living and the inanimate; it was a creature of genetic material and protein, but lacking the cell structures common to all life. Yet it took life wherever it found it. In this case, it fed on the nervous tissue of humans and animals it infected.

Both Mike and Casey knew that Kuru was a disease discovered among natives of New Guinea still practicing the ancient rites of cannibalism. Their particular brand of cannibalism included feasting on the brain tissue of an honored enemy or even of a favored member of the family. Inside the gray matter was a dormant seed—the virus—awakened when ingested by the living, to bring on the *shivering death,* or Kuru, a disorder somewhat akin to Parkinson's and Alzheimer's.

Tony Qunin lay in a room not ten feet away, the fast new virus literally eating him alive. But Tony showed no signs of giving in to it. In fact, he was barking at someone over the telephone.

He'd proved to be as difficult a patient as he had

warned. Mike had known that Tony would be impossible from the moment the reporter presented them with his list of demands to be met before submitting himself to quarantine. Topmost on his list was an open phone line; second was to be kept informed; and third, he refused any sort of sedative whatsoever. He was bearing the pain as stoically as a Buddhist priest, so far.

Meanwhile, other isolation wards, both at UCLA and elsewhere, were being filled with victims of the disease, and Mike had gotten word out to the healthcare community, describing the symptoms and the treatment to date, a treatment that had not prevented the deaths of Naldosa and Timmons.

Mike now had the comparison microscope loaded. On one side was a slide of the Kuru virus, on the other a slide he had prepared of the XK2 virus. He backed off after a long, thoughtful gaze and indicated to Casey it was her turn. "Meet the murderer."

Casey took an equally long look. What she saw took her breath away. Almost identical in configuration, the two viruses shared a common heritage. Casey could see tiny tendrils, like synapses in nerve cells radiating from the center. "The cannibal virus," she said, backing off, "but given even more virulence than in its normal state."

"We might have looked forever if it hadn't been for Tony coming up with these papers."

"Put it in a test tube and our XK2 virus is harmless," Casey said thoughtfully as she looked again into the microscope on the lab table. "Can't even make copies of itself. But give it an opportunity to reproduce in the host cell, and it could spread over the face of the Earth."

Mike understood only too well. He knew how viruses masked themselves and even evolved to look different to the cells they must immobilize and commandeer for their existence. He understood that the docking sites on cells served as receptors for hormones, enzymes, proteins and other vital substances, and that viruses learned to use these same docking bays for entry. By the time the cell knew what was happening, literally millions of viral genes could be produced.

The invader virus was only one sixteen-thousandth the size of a pinhead, consisting of a bit of double-stranded DNA, the master molecule of life. Once it penetrated the nerve-cell nucleus and inserted itself into a chromosome, it took over the cellular machinery, directing it to produce more of the XK2 viruses. Overcome by its alien product, the cell then swelled to bursting and died, but not before releasing a flood of new viruses to attack other cells.

In an attempt to ward off the killer virus, the body's T-cells and macrophages, sent in by the immune system, tried desperately to combat the virus. But the virus actually invaded its would-be destroyers too, and replicated in the T-cells and the macrophages as well. Nothing seemed capable of even slowing the process, much less stopping it. No cure was in sight.

"Horrible, to think of someone actually cultivating such an organism," said Casey.

"I guess neither of us knew Leo Copellmier as well as we thought. There's no doubt from these papers that Leo and the Robels were tampering with Kuru in an effort to make the virus even more deadly."

Mike looked at Casey, studying her weary eyes and features. "What luck have you had? Anything?"

"Just getting materials prepared to go out to Washington and Atlanta has taken hours. Both autopsies are completed, but I still had to fix the brains according to strict requirements. They're still soaking in formaldehyde and saline. Soon as they're ready, they will be sealed in cellophane and packed in ice for shipment by military transport, part to Washington, part to Atlanta.

"I've ordered every possible pathological test, but

frankly, Kuru never entered my mind. I'll report our latest findings now, of course. Meanwhile, I'm holding on to some cross-sections myself."

The door opened and both doctors looked up to see Dr. Herman Grogan enter. Grogan, carrying a file folder, introduced himself. "I have something important to share with you both," he added. "It may have some bearing on your strange disease. Can we talk?"

"Of course," said Mike. It was almost 4 A.M. "Let's get out of here for a while, Casey."

Casey nodded.

"My own independent investigation has led me to work exclusively with nervous tissue," Casey was saying as they followed the corridor to a lounge. "And Mike— Dr. McCain's investigation has led him to the same conclusion."

"I tried culturing the unknown virus in mice, guinea pigs, rodents and monkeys, as well as in tissue obtained from our two human subjects," explained Mike.

"In every case, it only grows in nerve cells," finished Casey.

Grogan was clearly fascinated, his eyes darting from Casey to Mike and back again. "Now that you've isolated it, any answers?"

Mike told him what they learned from the Robel papers and about the discovery that they were dealing with a genetically altered Kuru virus.

"Jesus God," Grogan said with a groan. The three had reached the doctors' lounge, and were now sitting around a small white table.

"Our plan, feeble as it is," began Casey, "is to somehow use the nature of the disease against itself."

"If my cultured viruses follow the route of the wild viruses, they might in time be tamed," continued Mike.

"In time? How much time?"

"Can't say, really . . . but . . ."

"But," continued Casey, "it's normally a process that takes much more time than we have."

"I've injected the cultured virus subcutaneously into a test monkey. We're watching him closely."

"Several others have already been sacrificed," added Casey.

"In time, as the virus is introduced over and over to other animals, it will, we hope, lose some of its virulence, producing a new strain, a less powerful strain, which could lead to a vaccine, a *tamed* virus."

"I see where this process takes time, all right," replied Grogan, sipping a cup of coffee. "So the papers we dug out weren't of much use?"

"On the contrary," said Casey. "They filled in a lot of holes, doctor."

"But there's still a lot more holes that need filling, huh?"

"I'm afraid so."

Casey pulled open a folder she had brought with her and spread it before Grogan. "You're a pathologist; take a look at this and tell me what you see."

Grogan studied the file a moment. It contained Casey's findings on Naldosa. Finally, he said, "This man died of massive internal dehydration, brought on by a brain disorder of an unknown nature."

"Not totally unknown any longer, but still, we know very little about how it works, how it does what it does," replied Mike.

"Dehydration while plugged into an IV for plasma and glucose, Dr. Grogan," added Casey, "and what do you make of the amount of steroids in the bloodstream?"

"I . . . I assumed it was part of your treatment . . ."

Casey shook her head.

"Then where are they coming from?"

"Part of the disorder," said Casey. "Disease strikes,

debilitates through dehydration in the organs and muscles and feeds messages to the brain to produce steroids . . . steroids of all kinds. This in turn puts incredible stress on the brain and certain other key glands."

"Little wonder these people are dying."

"Humor me, doctor, and tell me, when does a man stop growing?"

"Stop growing? Physically, you mean?"

"Yes."

"It varies, of course, but a youngster's growth hormones and bone structure . . . I'd say between sixteen and eighteen years of age."

"Naldosa was thirty-six, but his blood is indicative of a sixteen-year-old boy," Casey said.

"You might say he died of growth pains," added Mike.

"Growth pains?"

"Extreme growth in muscle tissue, limbs, organs, and bones."

"Everything was primed for growth, the glands had gone mad, pumping out hormones his body had once stopped producing long ago. His brain, affected as it was by the disease, was giving signals loud and clear to grow."

Grogan's face clearly showed his amazement, unable to comment on the information the doctors seemed anxious to share.

Mike spoke, "While all this is going on, of course, the body was dehydrating at an accelerated rate, so weakening the man as to throw him into shock."

"Hell of a way to die," replied Grogan. "Is that what's going to happen to Tony?"

Mike and Casey looked at one another, unable to respond.

"Guess so," Grogan murmured.

"It's a man-made virus with a definite liking for nerve

cells," said Mike after a moment. "The only thing that seems to slow it are steroids. In fact, it seems to trigger the production of steroids in the body in order to sustain the host body, so that it might grow."

"So it has time to feed before the body quits on it." Grogan was disgusted, a feeling he hadn't experienced since pre-Med days. Then his face lit as if someone had just turned on a Christmas tree. "So you can buy time for the patient by feeding the damned thing what it wants, by introducing steroids before the thing is in complete control."

Casey put a hand on Mike's arm and looked into his eyes, knowing what he was about to say.

"There are side effects."

"What's Tony got to lose at this point?"

"Increased discomfort," said Casey, biting her lip. "More pain."

"Hell, he'd be alive!"

"As it is he won't submit to sedatives, not even soundwave therapy."

"Don't you see, Dr. McCain?" replied Grogan. "Sedation may have been merciful, and was certainly called for in your earlier patients, when you didn't know anything about this bug, but now you must consider the possibility that those men slipped away that much faster because they were in a sedated state. I think the patient has to fight back, resist, so that you may be able to give him more time with the proper steroid treatment."

"Okay, assuming this might be a better way to proceed, what sort of treatment are we talking about?" asked Mike.

"Like everything else you're doing, it'll take some careful testing."

"And Tony's our next guinea pig," said Casey sadly.

"I'll work up a careful, conservative treatment," said Grogan, "and we'll see what happens."

"All right, we'll leave that part of the therapy to you, Dr. Grogan. But whether or not we use it is up to Qunin."

Grogan thought for a moment about Brooks and all the work awaiting him back at his own office, but quickly pushed those thoughts away. Then he recalled the reason for his visit to McCain and Sterns in the first place. "Doctors, I have brought something for you to see." He lay out a folder of his own, opening it to reveal an official-looking document. At the top of the form was the seal of the Los Angeles Medical Examiner's Office. Behind the report were a scattered handful of photographs of the claw-glove, and the skull it had shattered; one photo had the metal claw fitting into the blue-black lesions on some poor devil's severed neck.

Grogan explained to them where the metallic "monkey's paw" had come from. "I'm off to find Tobler," he finished. "See if he has any ideas on the steroid treatment. As for this report and the photos, I'll turn 'em over to the cops as soon as I can." Grogan knew he had first to keep his promise to Tony Qunin, and share these findings with him.

"What do you make of this robotic hand, Dr. Grogan?" Casey asked before he could get away.

"So far as I can tell, some madman is out on the streets stalking people from within one of these suits, ripping out their brains. Whether I can get a policeman to believe me . . . well, that's going to be another matter."

Grogan was gone as fast as he had come, leaving Mike and Casey shaken by this last new development.

fifteen

Hatred motivated its actions now, hatred and anger, directed at *them,* their wretched kind . . . those who had killed its young.

With the death of the young they had destroyed all hope for a final end to the pain. The horrid torture had returned, and was overtaking its body once again; a devouring pain, throbbing as never before. Was this its punishment for failing to protect its young, it wondered?

It had to feed, to push out the pain. Maybe then it would find the strength to prepare new nests, to lay the fragile sacs again. But this time it would watch over the young until they were born.

It climbed the metal pipes to a grate, peering out through a crisscross of bars. It stared across the cold, concrete world inhabited by *them.*

Sniffing for any hint of them, scanning in every direction, moaning uncontrollably with the pain that coursed through its being, it hefted away the grate. Doubling over with the effort, it climbed out.

Then it realized that overhead there was no sky, only more concrete. It had left the tunnels for an enormous concrete box filled with machines that sat silent, and waiting.

It darted for the blackest corner and nestled there, curled and waiting.

All around it were hard gray walls. It wondered how long it could wait before the pain would render it helpless. It knew it must feed and soon; that it must find—

A noise. The clumsy noise of one of them.

It looked out over the machines lining the walls and saw one of them carrying something big into a dark place, not too far off. Trying desperately to put the pain from its mind, it dragged its heavy limbs toward its newfound prey.

It moved across the floor and found the steps going down to a door where a small, naked lightbulb, faint, but bright enough to hurt its eyes, waved in midair. The door was ajar. Inside, one of them stuffed things into a hole. It heard metal clinking sounds, and then there was a machine-humming noise filling the small chamber. One of their weapons? Had the man-thing seen it? It remembered what they had done to its young.

The memory infuriated it, and it lurched onto the man-thing's back, tearing wildly at the head, its claws tangled for an instant in long, black hair. A final, stifled scream was ended as the jugular and vocal cords were severed. The body fell one way, the head another, rolling across the damp, dark floor, stopping inches away from the humming machine. It only hesitated a moment before the machine, grabbing the head and taking it a few steps away. It was wary of the big square machine, and expected it to explode at any moment.

But no explosion came, and it fed, fishing the juicy morsels out with its claw. Then a noise came from outside; one of them was calling the dead one, coming closer. . . .

Yes, come, it thought, pushing away the body, slinking into a dark corner with what remained of the head to hide there in the shadows.

The other one came closer, still calling out. "Melanie? Honey? Where are you?"

This one saw the pool of blood at the machine, the spatters covering the glass and metal. He froze, then began to back off, trembling. Had he smelled the dead one, it wondered? Or had he smelled *it*?

It moved spiderlike along the wall, below a table, preparing to pounce. But the man-thing backed out too quickly.

It went to the door, slithered up the stairs, and caught sight of its prey. The stupid creature was rushing blindly up stone stairs, tripping and shouting.

It leaped onto a rail that ran up the side of the stairs and caught hold. It scaled straight up along the railing, invigorated after the feeding. It moved with a lizardlike precision, reaching the landing just ahead of its prey, facing the cringing figure as the man-thing came up, his only scream cut short when the claw flew through the air and into its prey's cranium. The head opened like a melon down the middle. The body fell in a heap. Windows opened, doors slammed, and shouts sounded from everywhere.

It scooped out the brain and left the rest, then scuttled down to the concrete below amid shouting and dogs barking. It raced crablike back to the darkness near the grate and fell into the black corner, its claws halving the brain that lay in its lap.

The feeding had only just begun. . . .

It intended to gorge itself on them.

It curled up beneath one of the machine things in the dark, staring along a row of them that seemed to go on forever. An annoyingly sticky and heavy liquid leaked from above, dripping onto its back. It slithered to the next machine to curl up there.

But it was alerted again by noises coming toward it, the curious noises they made with their mouths.

It peeked out to see one pushing another as both came near. One tossed its head back and cackled irritatingly. It thought them disgusting creatures when alive.

It followed their ankles now, crawling from machine to machine, careful not to be seen by them. When they slowed, it slowed, and when they stopped before one of the machines, it was lying just beneath.

Here, the two divided, one pair of ankles going to the right, the other to the left. It speared out with its claws and latched onto the ankles of the one that had chosen the left, the claws instantly slicing through to the bone, causing this one to scream in agony. A moment later, a single, ruthless tug ripped the man-thing to the concrete floor. The head crunched resoundingly before the entire body was dragged below the machine.

The other one let out hysterical cries. "Randy! *Randy!* Damn you, this isn't funny, Randy!"

In milliseconds the claws mauled through its victim's skull, the long, square, metal fingers becoming sticky with the gray matter beneath. Then the long-haired one stooped and peered beneath the machine. Their eyes met and seeing the fate of the other brought on screams and a mad scramble to escape.

It left its food in pursuit of the live one, slithering like quicksilver beneath the cars. It came up behind its new prey and pounced.

It allowed this one to live longer than the others. Savoring each shiver beneath the iron grip. It wanted them to suffer more; to suffer as it had suffered. But the prey became limp, the fear-filled eyes lifeless now, robbing it of all pleasure.

The moment lost, it dragged the body back to feast.

Beneath the machine, it took the bodies apart, savored the best of these two beings, and having ample time, searched their corpses for more places where good tissue might be found.

This new feeding ground, within a few feet of an escape hole, appeared a good feeding ground; a good place to start over.

A warm feeling swelled its insides as it continued to feed, lounging atop the mutilated bodies. It had not fed enough, not yet, not until it once more felt the strange and awful power surge inside and sweep over it, to bring the young again.

It knew there was no returning to its lair, that a new one must be created. It knew that one must be prepared soon, near this feeding ground, if possible. Perhaps it could use these two bodies, take them to a safe place below, and turn them into the rich soil it required. There had been two at the other lair, but they had been placed too close together. This time, at least one of the birthing places would escape *them*.

Thoughts were interrupted by footsteps. Black boots suddenly appeared and a man dropped to his knees and flashed a burning light in its eyes. He had heard the screams and come to investigate, had followed the feeding noises and now stared at it, lying atop the two mutilated bodies. The man fell back, dropped his light, got up and ran.

Momentarily stunned by the light, unable to see, it scurried on instinct toward the sounds of its fleeing prey. In an instant, its vision regained, it leaped onto his broad back, sending the prey sprawling, speared beneath the two deadly claws.

This one it watched squirm, spiked as it was against concrete, under the metal claws. Its prey moaned, cried, pleaded, and blubbered, giving it real pleasure. It thought again of its young burning into nothingness, and the memory prompted it to act.

Slowly it moved its left claw through the squirming

neck, cutting the head cleanly away. This one would become a third planting ground.

There was much work to do . . . but it could wait until after this feast.

The major conditions Tony Qunin placed on his cooperation with the doctors was that he have a telephone line, access to the newspapers, a television set, and a radio. He operated out of his hospital bed like a Mafia boss from a prison cell, somehow keeping 3-CTV alive by remote control and making calls to as far away as Washington, D.C. Herman Grogan, in protective wear, found him on the phone when he entered with a hypodermic needle.

"Nice parable, General Bader," Tony was saying. "Does it have a moral? Like the Russians have the same technology *and* evil intent, while our intent is purely angelic?"

The man at the other end hung up so loudly, Grogan could hear him.

Tony pointed to the needle in Grogan's hand. "What's that, Vitamin E?"

Grogan could see from his perspiration that Tony was fighting off terrible pain. Already, his arms were almost completely covered by the brown, scaly lesions. So far, his face was not distorted much, although a number of lesions had formed there, too.

"It's something to help you, Tony."

"Oh? A cure?" he mocked.

"No, but—"

"I said no sedatives until you guys are ready to put me out for good."

"This isn't a sedative, Tony. It's a steroid treatment, especially designed for your size and weight, and if it works, maybe we can help the others that are coming down with this thing."

Tony thought about the patient who had just been

brought into the room next door. Tony could see him through a glass partition; he was just a little boy. He was resting, hooked up to that damned soundwave machine that induced sedation. Tony had wanted nothing to do with it, wishing to use all the precious time left him. He was working on the biggest story of his career, a story that would be certain to leave no doubt about Dr. Leo Copellmier's character, and to blow the lid off government-funded biological warfare research.

"Just what are steroids supposed to do for me?"

"Buy you time," said Mike, who'd just entered.

Tony considered his words. "You two sure of that?"

Grogan looked to Mike and back again. "As sure as we can be of anything at this point. Chances are it will cause some side effects, but it will give you more time, Tony, while the doctors keep searching for an answer to this thing."

"Time's all that matters now," he admitted. "What"— he stopped to gulp down pain—"what about the pain?"

"It probably won't help that," replied Mike.

Grogan told him about the possible side effects, beginning with periods of dizziness, disorientation and ending with sterility.

Tony shook his head. "Lot of great options opening up to me, huh? Okay . . . shoot me up . . . run your experiment," he said, holding up an arm to Grogan.

Grogan went to work, talking the entire time, bringing Tony up to date on his findings at the lab with regard to the metallic glove.

"Makes a hell of a sidebar to the story I'm working on. You suppose someone could go crazy with this disease, like that monkey that killed Timmons? Could the Brain Snatcher be a killer *and* a carrier?" Tony could not get the screeching sound he had heard emanating from the bowels of the CCDC ruins out of his mind.

"At this point, I wouldn't rule out anything," replied Grogan.

Mike had moved toward the bed, and noticed an elaborate map of the city streets of L.A. on the table beside Tony. The map was dotted with red circles. "What's this all about, Tony?" he asked.

Tony immediately began to fold the map, shrugging. "Just keeping busy, you know."

"Tracking the Brain Snatcher's movements?" asked Grogan.

"Trying to keep up, yeah, but whoever he is, he's fast . . . like this damned disease. In fact, the more I lay here, the more I believe they're related: the disease and the murders. . . ."

Leaving Qunin and Grogan, Mike found Casey with Dr. Tobler in the adjoining room.

"You two must come with me, now," Dr. Tobler announced. "You must have a look. It's astounding . . . quickly, out of those suits and to my computer room, hurry!"

Mike and Casey shed their protective wear and in a moment were in the presence of Dr. Tobler's supercomputer, the Cyber 250. Their attention was immediately caught by the large screen over the computer and the image projected there.

"A computer model of your killer virus, the XK2," said Dr. Tobler, triumphantly, "in three dimensions!" The colored image began to slowly turn. "This is the Kuru-twin, as cultured by you, Dr. McCain, in Naldosa's brain tissue. Marvelously and devilishly complex, wouldn't you say?"

"Incredible . . ."

"But how did you arrive at the model, doctor?" asked Casey.

"I fed the Cyber the findings from the electron microscope and asked a few questions. You're seeing the results." Tobler pointed at the screen and drew an imaginary triangle with his forefinger. "A careful look and you see the thing is multisided, much like a soccer ball, if you ignore the tendrils shooting from it at odd intervals. According to the Cyber, it is genetic material surrounded by a protective outer shell of twenty sides, doctors . . . *twenty*."

"And each side forms three triangles fitted neatly together, identical on each side," added Mike, staring in wonder, "like rhinoviruses.

"Unless I miss my guess each side has three proteins," agreed Casey.

"Yes, all that's been computed . . . no chance of error," replied Tobler. "Now, look at this."

Tobler punched in a new set of commands to the Cyber and suddenly the overhead screen, blipping zoomed into the model, going deeper and deeper until it reached the findings of the electron microscope at its highest magnification.

It became clear that there were odd features on the surface, that it was not smooth and regular at all, but pitted with valleys, holes and spiked mountaintops. The scene resembled an artist's conception of the pitted surface of the moon.

The doctors studied the screen in a near reverent silence until Casey said, "Antigens, Mike?"

"Antigens." He nodded. "Structures that antibodies seek out and attach themselves to, to eventually overpower the virus. Ineffectually in this case, it would appear."

"But this damned thing must have a weakness?" asked Tobler.

"See the deep crevices, the valleys, Dr. Tobler?" asked Mike, indicating the formations. "They're called *canyons*. They're receptor sights, like the grooves on a key . . . and they fit perfectly into the grooves on nerve cells . . . too perfectly."

"The virus uses the canyons to attach itself to the nerve-cell receptors," added Casey, tracing one canyon in particular. "The tendrils are quite possibly like feelers that seek out nerve cells."

"Finer than any fiber on earth."

"Dr. Tobler," said Casey, "I agree with you. There's simply got to be an effective antibody."

"No one's ever found a cure for Kuru," said Mike. "It would take a lab-designed antibody, something that doesn't exist, and that would mean more time than we have. Besides, the chances of creating an antibody to fit the grooves of this thing . . . well, it's impossible, Case."

"We have to try!"

"It could take years, and even then the damned virus will have mutated and—"

"We must try!"

"No, no, there's another way." He stood, shaking his head. "There's *less risk* of failure with the other approach!"

"Of course," she said, a look of deep concentration coming over her.

"Would you two care to share this *of course?*" asked Tobler. "What 'of course?'"

"Mike's talking about going after the canyons, finding an effective coating to shut them down, to fill the key grooves with cement."

"Can this be done?"

"With the help of your Cyber 250, a drug might be developed to effectively coat the receptors on the virus itself and leave the nerve cells unharmed."

"Sounds brilliant," replied the older man.

Casey smiled for the first time in days.

"Hold your praise. It'll take time and lots of work."

"So?" Tobler asked. "What else is new? But look, you two, you're not alone in this. You have a building full of concerned assistants. You have my help, Herman Grogan's, and the Cyber."

"And we can't tell you how much it has meant to us, Dr. Tobler, your understanding and help," said Casey. "Why this"— she indicated the computer model—"this is a miracle, to be able to see this awful thing as it really is."

"I'm not here for congratulations any more than you are, doctors. But you two must get some rest. If you fail from fatigue, well, you'll do no one any good. I know you're racing the clock, for Mr. Qunin, for the little boy, but you must delegate some of your tasks to others."

Casey, despite her fatigue, and the fact he was right, began to protest. "But there's so much to be done!"

"Dr. Tobler's right, Casey," said Mike. "Once we set up an initial trial on the drug, we're handing it over to him, his assistants, and his Cyber 250 here. Then we're going to take advantage of his hospitality and get ourselves some much needed—"

"—and much deserved . . ." added Tobler.

"—rest," finished Mike. "But for now, let's get to work feeding this computer. Know any good receptor coats?"

sixteen

It had returned to feed repeatedly in the large concrete arena where they kept their moving machines. It devoured twice as much as it needed, attempting to restore itself on the one hand, and punish their kind on the other. Still, its first concern was to regain its primordial urge to reproduce.

What would happen if it could not?

It pondered this grim thought until it ached.

Was all that remained despair and depression and feeding on *them*?

These were the feelings and questions swimming wordlessly about its mind when it began to sense a familiar feeling welling up; a warm, soft, insistent pain, unlike the other pains. It was almost imperceptible in its gentle nudge, as of a wishful memory. But it came again. More distinct, more directed. A new insistent feeling like none other. A new chance *was* coming. The feeling was too strong to be denied.

The preparations had not been made in vain. The waiting, fertile ground would receive the new sacs, and nourish them through the early stages.

It abandoned the upper world for the lower, moving with renewed vigor and purpose, knowing precisely where it wanted to go. Once in the tunnels it was there within minutes.

It had located a small, square cell, raised above the waterline beside metal steps. The little chamber was filled with pipes, metal boxes, discarded paper and wire. In a corner a large locker was now stuffed full with the body it had chosen. Scattered over the floor were the tools it had found inside.

It crawled past the tools to the locker, examining the body. The process necessary for fertilizing the egg sacs was not quite complete, the body not having laid there quite long enough. The brown ooze that creeped about the torn, dirty clothing went in strips and moved in unconnected fashion, not whole or complete as yet. It instinctively knew that any attempt to reproduce now could destroy the last hope for any young. It tried to encourage the separate splotches and brown strips to unite, but only managed to lift some off with its awkward claws.

It must be patient. Nature could not be forced.

The carcass lay atop pipe fittings and dirt at the bottom of the locker. It curled up next to the body, contracting with the pains, trying to hold back, to wait.

It wondered how long it would be before the young would come. Would the "earth" be ready to receive them? Could it then leave this world forever? Or must it live on to continue its agonizing life?

The pain of reproduction was not so insistent, not so strong as the first time, as if the new brood hadn't the health of the first. It knew they would not come so readily.

How long would it take? How long before it could deposit this new life, and end its own?

It seemed an eternity, but finally the corpse was covered in the brown teeming life, and finally, it gave birth to the second brood.

Exhausted far more than it had been the first time, it felt as if it were dying as the final sac was released, one of the hundreds that buried themselves deep in the brown ooze.

It had felt the sacs emerge, had known they would be engulfed by the brown membrane. A feeling it had felt only once before overwhelmed its mind, the pain of losing the first brood. It returned like a flood of bile. Fear for its young poisoned all desire for its own release from life.

It wanted to crawl away, to find a place to die. Or to seek out the creatures that it hated so vilely and attack them until their machines brought it a quick end.

It inched toward the opening of the cell, its mind warring with itself. It felt weak but its strongest urge pulled it back . . . back to its young. It knew it must wait longer, must protect the young. It sensed now how it must die: the young would cover it with their numbers and devour it whole. At some time in the future, when they were large enough, they would devour their parent as they would devour the corpse below their crawling forms. Then they would carry on the shared memory, all the knowledge it now possessed about *them*, particularly the knowledge of how best to kill and feed upon their choicest prey.

It was half-past 8 P.M. when Casey and Mike returned to the UCLA labs. They had set up the initial experiment to find a suitable coating to guard against the incursion of the nerve-eating disease, and while they rested, Dr. Tobler orchestrated a small army of researchers on the project.

Thanks to Jose Ortiz, Casey and Mike had had a change of clothes; Jose had run countless errands for them both. Casey was now dressed in snug jeans and a blouse, her hair tied in a ponytail, opting for comfort over fashion. Mike, in a polo shirt and tan pants, completed the picture of two graduate students out for an evening stroll across campus. Soon they entered Tobler's research labs.

"I just sent someone for you!" exclaimed Tobler on seeing them enter. "I believe we have something significant, doctors. Your theory must be working!"

"Let me have a look," Mike said, his voice laced with caution.

They took turns studying the culture under the powerful comparison microscope. On the right were healthy nerve cells, and on the left the diseased tissue, treated with Mike and Casey's coating. The diseased cells were fighting back, trying to ward off the attack, and despite the fact that many were losing the battle, it was a promising beginning.

"What next?" asked Tobler.

"We've got to increase the dosage, turn up the heat," Mike replied, as Casey looked into the microscope.

"It's a marvelous beginning," she told Tobler.

"Can it be made more effective?"

"Yes, I'm certain of it." For the first time, Casey allowed herself to hope.

"We'll attack from every angle," Mike began. He thought out loud as he paced the room. "Begin by tripling the dosage, then work *down* to the point of ineffectiveness. At that point, we'll know what strength we'll require, and then—"

"—try it out on Tony," Casey finished when he hesitated.

There was a moment's silence. "We haven't any time for testing. All our animals are dead, and with the time it would take to infect another . . . well, Tony would be dead by then."

"I'll go speak with him," she said.

"Maybe we'd better do it together, Case."

She nodded, and the two of them went toward Tony's room, stopping only to put on their protective wear. But the moment Casey looked through the glass on the door leading to the newsman's bed, she knew something was terribly wrong.

Tony's IV was disconnected, his sheet thrown over pillows in an attempt to hide the fact he was gone. Mike angrily snatched off the sheet, sending two small white tablets flying off the bed. Casey picked them up, and after a sniff said, "Cyanide pills."

"Damn! How'd he get those?"

"Ortiz, no doubt . . . but obviously, he didn't elect to use them."

"Unless he has more?"

Casey spied some of the paper and debris under Tony's bed, and picked up the map with concentric red circles. She saw that they radiated out from the area of the CCDC for about ten miles. "Maybe our investigative reporter has chosen another way to die. Look at this." She tossed the map on the bed in front of Mike.

"I saw this before," he confessed.

"And it didn't occur to you what he was up to?"

"I thought he was directing the movements of others; I never thought he'd go out there himself, that's all."

"We've got to find him, tell him there's hope for recovery!"

"Ortiz must've helped him escape."

"And they've got to be somewhere around here." She pointed to the circles on the map. "Bring the map, hurry!"

"We've got to tell Tobler first, Casey."

"There's no time!"

"We've got *other* patients, Case!" Mike pointed in the direction of the silent boy in the bed once occupied by young Dr. Timmons.

"Tell me what?" It was Dr. Tobler. Casey explained

everything, and Tobler took a moment to consider it all. "You two go after him. We know what you want, Mike, and my team can deliver it. Meanwhile, you take my car—it's the white Lincoln Town Car in the lot outside. I'll get the key."

Jose Ortiz and Tony Qunin stopped the 3-CTV news van just outside a large city parking garage, one of the few such structures in the city to have made it through the earthquake intact. The garage was dark and deserted, even of cars. Normally, it was packed to capacity, even at night. But only the day before, two Brain Snatcher victims had been found here; Jose didn't wonder at the scarcity of men and machines. He hadn't exactly been pleased to learn that he himself would be entering the garage tonight.

The headlight beams cast light into the depths of the garage, but they served only to make the black corners blacker. The light hit the attendant's booth, revealing that it, too, was empty.

Jose had done exactly what Tony had wanted. He had gotten hold of extensive maps of the city's drainage system. He had brought firearms: two fully loaded .44 Magnums. Jose had also brought walkie-talkies, and now, still wearing the protective suits which had also allowed them to escape the UCLA detention area without endangering the public, they were prepared to meet and slay the Brain Snatcher.

Now they stepped from the van, and Jose said, "I hope you know what you're doing, Tony."

"Nothing to worry about, my friend. Don't forget why we're here." Tony had filled Jose in on all that he had learned from the doctors while in quarantine, about the Robels, the CBWs, and the claw Grogan had found. The entire story was now on a desk in his apartment-turned-newsroom, waiting for the A.M. news. The gutsy woman in charge, Jill Amper, would use it, if he did not return.

"What exactly is your plan, Tony?"

"We know the last several attacks have been in this vicinity, Jose, within a few blocks of this garage; some right inside here. Now, unless I miss my guess, the killer's using this area as a base of operations—"

"And you think, he . . . he's living in the sewers?"

"Exactly."

"But the police, Tony, they've combed the sewers."

"Then they used a comb without enough teeth, partner."

"But what can we do that they haven't?"

"I've had time to study this thing. I tell you, the Brain Snatcher's here."

Jose looked uncomfortably around the empty blackness of the garage, as if to catch a glimpse of the murderer.

Tony found a manhole cover and said, "Here, help me lift this."

"I don't know, Tony . . . I mean . . ."

"Jose, please!" Tony choked on his words, pain obviously bolting through his body. Jose had noticed how Tony had struggled when he pulled himself from his hospital bed. But there was no arguing with Tony. Tony was like Jose's alter ego, his assertive self, the one with all the answers. Since Tony's illness, Jose had been afraid to even think of the possibility of losing Tony. He couldn't imagine life without his best friend, except for the knowledge that he would be alone—truly alone.

Jose noisily removed the manhole cover, secretly pleased that the sound, like the grating lid of a crypt, would chase off anyone, including a psychopath. Tony pushed a button on his half of the walkie-talkie set, testing it. The instrument had a police band frequency, and when the time was right, he planned to switch to it.

Tony then flashed his light down into the black hole, and saw a reflection in the brackish water covering the floor of the pit.

"Why not call the police now, Tony?" Jose asked. "I mean, this is crazy. What can you do?"

"I'm going to slay the dragon, Jose . . . or die trying."

"This is *crazy*, Tony!" Jose's voice betrayed fear.

"No, Jose. I'll tell you what's crazy. It's not fear of what's down there in the dark, or even fear of death. It's waiting here idle, dying by degrees, slowly and surely, while some man-made disease eats away at my mind and body. Dying in bed ain't for me, *amigo*."

Jose could not see his friend's face behind the visor over his head, and even his voice was changed by the suit. He wondered for a moment if Tony's mind hadn't already been effected by the disease. But the camera dangling around Tony Qunin's neck reminded him that for all Tony had been through, he was still a newsman, still determined to prove the existence of the Brain Snatcher and the insidious link to Leo Copellmier and the CCDC.

"Stay in touch on the radio," were Tony's last words before descending.

"Wait, I'm coming with you."

Tony stopped, and looked up at his friend from the ladder. "You've already done enough."

"We can cover twice as much territory."

"No, Jose. This is my story."

"You can't keep me from following you, Tony."

The newsman considered Jose's words. "Okay, but you go north, and I go south. And be ready to use your gun."

Jose slipped down the manhole after Tony, his shoulders butting the sides, his feet feeling for each metal step. Around Jose's neck dangled a second camera, his 35-millimeter with automatic flash. In one hand he held a wide-beam flashlight, and on his belt hung the other walkie-talkie.

The police had investigated this entire area the day before, finding only the mutilated remains of the Brain Snatcher's victims. But Tony could always sniff out a story, and Ortiz sensed that something was about to happen.

"Remember, Jose," said Tony, his words accentuated by the sloshing water that came up to his thighs, "remember, if anything happens to me, you tell them to find the goddamned camera, right?"

"Nothing will happen—"

"*Remember!*"

"Right, right, *amigo.*"

Had it heard new noises? Or was it just the natural flow of water in the surrounding pipes? In its underground world of metal, concrete and water, all kinds of sounds disturbed its rest. It only wanted to rest until the inevitable end, the death that must come with the frenzied feeding of the young. It welcomed its own end, and as much as its mind would allow it, looked forward to death.

The sacs now squirmed and swelled to bursting below it, like so many nubs of flesh without shape or form. A few developed more rapidly and these devoured their siblings whole.

An uneasy feeling persisted. Something was not right. Some deep, secret sense told it so. Out there, in the tunnels, something was coming for it.

Ears alert, nose twitching, it eased off the earth-brown corpse and slithered to the opening. It stared hard in the inky blackness in both directions for any sign of *them.*

Nothing there.

Had they powers it could not comprehend? A sense

that told them the young lay here? Had they some machine that detected the truth? They had come straight to its first lair. Were they coming to this one?

It must know. And yet, it feared leaving the helpless ones alone. But it had to know in order to be ready this time.

seventeen

Casey and Mike cruised slowly around the city garage, searching for any sign of Tony or Ortiz, when suddenly Mike spotted their van. He wheeled the Lincoln in a circle, stopping it outside the open gates. They both leaped out and rushed for the van, calling for Tony and Jose.

"Over there!" said Casey, her flashlight beam revealing an open manhole. "They must be belowground."

"Qunin! Ortiz!" Mike shouted down the black hole, his light cutting shadows in all directions. "Tony! Jose! It's me, McCain! We have good news for you! A cure for the disease! Come back up here!"

"There's no telling how far they've gone, Mike," said Casey. "I doubt they can hear you."

"I've got to go down after them then," said Mike.

A small, slithering, catlike noise came from one of the black corners of the garage. They both turned to look, and Casey clutched Mike's shoulder, as he had begun to descend to the sewer. "What was that?" Casey whispered.

"A stray cat, maybe."

"You're not leaving me alone," she said flatly.

"You're better off here, Case, waiting in the car. I won't be long. It's dark down there, and wet, and—"

"I can handle wet, and I'm not afraid of the dark so long as I'm not left alone."

"Casey, you're being stubborn. The car's the place for you, believe me."

"Come on, we're wasting time."

"I don't want you in danger."

"Neither do I, believe me. And right now, I feel safest with you."

Mike saw the determination in Casey's eyes, and knew it was useless to argue. "All right, but be careful."

When they reached the bottom, Mike flashed his light in either direction, wondering aloud, "Now which way?"

Then they heard something in the distance, coming from their left. "Guess it's this way," said Casey, pointing.

"Jose? Tony?" he called as they inched forward, sloshing water around their thighs. The inky blackness threatened to engulf them. Mike and Casey were chilled instantly, as the icy water soaked through their clothes. Foul odors assaulted their nostrils, and unidentifiable debris swirled about their legs, touching them as if wanting to touch something alive in this most lifeless of worlds.

Tony Qunin looked as if he were a medieval knight in his bulky protective suit, sloshing through the dark of a watery dungeon, his Magnum lifted before him like a sword. The camera on his chest looked like a curious talisman to ward off evil. He fully expected at any moment to see his dragon, the Brain Snatcher. He would use the camera if he could, the gun if he must. Like Jose, he felt that something was close at hand.

He moved cautiously, stopping at times to allow his

eyes to master the dark. With every ounce of his being he willed himself to ignore the horrid pains deep inside his own frame, to try instead to concentrate on any ripple in the water.

He saw a secondary tunnel and went slowly toward it. He stared down its length for some time. The tunnel seemed to be rising on a slow grade toward the surface. At the end of his line of sight, Tony thought he saw something odd dangling, almost as if floating on air. He squinted, blinked, rubbed his eyes, and stepped cautiously closer.

He pulled the walkie-talkie from his hip and tried to raise Jose. There was no answer. He tapped the mechanism several times, trying again and again before giving up. Perhaps Jose is out of range, or maybe his receiver is defective, Tony told himself. But he feared that something was terribly wrong.

Tony inched forward, his eyes never leaving the mysterious object ahead of him. More and more, it looked like a man's booted foot floating on the stagnant air. As he made his way toward it, however, he saw that rather than floating, it was sticking straight from the concrete wall. He raised the light and gasped.

It *was* a man's booted foot, and it wasn't going to float away. Tony made his way to it, and found a mutilated corpse stuffed in a small cubicle of stone, well above the waterline.

Tony had found another victim of the killer, left in grotesque pose, and covered with the same oozing brown life that he had seen in the tunnel with Grogan. He switched on the police band and began signaling for help, flashing an SOS.

Jose Ortiz was fighting for his life. He'd been taken so totally by surprise that his gun and walkie-talkie were lost forever at the bottom of the sewer. The hideous creature had wrapped itself around Jose's legs, and he tumbled into the water. Thrashing about wildly, Jose tried desperately to get some kind of hold on the awful thing, but each time he tried, the shredded skin he held onto tore away, leaving him with a handful of rotted flesh.

Jose felt *it* clawing apart the protective suit he wore, felt it climbing like a clinging vine up his body. He screamed and tried to pull away, but it had him. He thought he had gone mad when he saw the thing rise before his eyes.

It stared through the visor at him with blood-red bulging eyes, and let out a terrifying screech.

"Awwwaaatttaaaaaa!"

Jose grabbed blindly at some pipes overhead, and fastened onto one, pulling himself and the creature upward. He knew that he had merely delayed his death, that in a matter of minutes he'd again be at the mercy of the thing. It had already taken great bites and slashes out of his suit—in seconds the claws and teeth would be ripping at him!

Still Jose fought to live. Kicking and shouting, he flailed at it with one powerful hand, and held tight to the pipes with the other. Then he remembered the camera.

He fought to locate the shutter button but it was impossible to find under the bulk of the protective glove. Suddenly, however, the creature ripped a wide hole in the arm of the suit, and Jose's hand shot through, instantly hitting the flash. Light flared right in the enormous, bloated eyes, blinding the monster. It was momentarily stunned, and let Jose go, falling back into the darkness of the water. Jose had guessed right; the red, bulging eyes *were* extremely sensitive to light.

But like a shark in the sea, it remained circling underwater, regrouping for a final attack. One slice of its enormous claw could kill Jose, and his only weapon was the pitiful flash camera.

Then Jose heard voices shouting his name, and for a brief moment, he allowed himself hope.

He pulled his large frame up higher, seeking a ladder leading to a tunnel overhead. He prayed that he could escape through this route. As he struggled to get to the ladder, he shouted down the tunnel to his would-be rescuers to run, to save themselves.

Jose reached the ladder and grabbed at its rungs, pulling himself along with what seemed to him like agonizing slowness. He got near the top and reached overhead to push away the cover, then suddenly he saw the hideous eyes again, inches from him, the thing clinging to the ceiling in the dark.

The shock made Jose let go of the ladder, and he fell away, hitting the water with an explosive clap.

Ahead of them, Mike and Casey had heard Jose's cries and the struggle in the water. Now something thudded hard against Mike's thigh, something hard and compact. He reached for it, cautioning Casey back as both felt the chill of silence fall over the tunnel once more. Mike wondered which was worse, the horrible cries of the man in agony, or the disturbing quiet.

"What is it?" Casey asked Mike, who had picked up Jose's walkie-talkie. In answer, Mike frantically tried to get it to work, but all that returned to him was static.

"I'm scared," whispered Casey, clinging to him.

"You and me both. We were fools to come down here without any weapons."

The abrupt silence had intensified so that every trickle of water from the damp walls plucked at their nerves.

"We have to go back, Mike, now."

"I think you're right."

"Wait," she said, "what's that?"

He looked about. "Where? What?"

"Shine your light there." She pointed, and the light

reached the spot moments before Jose Ortiz's body disappeared below the water.

Casey screamed, tears welling up for Jose, and out of sheer terror.

"Come on, *now!*" He snatched at her and they splashed back the way they had come, but they were stopped by a chilling, animal cry wafting eerily toward them from straight ahead.

"My God, how many of them are there?" begged Casey.

"It knows these tunnels, whatever the hell it is, and it cut us off. This way, hurry."

Casey pulled back. Mike wanted to go directly to where Jose had met his end.

"It's our only hope. This thing *thinks*. It's expecting us to go back where we came from. It's waiting for us there."

Casey nodded, and they raced ahead into darkness, Mike still trying to raise someone on the walkie-talkie. "Tony's got to be nearby. We've got to warn him."

Mike helped Casey over a slab of concrete in their way. They followed a tunnel which ran toward the site of the center of the quake. Debris increased as the water level dropped, but there seemed to be no way out.

Out of breath, they rested for a moment amid the stones and concrete blocks, their only light coming from Mike's flashlight. Casey was shivering, and as he tried once again to contact Tony, Mike wrapped an arm around her. As Mike worked with the radio, Casey shone the flashlight in circles, searching for a way out.

Cables and pipes dangled overhead, but Casey followed one length of undamaged pipe back to a pile of rubble at their backs. She made out a T-connection in the pipe, leading, it appeared, into another tunnel.

"I think I see a way," she told Mike. "Come on."

"Wait, just a minute," he said, the static from the radio replaced by Tony Qunin's voice.

"Jose? Can you hear me?"

"Tony, Tony! This is McCain . . ."

"What?"

"What is your location?"

"To hell with you, McCain. Where's Jose?"

"Dead, you damned fool! Now listen to me!"

"Dead? Jose?" Even over the radio, his voice was choked by disbelief and sorrow.

"Whatever this thing is, Tony, it strikes lightning quick. Now get yourself to the nearest manhole and get the hell out of this trap. I'm getting Casey and myself out. The last time we heard the killer, he or *it* was at the location where you and Jose entered."

"You two get out fast," said Tony. "I'll keep the sonofabitch busy."

"No heroics, Tony—"

"I've located its lair, McCain!"

"Its lair?"

"Dammit McCain, shut up and listen! This thing's got larvae, a lot of them, crawling around on a corpse stuffed inside a tin box. I'm gonna burn them back to hell before I do anything else. The smell might draw the thing back to me, and you two—"

"That's suicide, Tony," shouted Casey.

"I got nothing to live for anyway, *doctor.*"

"But you do, Tony! We've found a cure!"

A moment's silence preceded Tony's reply. "I've got my own antidote now."

"He doesn't believe us," Casey told Mike.

"For God's sake, Tony, get out, hurry," Mike shouted.

"Cops are on their way," said Tony, "but don't stand around waiting for them. You two take care. Over and out!"

Mike looked to Casey. "Nothing we can do for him. He's determined, and with that thing between him and us . . ."

Casey swallowed hard, and shined the flashlight beam onto the ceiling, running it to the T-section where they saw a black hole in the debris. "This way, Mike, hurry."

As they made their way to the passage, they heard it in the water—the weird, gurgling noises being made, they knew, to frighten them, and having the desired effect.

Mike looked back over his shoulder and cast his light just in time to see the thing's mottled back sink again into the water. Despite what Tony said, it was coming after Mike and Casey, not him.

Tony had realized after pulling off a body in the entranceway to the concrete hole that this sentinel body had been stuffed there as a kind of protection, a wall to hide the more important corpse deep inside the small, debris-filled cave. Tony had climbed a ladder, peered in, and discovered the monster's secret. He was now crouching over the foul remains of a second body, one covered in the sticky brown soup, like those discovered below the CCDC. But all over this one the tiny, mucous-soaked creatures he'd seen popping off the body he had torched earlier were larger, partially formed, like so many slimey tadpoles. Some raised sharp, little incisors to rip other less formed ones apart, feeding on the gore.

The sight was both repulsive and fascinating. There was something oddly human in the shape of the heads, in the half-formed eyes.

"Got to burn these bastards," he told himself, rousing from his macabre reverie.

Tony pulled away as much clothing as possible from the dead man in the doorway. He opened his suit and reached inside a pocket for his lighter. Tony gathered his flammable materials together, preparing to destroy the grotesque life created here on the remains of the human torso in the tin box.

The teeming creatures inside the box began to make tiny squeals, as the feeding ebbed and flowed by degrees.

Tony wished fervently that this was all just some kind of nightmare . . . but he knew better. Jose was dead, killed by the progenitor of these awful creatures. McCain and Casey Sterns were fighting for their lives, and an entire city was at the mercy of the disease these mutations carried. For a moment Tony was chilled by the thought of a world populated by these freaks of Leo Copellmier's making.

Tony inched on hands and knees the final few feet to the metal coffin, his knees throbbing through the protective suit he wore. Unable to breathe easily any longer, he snatched away the head covering and tossed it over the corpse, along with the clothes salvaged from the other corpse. Tony draped a piece over the end of the Magnum and lit it. Allowing the flame to grow, he tossed the burning cloth onto the stack over the corpse, and watched to be certain it would catch.

He saw one of the small creatures climb out one side of the locker. He grabbed it as he might a live mouse, and tossed it back onto the burning mass. Another leaped out, and again he returned it to the burning corpse.

The odor of burning flesh and smoke engulfed the small room and Tony began to choke, suffocating. He backed out, saw a third creature leap from the fire trap, aimed his gun, and blew it to pieces with a feeling of satisfaction.

He caught his breath at the ladder, careful to breathe in shallow gulps. From his new position, he spied a manhole cover overhead which he hadn't noticed earlier. It offered him a quick escape route, and lucky, too, since he'd had no plans of escape, consumed as he was with his mission. But Tony feared that one of the infant creatures might yet escape the inferno. He must hold on until he was sure.

Using his walkie-talkie, he contacted Mike, telling him what he'd done.

"Get out of there, Tony! Now! It was following us, but I think it's turned, heading your way!"

"I have to be certain first!"

Suddenly, from behind Tony, the monster flew from the water straight at him, its horrible claws slicing through his back. He slid like a rag doll from the ladder and fell into the water. His ears were pierced by the ranting, banshee cry of the creature, as it realized the fate of its young.

Tony lay floating in the water, able to move just enough to reach up with the Magnum and point it at the mottled, black form that was picking over the burning remains of its spawning ground. It wailed in pain, searching for any survivors among its kind.

Seeing no life amid the fire and smoke, it turned with the most venomous hatred imaginable toward Tony, and leaped at him with a piercing cry.

Tony fired. The exploding .44 bullet shattered one claw, sending shards through the air. But the creature's left claw split Tony's skull almost at the same instant, killing him.

Mike and Casey heard Tony's final cry over the open channel. . . .

"Run *faster*, Casey," Mike pleaded.

The sound of the creature was no longer coming over the radio, but from down the tunnel. It had taken to the black waters again, propelling itself with the energy of hatred toward the remaining humans who had entered its cave and killed its young.

It was coming fast.

"There has to be an exit here somewhere!" cried Casey.

In all the debris, two exit routes had been unattainable. If and when they found another, Mike wondered if it, too, would be blocked.

"Go on ahead, Case," said Mike, stopping.

She stopped as well, gasping, "What is it?"

He pushed her away lightly. "Go on, look for a way out."

"I won't go on without you."

"I'm going to try to slow it up." He pointed to a precariously perched concrete slab overhead. "I'll try to push it down on the damned thing."

"I won't leave you."

They were both struck silent by a bubbling, gurgling noise in the water.

It appeared in the water, weaving from side to side, giving them time to hear it, to think about dying. It splashed toward them, the noise silencing their pitiful cries.

Enraged with grief, it was coming for them.

It didn't think about feeding on them, not now. It had left the last one all but intact; it was anxious now only for the kill, to fill the void of grief with bloodlust.

It lifted eyes above the waterline and looked at them in the near distance, running hopelessly. Their bodies were no match for it.

It wanted to take its time, to thrash about until they became so terrified that they could not fight back.

Killing them wasn't enough. Feeding on them was not enough anymore. It would torture them, as slowly and painfully as possible.

Casey and Mike heard the creature noises in the water and they seemed like a mutant language. But another noise wafted down to them from the street above. Overhead, they saw a dim light filtering through a grate. There was a ladder going up, an upended, lead-pipe fence.

"Come on," said Mike, "I'll follow you."

"I can't make it," she breathed painfully. "Get help, *go!*"

He shook his head. "I'm not leaving you." He pulled her up and forced her along the first rungs of the ladder.

"Help! Someone, *please,*" Casey called through the grate.

Mike slipped, and Casey screamed, certain he'd been pulled to the bottom by the monster.

"I'm okay, Case, keep going!"

Then Mike saw it. It was creeping along the ceiling, crawling upside down, red eyes alight, coming right for Casey.

"Back down, Casey, now! *Now!*"

Then she saw the malevolent form of the blackened creature crawling lizardlike toward her, arms and legs twisted and ropey. The charred torso dragged peeling layers of skin that sagged with its movements. Its eyes were fixed, shining with hatred, fixed on her. Huge, flaring nostrils and a twisted, gaping mouth breathed a horrible stench at her. Then the monster showed its evil claw like an enormous jewel, extending it outward to catch a glint of light. To Casey's eyes, it was a demon that had crawled out of hell.

Mike looked desperately for a weapon, anything that might serve, when his eyes fell on a section of steel pipe that lay nearby. He lurched for it, grabbed it, and raised it in one fluid motion just as the claw came down toward Casey's forehead. He struck the charred arm just before it reached her. Again the claw came, and again Mike interrupted its deadly course.

But Mike sensed that the monster was holding back, like a cat toying with mice; the creature seemed to be playing at killing.

"Run, Case! To the next exit! Hurry!"

Casey hesitated; her instinct was still not to leave him.

"Go, dammit, *now!*" He pushed her on, holding the pipe overhead, his eyes never leaving the monster's.

Casey, stumbling and crying, made her way along the tunnel. Mike watched the awful thing drop from the ceiling and back into the water, disappearing.

"Damn!" he hissed, circling and scanning the brackish water for the next sign of the thing, his hands slippery with sweat as he clutched the pipe. Mike couldn't see even a ripple in the water, and fearing the worst, he hurried after Casey, dragging the awkward pipe with him. He was terrified that at any moment the creature could lock around his ankles and send him toppling. But the thought that the monster might gain on Casey was far more terrifying.

Then, as if from far away, Mike heard the groaning keen of the creature: *"Aaaaawaaaaattttaaaaaa!"*

Mike's mind wanted to let go, to scream and rant, but he knew he must fight the desire to do so, that he must somehow remain in control. Yet, he knew that it was the creature that was in control now.

He again heard the keening and placed its source behind him, and for this Mike was grateful. He continued to fight his way through pools of water and debris, searching for a way out, stopping just long enough to look in the direction from which the keening continued. The flash revealed the back of the monster as it rose and dipped like a leviathan in the water, perhaps twenty yards distant. It was keeping him in sight, biding its time, as if it meant to draw out the hunt and enjoy it to the last.

Casey had gotten ahead of Mike, searching frantically for any sign of an exit. Alone now, her mind raced with fear, terror gripping her heart like an icy hand. An image of Mike viciously ripped apart by the demonic creature flashed through her mind, and she wondered how soon the end would come for her.

She had scrambled out of the water, clawing at a concrete wall, when a new tunnel opened up for her.

The unending maze was like a monster itself, a twisting, mocking world which Casey must escape.

Then she heard something coming. She stood frozen, afraid to make a sound.

"Case! Case! Keep going!" Mike was rushing toward her, daring to flick on the beam again.

"This way," she called, taking the new corridor. The passage rose in a gradual incline, the water level lowering as they went.

"*Awaataa . . . awaataa . . . awaataa . . .*" it chanted, not far behind.

Mike's flash sent a beam of light out in front of them as they ran. Then Casey saw another light, far ahead. "There!" she cried.

When they reached it, they saw that it filtered down from overhead, at the end of a narrow, concrete drain. Mike stared upward. "No guarantee we can get the grate off."

"We have to try."

Behind them the cry of the creature was closer.

"It's our only chance!" Casey pleaded.

"Once we're up there, there'll be no turning back. It could turn into a trap."

"We don't have any choice! We've got to risk it, Mike!"

They began the climb, almost straight up.

They were bruised and filthy, each with hair soaked and plastered against their skin. About halfway up, Mike whispered for silence, and the two of them tried not to breathe. They sensed the black thing below them, staring through the dark at them. Mike doused the light.

"*Aaa-wwwaaa-taaa,*" it groaned with what sounded like pleasure.

Mike, gambling, answered by turning on the wide beam of the flashlight, causing the creature at the foot of the drain to screech with the sudden pain to its eyes. He tried to follow the creature with the light as it withdrew, and in his haste, smacked the flash against a pipe. The light went careening down into the water.

"Hurry!" Mike shook Casey from a frozen stare, pushing her on to the top. Mike strained against the heavy, iron grate overhead, pushing and panting with more effort than he thought left in him. Through the bars of the grate he saw an enormous square pillar with red and blue paint and a large black stenciled number, G-2. "It's the ballpark," he whispered. "Dodger Stadium!"

"It's coming!" she said, hearing the metallic claw scratch over concrete.

With a final thrust, Mike pushed up the heavy grate and moved it aside, lifting himself up and out, then grabbing Casey's hands to pull her up. She screamed at the last instant when the claw swiped at her ankle, barely grazing it.

When Casey was up and out safely, Mike expected the creature to leap out at them. He was amazed when it did not. Where was the hellish thing?

It seemed too easy, this escape.

"Cover it, Mike, cover it!" Casey eagerly helped Mike return the grate. At a nearby concession stand below the bleachers, Mike found three heavy carbon canisters. He laid them across the grate.

But Mike remained ill-at-ease. He took Casey under his arm, and she leaned into him, releasing a deep breath of air, shivering with the thought of all that had happened.

"We've got to get out of here," he told her, and they started for an exit. With his free hand, Mike pulled out the walkie-talkie he had clipped to his belt. He clicked it to the police band and called for help, explaining their situation, unsure if anyone was reading him. But when he mentioned the Brain Snatcher, he got an instant reply.

It was Herman Grogan's voice. He was with the police at the city garage. They'd gotten an earlier message from Tony Qunin.

"Get a car over to our position, Dodger Stadium. Qunin's dead and—"

"We know. We fished out Ortiz's body as well."

"Careful, Grogan, it's not safe in those—"

Mike and Casey stopped and stared ahead of them. They had rounded the concrete circle below the stands, the entire place thick with the odor of the quake victim's bodies still covering the field. Now, crawling up from a second grate that rattled cryptlike over the stone floor, the misshapen form of the mutant rose menacingly before them.

Mike and Casey backed away in horror, neither of them able to take their eyes off the evil confronting them.

"Start moving, Case," Mike whispered, "slow . . . easy."

"McCain? McCain?" Grogan's voice came over the radio.

"Grogan, the damned thing's not twenty yards from us."

"We're on our way!"

The slouching monster dragged its limbs along the concrete, coming toward them. A snarl creased the furrows of its leathery, mottled face. The eyes bulged with recognition, and delight.

"Oh, God, no," moaned Casey.

Mike searched for a way out as they backed off, holding tight to each other. "Have to slow it up, divert its attention. Get back to where we came from. Those carbon cannisters might help."

She didn't understand his logic, but she agreed that they must do something.

"Now," he cried, "run!" Mike hurled the heavy

walkie-talkie at the creature with all of his might and raced after Casey.

The instant he reached the grate where they'd come out of the sewer, Mike raised one of the carbon canisters, turned and threw it at the charging creature, striking it a grazing blow. He repeated his effort with a second and a third canister, slowing the monster enough to get Casey ahead of him, through a passageway and into the stands.

Together, they stormed up the ramp and went into hiding amid the thousands of seats.

"*Awaataa . . . awaataaa*," it grumbled repeatedly as it moved about the seats around them.

Mike and Casey lay silent, not daring to breathe, between the dirty concrete and the seats. They couldn't see the creature, but they could hear its chant as it drew near.

Over the playing field a strange fog had spread, the product of tons of dry ice breaking down over the week-long emergency. It lay still and ominous over the dark body bags below. Mike stared out at the dry-ice fog and knew at once it meant cover, and perhaps a way out. But getting to it would be risky, and the creature would surely follow him into the cloud and away from Casey.

"I'm going to draw it away," he whispered, then rose up and pounded down the bleachers, bounding off the last row of seats and onto the playing field. He'd done it so quickly, Casey had been taken by surprise, unable to stop him. When she saw the monster tearing after Mike, she realized why he had done it.

Mike raced down a row of the dead, the grass slick, beaten down by traffic and workmen, none of whom had remained after the lights were shut down. Behind him, Mike sensed the awful black form in dogged pursuit, hidden by the fog. At least his desperate plan meant Casey was safe.

Then he slipped, sprawling face-first over the bulging body bags. Certain the creature would pin him here, he expected the ghastly end to come now.

The last Casey saw of Mike before he disappeared among the body bags was a glimpse of him losing his footing. As she searched for him again, she was chilled by the sight of the creature, hunched over the dead, crawling about the bags, sniffing doggedly for Mike.

Oh, God, I've got to get help! she told herself, and rushed back down the ramp the way they'd come, going for the exit. Coming suddenly around the refreshment oasis at the bottom of the ramp, she was startled by an ominous form blocking her path. Only when the man's flashlight was snapped on did she realize the brown uniform and cap in the dark meant a guard.

"Miss," he said in exasperation, "the morgue hours are posted on the gate! You have no business here!"

Mike lay still and silent, staring up at an enormous dry-ice fog, giving him cover, but also hiding the monster. He had stumbled on the stone-hard body of a quake victim as he had tried to maneuver on the slippery turf. When the monster didn't immediately fall on him, he had scrambled like a crab amid the rows of dead, his nostrils assaulted by the smell of decay. Somewhere in the maze of bodies, *it* was still emitting its chilling chant.

"*Awaataa . . . awaataa . . . awaataa . . .*"

Mike tried to stay ahead of the sound, knowing that his own movements made sounds that the creature could interpret and use against him. He needed a plan, but no clear thoughts would come. His only solace lay in the fact that Casey had gotten free.

The creature's cry told Mike that it could not be more than a few rows away. He knew he must act quickly, yet his entire body seemed numb and unresponsive. His muscles were becoming paralyzed by fear, while his

senses were fully alert. He could even hear the monster's
labored, staccato breathing, the clink of its metallic
claw. He imagined he could smell it above the stench all
around him. He wondered if it could sniff *him* out the
way a dog might, if it could pick out the wild beating of
his heart. Mike inched out from behind a stack of
bodies, fearing that at any second now the stalking
demon would be on him, tearing at his head and throat.
From his new vantage point, he saw the vague outline of
the dugout, perhaps fifty, maybe sixty yards off, the dim
outline of a doorway in its deep recesses. That door
might be his chance to escape . . . *if it were unlocked.*

"*Awaataaa!*" The cry came from directly behind him.
It was too close!

Mike was instantly up and sprinting, racing down the
wet rows of the dead, slipping as he hit the infield. The
creature keened madly behind him, bounding over the
bodies to get at Mike.

He knew it was coming in for the kill, and he
somehow found a sudden burst of energy that got him
to within a few yards of the dugout before he stumbled.
The creature had dived at his legs and toppled him, its
claw clamped onto his foot. Mike pulled, and the
monster tore away his shoe, bloodying his left foot
badly. But Mike was able to roll into the dugout.

He reached the bat rack, instinctively grabbing for a
bat for protection as he fell. An instant later, the killer
claw came down at his eyes, spintering the wood that
Mike held up as a shield. Part of the bat had jammed
into the monster's claw, and Mike scuttled to find a
second bat, this one with an enormous ring weight
attached to the end. With it, Mike jabbed ferociously at
the black flesh over him, stabbing at its abdomen,
causing enough pain to push it from the dugout.

Then Mike heard its scratching feet on the roof and
suddenly the claw came crashing through the top,
reaching for him. Mike battered the claw once, twice,

and a third time before the creature pulled it back. In an adrenaline rush of panic, he turned to the door and tried to push through.

It wouldn't budge.

He backed away and struck at it with the bat, hurling curses, but it was useless. Then he found a metal bat, and rammed it against the door.

He was trapped.

Somewhere overhead he heard the monster scratching, planning a new attack.

Then Mike heard the whine of a small engine. The sound caught the attention of the creature, and it suddenly leaped down from the top of the dugout. It loped out into the field, climbed atop some of the bodies, and stopped, staring.

Mike lifted his head out of the dugout, and in the distance, he caught a glimpse of a golf cart going at top speed. He squinted in order to follow it toward the outfield, where it disappeared in the fog.

The demon creature growled hideously, lifting up its claw, making a threatening gesture toward the cart.

At that sight, something in Mike snapped. He was gripped by an overwhelming anger, and his fists tightened about the metal bat until his knuckles shone white. He took firm steps toward the monster and began shouting at it.

"Now, you freak son of Satan, you're going back to hell! *You're* going to die!"

Mike's shouts caused the monster to turn slowly, revealing once more its bloated and blackened features.

It scuttled across the body bags and jumped onto the ground with a thud, facing Mike, answering his challenge.

Mike hefted the bat, carrying on his monologue. "No more running shit-scared from you . . . no more hiding. You're no demon, just a twisted lump of flesh, a life form that was never meant to be . . ."

It gave out a whining sound, as if in answer. *"Aaawaataaa . . ."*

Mike grimaced at the repugnant thing before him. "I'm sending you straight to hell," he repeated his threat, bringing the metal bat aloft.

Its ugly eyes responded, widening at his words as if trying to interpret them for the diseased brain beneath its creosote exterior. *"Aaaawaaataaa,"* it murmured, raising its claw.

Then, with ferocious intensity, it let fly with the hammerlike claw, ripping through one of the body bags. When the claw lifted again, Mike saw gray and white drippings at the end of it. The vile thing stuck the end of its claw into its mouth, trying to weaken his resolve.

Once more it dipped its claw into the ruptured body bag and displayed it before Mike's eyes, careful to watch each move Mike made in response. Its eyes dared him to come nearer for a closer look.

Mike knew he must avoid the claw at all costs, that a single blow from the creature would end the battle, completely disabling him.

Now Mike darted toward it, readying the bat. When he was within striking distance, he sent his weapon whizzing at the creature's claw, knowing he must disable it. But he missed as the thing jumped back and perched on the body it had so recently mutilated. Mike didn't hesitate a moment, coming off the backswing full-tilt, but the bat again missed, only to make a sickening thud against the corpse at the creature's ponderous feet. In an instant, one of its feet clamped down on the bat, holding it firmly in place. It lashed out at Mike with the deadly claw.

Mike ducked, yet held tightly to the bat, pulling it away when the creature's foot lifted. A second swipe of the claw came down at Mike, but he blocked it with the steel, the noise of claw against bat ringing around the ballpark. Again the claw swiped, and again the bat met it and held, but crimping dangerously.

Metal hit metal again and again, continuing the clanging chorus. A mighty blow from the creature swatted the bat from Mike's hand, and the monster reared back for the final blow. The claw went aloft, the creature screeching, "AAAAWWWAAAATTTTAAAA!"

But the victorious screech turned suddenly into a cry of terror and pain as the field was flooded in blinding, glaring light, which sliced laserlike through the strange fog.

"Casey!" Mike cried, realizing now that she had gone to the scoreboard.

The hideous monster was even more repugnant under the light. It reeled about in a blind rage of pain amid the body bags, seeking any corner of shadow. It was as if its entire body hurt from the intense lights directed on the field.

As it circled in confused pain, screeching, shots rang out from all sides, and the beast absorbed shell after shell, flinching and writhing with the gunfire. The park was filled with policemen. They had launched their barrage the instant they were able to see their target.

The creature had fallen over a stack of bodies, and now lay still. Mike found himself praying it was finally dead.

Still in near shock from his experience, Mike stared blankly at the misshapen mound of black flesh that was the remains of this creation of man. All around him, unbelieving policemen still held their weapons poised for another barrage.

But it didn't come . . . and the silence in the creature was indeed the silence of death.

Casey raced up to Mike and took him in her arms, tears flowing. They embraced tightly, needing to reaffirm the fact that they had lived through the horrors of the past few hours.

"Dr. McCain! Dr. Sterns!" It was Herman Grogan. "Thank God you're alive."

Mike and Casey separated, but continued to hold firmly to one another's hands.

"I think you might want to see this," continued Grogan.

Mike and Casey stared at a small tuft of jet black hair that the coroner held in his hands.

"What the hell is it?"

"Unless I miss my guess, this will test out to be a strand of human hair, very likely Marie Robel's."

"But where—?"

"Jose Ortiz gave it to me."

"But Jose's dead . . . we saw his body," said Mike.

"Yes, so did I," Grogan agreed. "Jose had these strands clenched in his hand. The mutant had to be one of three people. I saw the Robels' files, and only Marie had black hair. The two bodies we found under the CCDC were Arthur Robel and Leo Copellmier."

Mike and Casey stared at the deflated creature, lying in a heap nearby. "Then that thing," he said, pointing, "was once Marie Robel?"

"*Was* is the operative word, Mike. Marie died in a very real sense long ago, in that chamber with Copellmier and her husband. But out of her death—or what remained living inside her suit—*that* crawled out into the world."

"To spread a terrible disease," said Casey.

"And to feed on men," Mike added, a cold chill tickling his spine. "Thank God it's finally over."

epilogue

Far below the recovering city, in the vicinity of where Tony Qunin had died, something moved.

A small shape darted near a pile of soggy debris, burrowing for signs of food. Finding nothing, it skittered off, stopping to investigate an enormous metal claw with a distinctive odor so powerful that not even the water could erode it entirely.

The tadpolelike creature had thick, crusty scales, below which throbbed elastic muscle, which often pulsed with paralyzing pain.

Not too far from the claw, it found another interesting shape submerged, a shape that meant something to it, but it was unsure what. It rounded the smooth outer edges of the form, rose and dipped along its perimeter, and then fantailed in and out of the empty eye sockets. The shape was somehow imprinted on its primitive mind as a form from the past. . . .

It darted up for air, spiraling and shooting from the dark water to beach itself on a barren slab of concrete. It lay there unmoving. In its belly the pain gnawed at it as if it were being eaten alive from within.

It squeaked an odd sound through sharp-pointed incisors.

"Awwa-taa . . ."

Then a rat came toward it, creeping on all fours, sniffing the air, its hair prickly with all senses alert. The creature lay motionless until it was within striking distance. In the blink of an eye, the instinctual snapping of its jaws clamped with deadly accuracy around the rat's throat and severed its head.

The creature curled up with the rat head on the stone slab.

In a short time, it had finished feeding, and once more it lay still, waiting . . .

. . . waiting for something to come along . . .

. . . preferably something larger. . . .